Lords of Disgrace

Bachelors for life!

Friends since school,
brothers in arms, bachelors for life!

At least that's what "The Four Disgraces"—
Alex Tempest, Grant Rivers, Cris de Feaux
and Gabriel Stone—believe. But when they meet
four feisty women who are more than a match
for their wild ways, these lords are tempted to
renounce bachelordom for good.

Don't miss this dazzling new quartet by

Louise Allen

His Housekeeper's Christmas Wish
His Christmas Countess
The Many Sins of Cris de Feaux
The Unexpected Marriage of Gabriel Stone

All available now!

Author Note

Gabriel Stone, the Earl of Edenbridge, is the fourth of the Lords of Disgrace, whose stories I have been chronicling. Gabriel always was the wildest of the friends, but at first I had no idea what lay behind the dangerous rake's facade. His story, I discovered, was far darker than I had ever imagined, but neither his past nor his present hedonistic lifestyle prevents him from becoming entangled in the affairs of Lady Caroline Holt.

Innocent Caroline will do anything to save her young brother's future—even bearding a dangerous rake in his lair. Gabriel discovers to his horror (and the amusement of his friends) that he'll do whatever it takes to rescue Lady Caroline from the dangers she faces, even if that involves masquerading as a Welsh hermit. As I explored, I found that Caroline, innocent or not, is more than a match for her reluctant rescuer, even when his past, and the long arm of the law, catches up with him!

I hope you enjoy Caroline and Gabriel's story as much as I enjoyed writing it.

Louise Allen

The Unexpected Marriage of Gabriel Stone

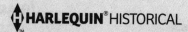

If you purchased this book without a cover you should be aware that this book is stolen property. It was reported as "unsold and destroyed" to the publisher, and neither the author nor the publisher has received any payment for this "stripped book."

Recycling programs
for this product may
not exist in your area.

ISBN-13: 978-0-373-29888-4

The Unexpected Marriage of Gabriel Stone

Copyright © 2016 by Melanie Hilton

All rights reserved. Except for use in any review, the reproduction or utilization of this work in whole or in part in any form by any electronic, mechanical or other means, now known or hereinafter invented, including xerography, photocopying and recording, or in any information storage or retrieval system, is forbidden without the written permission of the publisher, Harlequin Enterprises Limited, 225 Duncan Mill Road, Don Mills, Ontario M3B 3K9, Canada.

This is a work of fiction. Names, characters, places and incidents are either the product of the author's imagination or are used fictitiously, and any resemblance to actual persons, living or dead, business establishments, events or locales is entirely coincidental.

This edition published by arrangement with Harlequin Books S.A.

For questions and comments about the quality of this book, please contact us at CustomerService@Harlequin.com.

® and TM are trademarks of Harlequin Enterprises Limited or its corporate affiliates. Trademarks indicated with ® are registered in the United States Patent and Trademark Office, the Canadian Intellectual Property Office and in other countries.

Printed in U.S.A.

www.Harlequin.com

Louise Allen loves immersing herself in history. She finds landscapes and places evoke the past powerfully. Venice, Burgundy and the Greek islands are favorite destinations. Louise lives on the Norfolk coast and spends her spare time gardening, researching family history or traveling in search of inspiration. Visit her at louiseallenregency.co.uk, @louiseregency and janeaustenslondon.com.

For the Quayistas—
and the lovely staff at Hartland Quay Hotel.

Chapter One

London—June 1st, 1820

'There is a young lady to see you, my lord.'

Gabriel Stone, Earl of Edenbridge, swung his feet down from the fender and sat up in his saggingly comfortable armchair to fix his butler with a quizzical look.

'Losing your touch, Hampshire? Young *ladies* do not come calling on me, not even with a bodyguard of chaperons.'

'Quite so, my lord. However, this is indubitably an unaccompanied lady and a young one at that.'

'Does this mythical creature have a name?'

'Lady Caroline Holm, my lord.'

'Holm?' That rang a bell. A very faint and slightly muzzy chime, given that Gabriel had been playing cards and drinking brandy into the small hours at a cosy hell in St Christopher's Place. He glanced at the clock and found it was now eleven o'clock in the morning. He really must summon up the energy to go to bed.

It had been a profitable night and the crackle of promissory notes in his pocket told him so as he lounged to his feet and stretched all six foot two inches of weary body.

Profitable to the tune of several hundred pounds, a very nice signet ring and the deeds to a small estate in Hertfordshire.

The estate... 'Ah, I have it, Hampshire. I presume Lady Caroline is the daughter of Lord Knighton.'

'The eccentric earl, my lord?'

'A euphemistic description, Hampshire, but it will serve. The man appears to suffer from occasional bouts of gambling fever and is notoriously obsessional about improving his estate in the intervals between his binges. Of his other peculiarities I have no personal experience, I am thankful to say.'

Gabriel turned to look in the over-mantel mirror and was confronted by a vision of unshaven, rumpled dissipation, guaranteed to send any gently born lady fleeing screaming from the house into Mount Street. That would be an excellent outcome, although possibly without the screaming. He had some consideration for his neighbours. 'Where have you put her?'

'The drawing room, my lord. Should I bring refreshments?'

'I doubt she'll stay long enough. Have my bathwater sent up, will you?'

Gabriel sauntered out of his study towards the drawing room, the details of the night before gradually becoming clearer. Knighton was the man who had lost the Hertfordshire deeds to him as a result of one ill-judged hand after another. He hadn't appeared particularly concerned at the time, certainly not to the extent of sending his innocent and respectable daughter to the home of one of London's most notorious rakes and gamesters to buy back the stake.

The innocent lady in question was standing before the unlit grate and turned at the sound of the door opening. Gabriel had time to admire a slim, unfashionably tall fig-

ure in a blue walking dress before she threw back her veil.
The move revealed a chip-straw bonnet over neatly dressed
blonde hair, a pair of admirable blue eyes a shade darker
than her gown, a severely straight nose and, to balance it,
a mouth erring on the side of lush.

Not a beauty, not with that determined set to the chin,
but striking. *Tempting.* 'Lady Caroline? I am Edenbridge.
To what do I owe the pleasure of this visit?'

She dropped a hint of a curtsy, nicely judged to reflect
both his rank and his dishevelled state. 'You played cards
with my father last night.' Her voice was normally warm
and mellow, Gabriel suspected. She sounded anything but,
just at the moment.

'I did. To save time, yes, I won the deeds to an estate
in Hertfordshire from him in the process.'

'I know. I overheard Papa telling my elder brother about
it this morning.'

'You have not come to tell me that it is your dowry, I
hope?'

'It is not.' She took a few steps away from him, turned
and marched back, chin up, apparently using the few seconds to marshal her words. 'It belongs to my younger
brother, Anthony.'

'I regret to disagree, it now belongs to me. It is an unen-
tailed estate, I gather, one that may be legally disposed of.'

'Legally, yes, morally, no.'

'Lady Caroline, I have very little time for morals.'

'So I understand, my lord.' A sensitive man would have
flinched at her tone. 'My father is…'

'Eccentric.'

She seemed to weigh the word for a moment. 'Yes. And
obsessed with both his title and Knighton Park, our home.
That *is* entailed of course and my brother Lucas, Viscount
Whiston, will inherit it. Anthony is only sixteen. Papa has

decided that he will become a clergyman, installed in one of the livings at his disposal, and therefore he has no need of lands of his own. He doesn't understand Anthony like I do. I virtually brought him up and—' She must have realised she was losing his attention and her tone became brisk again. 'Springbourne is ten miles from Knighton Park, too far for it ever to be integrated into the main estate, so Papa thinks little of it.'

'The church is a common career for a younger son,' Gabriel observed. His own brothers seemed happy enough with their respective roles, but they hadn't been born first and saddled with the responsibility of title, tenants and lands. Let alone brothers. *Promise me, Gabriel...*

With the ruthlessness of long practice he pushed away memories of childhood and thought of his brothers now. Ben, the elder, a blood-and-thunder cavalry major, George, newly ordained as a vicar, a mild soul who tended to flinch when he encountered Gabriel, and Louis, painfully studious and conscientious and both sensitive and pugnacious, a difficult combination to handle. He was a student in his final year at Cambridge where he was reading law before taking over the family's business affairs, an outcome Gabriel was looking forward to immensely.

Now they were adults Gabriel gave them money when they asked for it, had introduced each to a good clean brothel when he judged them mature enough, warned them about predatory young ladies and their even more predatory mothers and beyond that managed to avoid them for months at a time. It was better for all of them that way.

'It may be usual,' Lady Caroline said in a voice that made him think of lemons inadequately sprinkled with sugar, 'but it is quite unsuitable for Anthony.' She glanced at him, then looked away hastily. It might have been the morning light shining directly into her eyes, it might have been the sight of him. The blue gaze flickered back, she bit that full lower lip and the hunting cat in him stirred, twitched its tail and began to purr. 'Anthony loves Springbourne. He isn't studious or intellectual. He is a natural farmer and countryman and it will break his heart to discover it has gone.'

'And you expect me to hand it back to you, just like that? Sit down, Lady Caroline. I have had a long, hard night and I cannot sit until you do.' Besides anything else, he wanted to watch her move.

With a small sound he assumed was exasperation, she sat on the nearest chair and studied her clasped hands as he subsided into the seat opposite. 'No, I do not expect you to do anything so altruistic as to save my little brother's dreams and future for no return.'

'Perceptive of you,' he drawled and was rewarded by a hiss of anger before she was back to being the perfect lady again. 'Do you intend to buy it back then?' He pulled the mass of vowels out of his pocket and sorted through the IOUs until he found the one scrawled in Knighton's hand. He held it up for her to see. 'That is the value your father put on it.'

Lady Caroline winced. 'No, of course I cannot buy it back. You must know that as an unmarried woman I have no control over my own money.'

'Then what do you propose?'

'You have a certain reputation, Lord Edenbridge.' Those gloves must be fascinating to require such close scrutiny.

'As a gambler?'

She closed her eyes, took a deep breath, then opened them and sent him a defiant stare before her gaze skidded away to settle on the fire irons. 'As a man of amorous inclinations.'

Gabriel tried not to laugh, but it escaped in a snort of amusement. 'That is one way of putting it.'

'I am a virgin.'

And one who blushed delightfully. 'So I should hope,' he said piously. The lush mouth compressed into a hard line and he had a sudden urge to capture it beneath his, tease it into softness and acceptance. Into pleasure.

'I propose an exchange, my lord.' She addressed the fire irons. 'My virginity for those deeds.'

Gabriel had always thought himself sophisticated in his dealings with women. After perhaps half a minute, during which time Lady Caroline's cheeks turned from light rose to peony and he revised his opinion of his own unshockability, he said, 'I am not in the habit of deflowering virgins, respectable or not.' *But in your case...*

'Perhaps you would consider making an exception? I understand men are almost obsessed with virginity, which seems strange, but then I know very few men.' And, by the sound of it, wished to keep it that way.

He flicked the IOU with one finger, making her start at the sharp sound and glance at him again. 'This debt is not your problem, Lady Caroline.'

She bit her lip and Gabriel drew in a steadying breath. Even talking about making love to her was having an uncomfortable effect on him. He could understand that men wanted a virgin bride because they needed to be certain their heirs were from their own seed. But maidens held no attraction for him. Forcing women was revolting and a willing virgin was doubtless a great deal more trouble than she was worth—tiresomely inexperienced with a price to pay in the form of a maddened father with a shotgun. Besides, he expected expertise and sophistication from his lovers.

And yet, this one... It has nothing at all to do with her

virginity. Those blue eyes and that mouth and the stubborn, innocent courage of her... Damn, she is not safe out when she has no idea the effect she has on a man.

'Oh, but it is my problem.' Lady Caroline was becoming animated now, her blush disappearing as she leaned forward earnestly, trying to convince him, or, perhaps his disordered neckcloth, which is what she was now fixed upon. 'Mama died ten years ago. Anthony is my little brother and I promised her I would look after him. I love Papa, of course, but he is…difficult. He would regard paying you to buy back the deeds as a waste of money that should go into Lucas's inheritance, or towards improving Knighton Park.' When Gabriel did not respond she said fiercely, 'Anthony is the only one of my family who truly loves me and I love him as though he was my own child, not just my brother.

'You have brothers, I know you have because I looked you up in the *Peerage*.' For some reason that brought the colour up again in her cheeks. 'This morning, I mean. I know, as a man, you can't feel about them as I feel about Anthony, but you would do anything you could to help them, wouldn't you?' It was more a statement than a question.

Yes. 'No.' He was not going to encourage her in this, allow her to see that her promise to her mother meant something to him. What his duty was as a man, as the eldest son, was quite different from hers as a daughter, a woman. 'Listen to me, Anthony is a boy. He'll find his own way in the world eventually. He isn't a child, your responsibility, any more. Your older brother will look after him.'

She was finally staring at him, although her expression suggested that it was because he had grown two heads. 'I do not understand you. I love him for himself, but Anthony is also all I have left of Mama. I know from the *Peerage* that your mother is dead too. Have you no affection for your own family? Don't you see your parents when you look at your brothers? Surely they are the most important thing in the world to you, even if sometimes you fall out with one of them?'

All I have left of Mama, she had said. He understood that too well. The blackness swirled down, the memories clamouring. *Promise me...the still white hand, limp beside the bottle...*

Gabriel shrugged the images away, unable to acknowledge what lay at the heart of them. He would kill...he would protect his brothers, of course he would. He had. They were his responsibility, his trust. He shrugged again. 'It is my duty. But I am a man and head of the family.'

'I am so sorry you feel like that, you must miss so much,' Lady Caroline murmured.

For an appalled moment Gabriel thought she was going to cry, she looked so upset. 'You are *not* going to sell yourself to me in exchange for those deeds. What will your husband say?' The heavens only knew where this impulse to decency was coming from.

'I do not have one. Yet.' Lady Caroline's expression changed from sad to rigid.

'You will, soon enough.' She must be in her early twenties, he guessed. Twenty-three, perhaps. 'And a husband means a wedding night.'

'Papa has a number of men in mind for me, but he hasn't made up his mind yet which would be the most advantageous match. Frankly I would be delighted to give any one of them a shock on the night.' She seemed to have recovered her spirit, but her gaze had slid away to the fire irons again.

'You do not have to obey him.'

'He is my father, of course I have to obey him. I have no choice.'

'Your duty, I suppose.'

She nodded, one sharp jerk of her averted head. 'Duty and lack of other options. My father tends to discourage suitors who do not match his wishes for me.'

'You don't really want to have sex with me, do you?' Gabriel smiled as she looked back, startled at the deliberate crudity of his words. He made the expression more wolfish than reassuring and ran one hand over his morning beard, drawing her eyes to his mouth. She stared and then swallowed and his arousal kicked up another notch. *Damn it.*

'To be frank, rather you, my lord, than Sir William Claypole or Mr Walberton. Or Lord Woodruffe.'

'Hell's teeth! Has your father made a list of every middle-aged bachelor in society?' If he had sisters he would not have been willing to match one of them to any of those men, least of all Woodruffe.

'Only of those with lands close to ours who would be willing to exchange them for me.' When he did not respond she said urgently, 'Please, Lord Edenbridge. I know you are supposed to be hard and cynical and to care for nothing and nobody, but deep down you must have family feeling. You must, surely, understand how desperate I am.'

The first part of that description was more or less accurate. 'You have managed to do a remarkable amount of research on me, considering that it is not yet noon.'

Lady Caroline blushed again. 'I have seen you about at balls and so forth. People talk.'

And you have been interested enough to ask about me? Gabriel laughed inwardly at himself. *Coxcomb. Flattered because some attractive girl has noticed you?* Women tended to look at him, just as he looked at them. But not well-bred virgins. He had a highly developed sense of self-preservation.

'I will take you up on your offer,' he said. She gasped

as though she had not expected it and the colour fled from her cheeks. 'I will send the deeds to you when I receive them from your father and you will give me an IOU for your maidenhead, to be surrendered when your marriage is definitely arranged.'

'But…'

'I may be a gamester and a rake with a shocking reputation, Lady Caroline. But I am a gentleman. Of sorts.' *Just enough of one not to barter your innocence.* On the other hand, if she thought they had an agreement it would prevent her doing anything else reckless in order to raise money to pay him. He could simply hand her the deeds and he *should* do just that without any conditions. But the hunter in him enjoyed having her between his paws. Not to hurt, just to play with a little. He was so damnably bored these days. 'On my honour I will speak of this to no one. What is your decision?'

She had expected to be sent packing with Lord Edenbridge's derisive laughter ringing in her ears, or to find herself flat on her back in his bedchamber, and had not been able to work out which of those was the worst of two evils. What she had not expected was this reprieve. Which was not a reprieve after all, merely a postponement, she realised as his words sank in.

'I accept.' Caroline wondered if she was about to faint. She was not given to swooning, but the room seemed unexpectedly smaller and there was a strange roaring in her ears that must be the sound of her blood.

'Please send the deeds to this address.' She found her piano teacher's card in her reticule and handed it to him without meeting his gaze. She had tried not to look at him, partly because the whole situation was so mortifying, but also because she knew she blushed every time she saw that rangy, carelessly elegant figure. Looking at his face, so close, would be too disconcerting. 'Miss Fanshawe understands the situation at home.'

'She is used to acting as a go-between for your illicit correspondence, is she?' The earl moved away towards a writing desk and Caroline realised that she had been holding her breath. A hasty glance at his back made her shiver. He was far too large and male and *animal* to be so close to. Whenever she had seen him before it had been across a ballroom floor at a safe distance and there his dark hair and the slight carelessness of his formal evening attire had been attractive.

This near, in the same room with him, his casual disregard for the niceties of fashionable male dress and grooming was shocking and more than a little unsettling. His hair was thick, slightly waving, rumpled as though he had run those long fingers through it. His face was shadowed by dark stubble, his neckcloth was pulled askew and his collar had been opened, exposing the base of his throat. He smelled of brandy and smoke and something faint and musky and his eyelids drooped with a weariness at odds with his drily intelligent voice. She wondered what colour his eyes were. Dark blue, brown?

At a safe distance he had attracted and intrigued her. The gossip about him was both titillating and arousing to a well brought-up young lady and she had fed her fantasies with it. Of course, she'd had no expectation of finding herself within ten feet of the object of her lurid imaginings. Aunt Gertrude, her chaperon, would have hysterics at the thought that Caroline might actually *speak* to Gabriel Stone.

His reputation was shocking and yet no one accused him of being vicious. He was amorous, said the whisperers, dangerous to a lady foolish enough to risk her heart with him and he was far too good at cards for the health of anyone reckless enough to cut a deck in his company, but

Caroline was not hazarding her allowance. Nor her heart, she told herself. In the shock and anger of discovering just what Papa had done last night, Lord Edenbridge had seemed like the answer to her dreams—amoral, unconventional, sophisticated and possessed of his own particular brand of honour. The man had disturbed those dreams often enough, so surely the bargain she was proposing would not be so very unpleasant to go through with, given that one had to lose one's virginity some time, to someone? Lord Woodruffe's stomach wobbled over the top of his breeches. She shuddered. *I will not think about Woodruffe. Think about this man.* Nothing about Lord Edenbridge wobbled physically, nor, apparently, mentally.

Caroline gave herself a mental shake. 'I do not have any illicit correspondence,' she said. 'But Miss Fanshawe is a friend.'

'Not much of one if she is encouraging you to come here.' He pulled back the desk chair for her.

'She has no idea what I am doing.' Caroline eyed the pen stand warily. She was not at all certain she knew what she was doing herself. It had seemed such a good idea at nine o'clock that morning. 'What should I write?'

'Whatever you feel covers our agreement.' The wretched man had a perfectly straight face and his eyes beneath those indecently long lashes were veiled, but she suspected that he was amused.

'Very well.' She dipped the nib and began, choosing her words with care. She was not, whatever he thought of her, completely reckless.

I agree to pay Lord Edenbridge the price agreed
upon the arrangement of my betrothal.
Caroline Amelie Holm
June 1st, 1820

She sanded the paper with a hand that shook only a little and pushed the note towards him. 'Will that do?'

'Admirably discreet.' He folded the paper and slid it into his breast pocket. 'This will reside in my safe, most securely.'

'Of course.' Strange that she had total confidence in his discretion and his honour—in keeping this a secret, at least. He would not be bragging in his clubs that he had made a conquest of the retiring and virtuous Lady Caroline Holm. *Would he?*

'Why do you trust me?' he asked abruptly, the question so near to her thoughts that she stared at him, wide-eyed, convinced for a moment that he could read her mind.

'I have no idea,' she confessed. 'Only my own impressions and the fact that everyone says how shocking and ruthless you are, yet you are never accused of dishonourable behaviour.'

'It is easy enough to be honourable if one is never tempted.' His voice was dry and his smile held little amusement. 'I confess that it is a novelty to be trusted quite so implicitly, Lady Caroline.'

The heat that had been ebbing and waning throughout this entire outrageous interview swept up her cheeks at the thought of what tempting this man might involve. She was innocent, certainly, but not ignorant. 'Obviously I have not tempted you beyond reason, my lord, given the very businesslike way we have concluded our bargain.'

'I did not say that I am not tempted, Lady Caroline.' He took her hand, raised it to within a hair's breadth of his mouth and held in there for a moment. His breath was warm, his fingers firm. She braced herself for the brush of his lips.

'How did you come here?' Lord Edenbridge asked,

releasing her without the slightest attempt at a kiss. He walked to the fireside and tugged the bell pull.

'In a—in a hackney.' *Damn him for making me all of a flutter, for making me stammer. For disappointing me.* Behind her the door opened and she bit back any more stumbling words.

'Hampshire, find the lady a hackney with a reliable-looking driver. Good day, Lady Caroline. I look forward greatly to the announcement of your nuptials.'

Her last glimpse of the earl was of him pulling his neck-cloth free and beginning to unbutton his shirt. Caroline did not deceive herself, her brisk walk down the hallway was as much a flight as if she had run.

Chapter Two

It had seemed such a good idea at the time. It had seemed the *only* idea at the time. Caroline took her place at the dinner table and wondered if the sinking feeling inside was guilt and shame or…anticipation. More likely, she thought as she made herself sip her soup, it was all three plus very sensible fear at what would happen if her father found out what she had been doing that morning.

'Something wrong, Caro?' Lucas, her elder brother, glanced across at her.

Her father, who was unlikely to notice anything amiss with anyone else, short of one of the party spontaneously combusting, ignored them. He had always been self-centred and selfish and she had given up years ago expecting any parental warmth and attention. She just prayed that Lucas would find a wife soon, someone who would stop him becoming just like his father.

'This soup is a trifle salty. I must speak to Cook about it.' Apparently her face did not convey the depth of her feelings, for Lucas merely nodded and went back to discussing with their father a planned visit to Coade's Artificial Stone Manufactory in Lambeth in pursuit of statuary for their latest landscape project.

She had noticed before that once her father had sustained a major loss he would stop gambling abruptly. It was as if the bubble of gaming fever that had built up in him had been pricked and he was back to normal, until the next time. At least he did not continue throwing good money after bad for very long, but the irrationality of his behaviour, the wild swings of mood, were an increasing worry.

'What new feature are you planning, Papa?' she asked as the soup plates were cleared.

'A hermitage. I will adapt the Gothic chapel that is already almost complete. The position where the path through the plantation has the view of the small lake is more suitable for a hermit's cell than for a church.'

'A hermitage there would be very dramatic and atmospheric,' Caroline observed dutifully, not adding *and damp*. That location faced north and the trees dripped moisture on to the mossy bank. But years of experience had taught her what to say to keep her father happy.

'Finding the hermit may take some time,' he commented, gesturing impatiently for Lucas to add more of the capon he was carving to his plate.

For a moment, despite all her years of experience with him, Caroline thought her father was joking, but he sounded perfectly serious. 'That might be challenging, I can see.' Somehow she kept her voice steady. 'I doubt the usual domestic agencies would be of any use. Perhaps an advertisement in the newspapers?'

'What kind of hermit had you in mind, Father?' Lucas was apparently fully behind the scheme. 'As it is a Gothic chapel then a Druid would be unsuitable.'

'I envisage a reclusive scholar,' their father declared. 'Once a monk, then expelled from the monastery by King Henry, now living alone in the ruins with the books and manuscripts he has saved from the Dissolution.'

'You intend him to actually live there, Papa? That way of life might be too rigorous for a modern applicant to accept,' Caroline ventured.

'Of course I have considered that. The chapel exterior will disguise a one-roomed cottage, just as I built accommodation for the gamekeepers into the folly tower.'

'And his duties?' What did a hermit do anyway? Herm, perhaps. Somehow she managed not to give way to her feelings. It would be all too easy to collapse into hysterical laughter this evening.

'I will want him simply to be there when anyone passes by. He must keep the hermitage in good order and maintain the area around it. I have no objection to him carrying on his own work—studying, writing and so forth—if he is a genuine scholar.'

'Will we be returning to Knighton Park soon, Papa?' Headlong flight down the hallway to the Earl of Edenbridge's front door was not enough, it seemed. Headlong flight out of London was beginning to feel much safer. 'The Season is drawing to its end in a few weeks.'

It had been the familiar round of socialising, of eligible young men who flirted and danced and then sheered off as soon as they encountered her father. Her looks were passable, her breeding acceptable, her dowry reasonable but her parent was the kind of father-in-law that bachelors were warned about. If she had ever met anyone who had wanted her for herself, loved her, then that would not have mattered, she supposed. But that had never happened and she was well aware of the whispers that Lady Caroline Holm was perilously close to being on the shelf. *Such a pity,* the old cats gossiped, *such a charming girl. But...* And then she had seen Gabriel Stone.

'We will stay in London for June,' her father said, jolting her out of her reverie. 'That will give the builders time to finish the hermitage while Lucas and I select the ornamental details and find the hermit.'

No escape then. Unfortunately it was not Lord Edenbridge from whom she felt she needed to escape, it was her own absolutely irrational desire to see more of him. *Playing with fire*, Caroline thought. *He is dangerously attractive and he is not for me. The man is downright wicked. As well as beautiful in that wild gypsy manner.*

Her food was becoming cold. Caroline applied herself to it and told herself she was suffering from an attraction that was as ridiculous as any schoolgirl's *tendre* for the music master. Only that was usually a hopeless passion, quickly forgotten. This was something that was going to lead her into the man's bed and might, if she was not very careful, end in scandal.

'The post, my lord.' Hampshire proffered the salver with so much silent emphasis that Gabriel picked up the pile of letters immediately, intrigued to see what had interested the butler.

The letter on top, of course. Sealed with a plain wafer, posted in London and addressed in an elegant feminine hand. He lifted it to his nose. Unscented and good quality paper.

The note inside was to the point. *The package has been received. I am most obliged for your prompt attention to the matter.* There was not even an initial.

'My *prompt attention*, indeed.' Gabriel tapped the note on the table. Lady Caroline would have done better to have written begging him to reconsider their agreement. He was in half a mind to stop playing with her, tear up her IOU and send it back to her via her obliging pianoforte teacher. He would never act on it.

Would I?

As a gentleman he most certainly should not, but part of him admired her outrageous logic. It was certainly one sure way to hit back at her father's schemes to marry her off advantageously whatever her own inclinations. Not that losing her virginity was going to save her from marriage, not unless she was prepared to inform her hopeful suitors in advance of the ceremony.

Yes, he should tear up the note and forget her and she would spend her entire married life giving thanks for a narrow escape. On the other hand he was bored, the situation was novel and a little internal devil prompted him to see just how this game played out a little longer.

He opened the next letter in the pile, noticing that it was from his old friend Crispin de Feaux and that the wax was impressed, not with the Marquess of Avenmore's usual seal, but with the discreet abbreviated version. Cris was up to something.

Not only that, he discovered, but requiring Gabriel to get himself involved as well. 'Collect information about Lord Chelford's debts…obtain a sedan chair and bearers… send to Stibworthy, North Devon… *North Devon?'* What the blazes was Cris up to now?

The study bookshelves returned no answer to his questions. This was too intriguing to deal with by post. Gabriel tugged the bell pull. 'Hampshire, I am going into Devon by way of Bath. I will want my travelling coach.' He glanced at Cris's letter again and smiled. 'Tell Corbridge to pack for action rather than amusement, I think.'

By the time he got back from whatever was brewing on the wilder western shores of England he would have located his better nature. He would do the right thing by the innocent Lady Caroline immediately and he would not yield to the temptation to discover just what the delicate skin at the base of her throat tasted like. Strawberries, perhaps...

June was drawing towards July, complete with sunshine, roses in bloom, a flurry of fashionable parasols—and no indication from her father that he would be leaving for the country for at least another week. Caroline could only be grateful because she had just realised the great flaw in her scheme, the gaping black hole in the centre.

She had the deeds, so Anthony's future was assured, she had told herself. Then, when she was locking them away in the base of her jewellery box, she realised that in solving one problem she had created another—or two, if she counted the looming shadow of Lord Edenbridge and her promise to him.

Anthony's estate was safe, but estates had to be managed. Plans must be made, orders must be given, wages paid, staff supervised, income banked and invested. Somehow Springbourne had to function for five years until her brother reached his majority and could take control. Meanwhile, she had no resources, no experience and no legal standing in the matter. Anthony was a minor, so neither did he. And if either of them tried to employ a solicitor or a land agent to act on their own behalf the first thing the man would do was consult their father.

Lord Edenbridge. Papa thought the earl was about to take over Springbourne and doubtless he had already notified all concerned. If Lord Edenbridge took nominal control it would solve everything. Would it be a huge imposition? Perhaps she could offer him a percentage of the income, or might he be offended by that? She needed to ask his advice.

It was the day she realised that she must speak to him

that Lord Edenbridge disappeared from London. She looked for him in vain at balls and parties, she heard no gossip about him and, when she contrived to have the barouche drive along Mount Street, she saw the knocker was off his front door.

There was nothing for it, she would have to write to him. Caroline sat in the little room optimistically referred to as her boudoir, chewed the end of her pen and racked her brains for a tactful way of phrasing a request that a virtual stranger take on the supervision of an estate she had extracted from him in return for the dubious value of her own virtue.

The knock on the door was almost a relief.

'Yes, Thomas?'

'His lordship requests that you join him in his study, my lady.' The footman had doubtless translated a grunted command to *fetch my daughter* into a courteous message, so she smiled at him, even though he had thrown what little she had managed to compose into disorder.

As she went downstairs she wondered what Papa wanted. Perhaps he had decided to go back to Knighton Park, in which case life would become immeasurably more complicated, for not only would all her correspondence with Lord Edenbridge have to go via Miss Fanshawe, but then be posted on to her in the country.

'You sent for me, Papa?'

For once he was not buried in a pile of plans and estimates, sparing her only a glance. To be the focus of his attention was unnerving. 'Sit down, Caroline. I have good news for you.'

That was *definitely* unnerving. 'Yes, Papa?'

'I have received an offer for your hand in marriage from Edgar Parfit, Lord Woodruffe. What do you say to that?'

'Lord Woodruffe? But he's…he's…'

'Wealthy, a good neighbour, in excellent health.'

'Forty. Fat. He thinks of nothing but hunting. His first wife died only a year after they were married.'

'It is hardly his fault the foolish chit fell off her horse.'

'Miranda was frightened of horses and she hated hunting. He forced her to ride, to follow the hounds. He is a bully.' *And he frightens me.* She managed not to say the words, for she had no justification for them, simply instinct.

'He is a well set-up, mature man who expects loyalty from his wife.'

'He can expect it of someone else, then.' Caroline found she was on her feet. 'I will not marry him.'

'You do not tell me what you will and will not do, my girl! Your duty is to accept this most advantageous offer that has been made to you.' Her father's face was already darkening with building rage at her defiance.

The match was far worse than she had been dreading and advantageous only in what Lord Woodruffe would be offering in the way of land to increase the Knighton estate. But she could do nothing until she had spoken to Lord Edenbridge, secured Springbourne for Anthony.

If Mama was still alive she would not let you do this. The words were almost out before she could control them. Mention of his late wife always triggered her father's worst rages. 'Yes, Papa.' She forced herself to meekness. 'But I hardly know Lord Woodruffe.'

'That didn't stop you spouting nonsensical opinions a minute ago,' he grunted. 'There's plenty of time to get to know him, no need to rush things. I'm too busy at the moment to worry about details like weddings and settlements.'

Reprieve...

'Next month or so is soon enough. We'll go down to

Knighton in a week or two, Woodruffe can do his court-ing, wedding in September.'

September? She had been hoping for six months, not two. The thought of the baron's *courtship* made her feel queasy. 'Yes, Papa.' It sounded weak, defeatist, but it calmed him. He was unused to defiance from her, she re-alised. Perhaps there had never been anything to make a stand about. Rebelling over being ignored and underval-ued or complaining about her marriage prospects would have been pointless. But this was different and she had just won a little time to think.

First she had to locate Lord Edenbridge and settle An-thony's estate safely, then, somehow, she had to find a way to escape from this marriage. Her brave words about los-ing her virginity and giving her husband a shock on their wedding night were wishful thinking, she realised now. Edgar Parfit's response to finding that his bride was not what he expected was likely to be extreme: she had no il-lusions about the man, only fears that seemed worse be-cause of their very vagueness.

'Will Lord Woodruffe be at Lady Ancaster's supper dance this evening, Papa?' She infused as much interest into her voice as possible.

'Doubt it.' He did not glance up from his papers. 'He's still in the country as far as I know.'

A small mercy, she thought as she let herself out of the study. If only Lord Edenbridge was at the dance, too, then she had some hope of settling Anthony's future and with that done, and her promise to Mama fulfilled, then per-haps she could find some way out of the mire for herself.

'You look very well, Caroline.' Aunt Gertrude, the Dowager Countess of Whitely, was normally sparing in her praise, but tonight, perhaps prompted by the news that

Caroline was to receive an eligible offer, she was positively gracious.

'Thank you, I was rather pleased with this gown, I must confess.' It was an amber silk with an overskirt of a paler yellow and she was wearing it with brown kid slippers and her mother's set of amber jewellery.

'The neckline, however, is verging on the unacceptable.' Her chaperon leaned forward in the carriage, the better to glare at Caroline's bosom.

'I believe it is well within the current mode, Aunt.'

'Humph. And you are somewhat pale.'

It was a miracle that she was not white as a sheet with tension, Caroline thought as she set her lips in a social smile and prepared to follow her aunt out of the carriage and into the Ancasters' Berkeley Square house. At least the necessity to act in a certain way prevented her from simply sitting down and having a fit of the vapours. She'd had to dress, have her hair styled, talk to her maid, choose her jewels, pay attention to Aunt Gertrude and now enter the Ancasters' ballroom looking as though she had nothing on her mind except pleasure.

'Good evening, Lady Farnsworth... Yes, Lord Hitchcombe, the floral decorations are charming... No, Aunt, I will be certain not to accept more than one dance from Mr Pitkin... Thank you, Mr Walsh, a glass of champagne would be delightful.' She smiled and prattled on, just like every other young lady in the crowded, hot room, while all the time she expected to open her mouth and find herself announcing, 'I have offered my virginity to Lord Edenbridge. I am deceiving my father. I am plotting to...' *To what? Ruin myself, most likely.*

And there, strolling along on the other side of the room as the company began to take their places for the first dance of the evening, was a tall, black-haired figure. *Eden-*

bridge. He turned and went through a set of double doors that Caroline knew led to several sitting-out rooms and the ladies' retiring room.

She murmured in her aunt's ear.

'Oh, for goodness sake, Caroline! Why on earth didn't you visit the closet before we came out?' Lady Whitely demanded in a penetrating whisper. 'The first set is forming and you do not have a partner yet.'

'I really must,' Caroline whispered back. 'The rhubarb posset…' She escaped before her aunt could reply. With any luck she would attribute her niece's haste to natural urgency, not the desire to go chasing after wicked bachelors.

She was moving so fast that she almost cannoned into Lord Edenbridge around the first corner of the corridor. He was standing with one evening shoe in his hand, prodding at the inside with a long finger and frowning.

'Lord Edenbridge, I must speak with you. Where have you been? I have been looking for you for days…'

'And good evening to you, Lady Caroline.' He inclined his head in an ironical half-bow, shook the shoe and held up a small tack between finger and thumb. 'I will have words with Hoby about this.'

'Never mind your bootmaker, my lord, this is urgent.' At any moment someone could come along the passageway and find them compromisingly tête-à-tête.

He winced. 'You utter blasphemy.' But he replaced his shoe and opened the door opposite them. 'As I recall… Yes, excellent, and a key in the door. How accommodating of dear Hermione.'

He meant, she supposed, that this might be a refuge for lovers. There was certainly a *chaise longue.* Caroline pushed away speculation about how Lord Edenbridge knew this room was here and waited while he turned the key.

'Now, Lady Caroline, how may I help you? I have been

down in Devon,' he added. For all his light tone and the smile, she detected a wariness about him. From her urgency he must think she was pursuing him, which was embarrassing, to put it mildly.

She sat down squarely in the middle of the *chaise longue*, spread her skirts out on either side in a way that made it quite clear she was not expecting him to join her and almost smiled at the rueful twist of his lips. 'Perhaps you have misjudged the situation, my lord?'

'Perhaps I have.' He lounged across and propped a shoulder against the mantel-shelf looking for all the world like a Romany who had, for reasons of his own, donned an evening suit and strolled into a *ton* ball. She half-expected to see a glint of gold in his earlobes. His eyes, she realised, were brown. 'I do wish you would stop addressing me so formally. Call me Gabriel, Caroline.'

'And risk letting it slip out should we meet in company?' *Gabriel.* She liked the sound of the name and she liked her own name on his lips even better. Perhaps not such a gypsy after all, she thought, watching him from beneath her lashes. His hair had recently been cut, although it was still on the long side, he had shaved to perfection and it was only the carelessness with which he wore his expensive clothes and the feline ease with which he lounged that spoiled the picture of the fashionable aristocrat.

'Your chaperon would run me through with a hatpin before I got within conversational range of you, Caroline, so I think we are safe. Now, having established that you do not desire me to deflower you in a retiring room at Hermione Ancaster's dance, which I agree would be unwise, however informal she insists the occasion is—'

'Oh, do not make me laugh! Not that there is anything to laugh about. I must be hysterical.'

'Just very anxious, I think. Ask me what it is you want

to know.' He sounded not bored, precisely, but certainly reassuringly unexcited by being dragged off for an intimate chat. The coolness was bracing. Then she met his gaze and saw heat and a raw masculine awareness of her as a woman. No, he wasn't cool at all, simply controlled and that very control was almost as arousing as the heat.

She could be controlled, too. She must be or he would read the utterly immodest carnal desire that was making it so hard to breathe. *Inhale.* 'How burdened are you with the management of your own estates, Lord Edenbridge?'

He straightened up, hooked an upright chair away from the wall and sat down. 'I am not easily surprised, Caroline, but I must admit that our meetings are presenting me with one novel situation after another. Would you care to explain why you wish to discuss estate management?'

'I have realised that securing the deeds to Springbourne for Anthony is useless unless there is some way we can run the estate. I cannot do it. As an unmarried woman I will never be able to open a bank account without my father's permission and Anthony is under age.'

'That is so. I have to admit, this had not occurred to me when I gave you the deeds back.'

'If I hand them back to you, will you manage the estate for Anthony until he is twenty-one?'

The silence seemed to go on for a very long time. Then Lord Edenbridge said, 'No.'

Chapter Three

'Naturally we could not allow you to be out of pocket, Lord Edenbridge. Perhaps your man of business could find a suitable manager and the estate would meet all the costs. It is perfectly solvent, I believe.' Caroline kept her tone as brisk and efficient as she could in the face of his frowning refusal.

'Money is not the point, Caroline. It is irrelevant.'

It is? How nice that would be, for money to be irrelevant.

'I employ perfectly competent people to run my own estates and my business matters. My own involvement will become even less as soon as my brother Louis leaves university. I can certainly add your brother's property to the portfolio and extricate it again when he reaches his majority, but you are asking me to assume a position of trust, to be responsible for another man's estate and income. That is a considerable responsibility. Who is going to audit the revenues and financial transactions?'

'Why, no one. I trust you. You are a gentleman.'

He ran both hands through his hair, turning it into something disordered and wild, then leaned forward to emphasise the words that emerged through what sounded like clenched teeth. 'Then you are an idiot, Caroline, and I had thought you innocent and trusting, but not empty-headed. You do not know me. I gamble and that in itself should raise warning flags. What if I suffer a big loss and see an easy way to *borrow* some funds?'

'I am not completely air-headed, Gabriel,' she retorted. The name was out before she realised what she was saying. He lifted his head, looked at her and the tight jaw relaxed as he smiled. Nettled by that little sign of male smugness, she pressed on firmly. 'I am a good judge of character. I told you I have heard the talk about you and no one accuses you of deceit or dishonourable behaviour, even the people who have no cause to love you. I was reckless going to your house the other day, proposing what I did. You could have taken advantage of me then and you did not.'

'You should not confuse financial probity with an unwillingness to pounce on young ladies when I am half-asleep and three-parts drunk.' His smile deepened, suggested that now he was not tired or drunk he might reconsider pouncing.

'Were you really? Goodness, I would never have guessed.'

'You thought I look like that stone-cold sober and after a good night's sleep, a bath and a shave? I am wounded, Caroline.'

'No, you are not, you are teasing me. And, yes, I do understand that I am asking you to shoulder a significant responsibility, even if it makes little actual work for you personally and involves no financial loss. How can I recompense you?'

The amusement faded out of the deep-brown eyes and they became harder than she could ever have imagined. 'I already hold one too many of your IOUs, Caroline. I will undertake this for you because you asked and because you are doing it for your brother, not because you have got yourself into this ridiculous mess.'

The smile edged back, curving the corners of his mouth, but not warming his eyes as he moved to stand beside the *chaise*. 'I have spent my youth and my adult life being disgraceful. A gambler, a hedonist. Being responsible is a bore. And yet now I find myself having to be the sensible one. This summer I have been attempting to talk a close friend out of a totally unsuitable marriage and now I am resisting the urge to take you up on your reckless offer. I do not know what is coming over me. Old age, possibly.'

Old age? Nonsense. Surely he cannot be above twenty-eight or nine? 'You still have my promise.' Somehow their fingers met, brushed, then hers curled into his. Not quite a hand-clasp, not quite a caress. She looked up and met Gabriel's unreadable gaze as his fingers tightened. 'And Papa tells me he has given Lord Woodruffe permission to court me.'

'Edgar Parfit?' Her hand was her own again and Gabriel was three angry strides away. 'That per— Is your father insane?'

She had often wondered what would be the verdict on her father's behaviour if he had been simply plain Mr Henry Holm, a shoemaker, perhaps. What in an earl was eccentricity would, surely, be treated rather differently in other circumstances. The obsessions, the mood swings, the recklessness and the utter disregard for other people were not normal, she knew. But to say the words was a step too far.

'No one has ever suggested my father is not legally competent,' she said carefully. 'Many in society would say Lord Woodruffe is an eligible match…'

'Well, quite obviously you cannot marry him. Besides his unpleasant preferences, he is probably diseased—'

What does he mean, diseased? Horrible suspicions presented themselves and she pushed them away, knowing they would come back to haunt her dreams. The atmosphere of closeness, of something trembling on the edge of desire, vanished in the cold chill of reality.

'What do you mean, *preferences*?'

He shook his head.

'Tell me! Preserving my innocence until I am actually married to the man is not going to help.'

'Some men enjoy pain as part of sex. Some want to receive it, be beaten.' His face tightened as though at some unpleasant memory. 'Others enjoy inflicting it. Woodruffe has a reputation for the latter.'

'Oh.' She felt sick as she recalled Miranda, Woodruffe's first wife. The bruises because she was *so careless*. The days when she did not leave her room because her health was *fragile*. Bullying her into riding despite her fear of horses had been the least of it.

But what could she do? 'Lord Edenbridge, listen to me. Your friend who is contemplating an unsuitable marriage is, I assume, male. He can choose. He is independent, free. I cannot choose and I am not free. Not legally, not financially and not emotionally. I have a family and I promised Mama I would somehow look after them.' *My brothers at least. Heavens knows if anything can be done for Papa.* She found she was on her feet. 'I will send back the deeds and I am truly grateful for your help. Please will you open the door now?'

'Caroline, this is the year 1820. Your father cannot force you to the altar.' Gabriel stood, unlocked the door, but kept his hand on the handle.

'Not physically, no,' she agreed, even as she wondered what bullying and bread and water might reduce her to if she defied Papa. Somehow she was going to have to per-

suade him because the alternatives, marriage to Woodruffe or fleeing her home and leaving Anthony, were too
horrible to contemplate.

She reached the door handle and he caught her fingers
in his, pulled her close until her skirts brushed his legs and
she could smell him—clean, warm man, starched linen,
brandy, a careless splash of some citrus scent, that hint of
musk again.

'Infuriating, stubborn woman. I do not know whether
to shake you or kiss you,' he said, his tone suggesting that
neither was very desirable.

'Kiss me then, for courage,' she said, seized with recklessness and something that must be desire: a hot, shaky
feeling, a low, intimate ache, a light-headed urge to toss
common sense out of the window. No other attractive man
was ever going to kiss her, it seemed. She must seize the
opportunity while she had it.

Gabriel lifted one hand, cupped her jaw, stroked his
thumb across her lips and the breath was sucked out of her
lungs. 'Have you ever been kissed before?'

She shook her head and he bent to touch his lips to hers,
caught her around the waist with his free hand and pulled
her, unresisting, against him. His mouth was warm, mo-
bile, firm. He pressed a little, shifted position, his hand
came up from her cheek to cradle her head and he made
a sound of satisfaction when he had her as he wanted.
Then she felt his tongue and the heat of his open mouth
and opened her own in response as he slid in, exploring
and stroking.

It was incredible and strange. It should be disgusting
and wet, but she found the taste of him exciting, the heat
inflammatory. She sensed his restraint, that he was holding back, toying gently with her, and she stepped forward

until their bodies were tight together, wanting more of this strange new intimacy.

His body was hard against her curves and there was the urge to rub against him, as a cat might burrow into a caress. But he was still and perhaps he would not like it if she did that…

Far too soon Gabriel ended the kiss, took his hands from her body, stepped back. 'Enough. Enough for your safety and more than enough for my comfort,' he added mysteriously, as he pulled open the door and looked out. 'Quickly, while there is no one about. Turn down Woodruffe, Caroline. Send me those deeds, then stay away from me.' He almost pushed her out into the corridor. 'Now go while I can still listen to what passes as my conscience.'

Gabriel had kissed her and now he did not want her. *Of course not, no doubt I was clumsy in my inexperience.* So what was that caress for if he did not desire her? There was something that had driven him to kiss her, something that had made that relaxed body tense. *I want him, perhaps he could come to want me? Madness.*

'Well, if you do not want me I shall not burden you any longer, Lord Edenbridge.' She made to sweep past him, annoyed that he could make her feel so much and yet obviously feel nothing himself.

There was a flurry of skirts, the muffled sound of a collision and a feminine voice said, 'I do beg your pardon, sir.'

Gabriel half-turned to confront the speaker and Caroline caught a glimpse of a tall young lady dressed in an exquisite sea-foam-green gown.

'Oh. Lord Edenbridge.' The stranger did not seem overjoyed to see him and he did not even respond to her.

Caroline stepped away, her hand to her mouth, not certain whether she was stifling a sob or trying to hide her face.

'Come back!'

She stopped, looked back.

'Don't be a fool,' Gabriel said. 'You do not have to marry him and you do not have to... Damn it, I've burned the thing.'

He had only been teasing her then, demanding that IOU that day at his home. She had gone through a maelstrom of emotions, through shame and fear and excitement and triumph that she had somehow rescued Springbourne for Anthony in return for that pledge, and all the time Eden-bridge had never intended to take her up on it.

'A promise is a promise,' she said, chin up. 'But if you do not want me—' She shrugged, turned and walked away, gathering the rags of her dignity around her.

Gabriel swore silently, then turned to confront the other female bedevilling his life, the widowed Mrs Tamsyn Per-owne, who was tying his friend Cris de Feaux, Marquess of Avenmore, in knots.

'What in Hades are you doing here?' he demanded 'Does Cris know?'

'Certainly not. I do not need Lord Avenmore's permission to visit a relative.' The wretched female looked down her sun-browned nose at him.

'Come with me.' He took her arm and swept her back into the main reception room. There, thank goodness, were Alex, Viscount Weybourn, and his wife, Tess. They could help him deal with Mrs Perowne.

Goodness knew who or what was going to help him with Lady Caroline because that clumsy kiss had made him realise that he could not cynically despoil an innocent, nor was it fair to tease her. And yet she had somehow got under his skin. *Damn it, she is not my responsibility.* Knighton could never force her to marry Woodruffe if she refused. *Could he?*

* * *

The deeds came back to him three days later with a brief, rather hurried-looking note.

I am about to leave for the country. I doubt very much if I will be able to receive or send any correspondence from there as I have grievously annoyed my father, but I know I can rely on you to look after my brother's interests in the estate.

Thank you, you cannot know how much it means to me to have Anthony's future safeguarded.

So Caroline had refused Lord Woodruffe. That could be the only explanation for her *'grievously'* annoying Knighton. *Good for you, my girl,* Gabriel thought. He pulled paper and pen towards him and began to draft instructions for his man of business and solicitor to set in motion all the things that must be done to manage the estate and preserve the income for the young man.

None of it was very taxing, it merely required logical thought and meticulous attention to detail. His solicitor might well advise setting up a trust to safeguard both parties, but that was straightforward enough. Yet there was something niggling at the back of his mind, some sense that everything was not as it should be. Whatever it was, it was more than the memory of that innocent first kiss he had claimed, which was now wreaking havoc with his sleep. He reached for the brandy.

He had still been brooding when he fell asleep that night and he woke with a crashing headache and a feeling of unease. Corbridge, his much-tried valet, came in on silent feet and left a glass with something sinister and brown beside the bed, then wisely left without speaking.

Gabriel hauled himself up in bed, swigged back the potion without letting himself smell it, fought with his stomach for a moment, then lay back with a groan. His life was changing. Two of his closest friends were married now, Cris soon would be. Where there had been four, now there would be seven. He liked Tess and Kate. He would probably like Tamsyn when he got to know her. But the change to that close foursome only made his dissatisfaction with life worse.

He had been aware of being unsettled for months. He was bored with his life, no longer content with an existence in which winning was all that counted. Jaded, that was the word. He had a title, lands, money far beyond his needs or wants. What was he doing it for? Damn it, he had toyed with the idea of ruining a respectable young lady just for the novelty. He didn't much like the man who could do that. Perhaps it was time to change. But if he didn't spend his time gambling, socialising, drinking, what was the point to his life?

His three friends had been closer than his family, closer than he had ever dared allow his brothers to be. Cris, Alex and Grant had come into his life when he had been at his most desperate and vulnerable, at a time when they all needed the help that only others who had been wounded could understand. They knew his secrets, all but one of them—he could not burden them with the lies he had told the day his father died. That burden was his to carry, ever since he had made a promise to his mother, a woman so desperately unhappy she had taken her own life.

If he loved anyone, it was his friends and he knew they returned the sentiment, even if they would have died rather than admit it. From the hell that had been his childhood he had met them and learned that friendship gave what family never could, an equal give and take.

'Good morning, my lord.' Corbridge came in with hot water. Obviously he judged Gabriel to be back amongst the living,

'Is it?' Gabriel got out of bed and strode, naked, into the dressing room. 'What's the point of it all, Corbridge? Life, I mean, because I'm beginning to wonder.'

'My lord…is anything amiss?'

Gabriel was aware of the valet laying one hand protectively over the razors and, despite himself, grinned. 'It is all right, I'm not about to cut my throat, blow my brains out or otherwise put a period to my existence. I am simply wondering what I am doing with my life.'

'My lord, you are an *earl*,' Corbridge said repressively.

'That is a title, not a job description.' Although perhaps it was.

Manage the estates, look after the dependents, take my seat in the House, marry well, have heirs, teach the next generation to do it all over again… Focus on the title and not myself. Give up taking lovers? Step back and pray I can manage not to make a disaster of heading a family? But who would listen to my *prayers?*

He grimaced at his reflection and reached for the soap and sponge. He did everything he needed to do to keep the wheels of the earldom turning, but he did it at a mental distance that felt as though he had preserved it in ice. When the frost melted would he find something fresh and new to engage with or find only the rotted carcase of the past?

A disgusting image. He shook off the ghoulish thought with an effort. 'I'm getting old, Corbridge.' Is that why it was so hard to accept how his life was changing?

'My lord, you are not even in your prime yet, if I may be so bold.' The valet began to work up a lather with the shaving soap.

Gabriel grunted and scrubbed his toothbrush into the

powder. What he needed was a purpose and he supposed the obvious one was his earldom and, heaven help him, his brothers, although they would probably think he'd got a brain fever if he suddenly turned up showing a keen interest in their lives and welfare. It would certainly unnerve them thoroughly.

'I'm at home until this afternoon, then I'll be riding. I may as well put on buckskins and boots now.' There was business to finish, then he'd blow away the cobwebs with a good gallop and try to work out how to finally come to grips with his inheritance, all of it, on his own terms. His identity had been that of the care-for-nothing rakehell for so long that he wasn't certain he knew who the man underneath that mask was.

It was not until the evening that he sat down and began to sort through the jottings he had made on young Mr Holm's inheritance. He picked up Caroline's message again, feeling the same prickle of unease as he had experienced the day before. Something was not right with it. He rummaged in the papers until he found her first note and laid them side by side. Same paper, same ink, but while the first was neat and elegantly written, the writing in the second was uneven, straggling, untidy. It looked as though it had been produced in haste and by someone who was either not themselves or who found it difficult to hold the pen. One corner of the page was distorted and he picked it up to study it more closely. A water splash. Or one fallen tear…

I have grievously annoyed my father. Father, not Papa as she had always referred to him before. Something was wrong, very wrong. He had encouraged her to defy Knighton over the marriage and now she was exiled to the country, perhaps mistreated in some way, until she gave in. In his mind he heard the crack of the riding whip, felt the shock of the pain. He had withstood it, pride and sheer bloody-mindedness had seen to that. But a woman…

Surely Knighton wouldn't beat his daughter? Yet he wanted her to marry Woodruffe. Surely he realised what the man was? Or perhaps he really was so obsessional that he could ignore the man's reputation?

Just because his own father had been utterly ruthless in imposing his will did not mean that Caroline's father was. Gabriel pushed away the old nightmares, studied the slip of paper for a long moment, then folded it and put it in his breast pocket. He was imagining things were worse than they were, surely. Even so, he could not rest easy. The paperwork for her brother's estate was soon completed and he bundled it up to go to his lawyer, then got to his feet. He had a commitment to help Cris and that might take a day or so, but then he was going to find Lady Caroline Holm and undo whatever damage he had caused.

He imagined his friends' expressions if they knew he was contemplating involving himself in some chit's family dramas. But Caroline was not *some chit*, she was intelligent, courageous and determined, and he felt guilty about the way he had teased her, he realised. That was novel enough to provoke him into action. What that action might be he had no idea, but at least he was not feeling jaded any longer.

Chapter Four

Hertfordshire—August 1st

August was usually a month Caroline enjoyed, especially if she was in the country. Now Knighton Park was a hot, stuffy prison and the sunlit gardens and park outside were a bright, tantalising reminder of just how trapped she was.

It was not my fault, she told herself for perhaps the hundredth time. It was not her lack of duty, not her wilfulness, not her foolish whims—all the faults her father had thrown at her. *It is his. His tyranny, his temper. His lack of love.*

It had started mildly enough. Her father announced that they were moving to Knighton Park and, recklessly, she had chosen to make a stand, to announce that she would not marry Woodruffe, or any of the middle-aged suitors he had considered for her.

The bruises on her right cheek had finally vanished. She studied her reflection in the mirror and clenched her teeth. There was some soreness and a molar was still rather loose, but she thought if she was careful it would grow firm again. The marks on her arms had almost faded, too. She could write long letters to Anthony without discomfort. His future, at least, was safe now.

The image of her face faded and the scene she kept trying to forget swam up in its place.

'You will do as you are told, you stupid girl!'

'I am not stupid. I am not a girl. I am of age and I will not be bartered to some man for whom I have nothing but contempt for the sake of your obsessions.' Caroline had no idea what kept her voice so steady, what kept her standing there as his face darkened with rage.

Her father was a believer in corporal punishment for his children, although Lucas, the favoured elder son, always seemed to escape with only the lightest of canings. As a girl, her governess had been instructed to strike her once or twice on the palm with a ruler for laziness or inattention, or whenever her father deemed her deserving of punishment, which was often. But she had never been hit by him.

Her father had grabbed her arm, held her as she'd pulled back against his grip, her righteous defiance turned in a second to stomach-churning nausea.

'You will obey me.' He'd jerked again as she fought against the pain in her arm. It felt as though the bones were grinding together.

'No,' she'd managed. 'Woodruffe is—' But she didn't have the words for what Gabriel had told her. And then her father had hit her across the face, backhanded, knocking her to the ground to land in a painful sprawl against a wooden chair. She had no clear memory of being taken upstairs, only of coming to herself to find her maid bathing her face. There was a bandage on her arm.

Now, with the bruises gone, she had permission to leave her rooms, go downstairs, allow herself to be seen, provided she maintained the fiction of a virulent sore throat that had laid her up for almost two weeks. She sat down in the window seat and searched for some courage. There were tales of how prisoners were afraid to leave their cells and the security of a familiar confined space and now she could understand how they felt. But she was desperate to get out, away from the tedium and anxiety, away from the circling thoughts and desires for Gabriel Stone.

She should be ashamed of herself for having carnal thoughts about a man, because that was what they were. She couldn't deceive herself that these were romantic daydreams about love and marriage and family. This man was never going to be domesticated and when she imagined herself with him what she saw was a tangle of naked limbs, what she felt was the heat of his body and the pressure of his lips. Beyond that she was too inexperienced to imagine detail. All she knew was that this was shocking, sinful and impossible, because when she had offered herself to him on a plate even this hardened rake had not wanted her.

She had to stop thinking about him. *I am the only person I can rely on, no one is going to help me if I do not help myself.* And she could achieve nothing shut up inside, Caroline knew that. Her old world of certainties and duty and acceptance of the limitations of a lady's powers lay in ruins. She would not submit to marrying Woodruffe and that meant she must act.

She had even thought through a strategy over the past few days: go downstairs and assess Pa… *Father's* temper and intentions. If he had no intention of yielding, then gather money, jewels, information and escape. Somehow. There would be no help from Lucas, for although he had been shocked by their father's violent outburst, he still shared his opinion that Caroline should marry as he directed.

But Anthony was a constant worry. What if he did something to arouse such violence in his father? And if she left home it was going to be horribly difficult to meet with him. *One thing at a time*, she told herself. *If I am mar-*

*ried to that man I would be equally helpless to look after
Anthony. This way I can write, I could see him when he is
at school perhaps.*

She dressed with care and went downstairs. Her father
and Lucas were at breakfast, the table littered with news
sheets and the scattered pages of opened letters. Lucas
stood up as she came in, her father merely grunted and
went back to his reading.

Caroline found a soft roll and some scrambled eggs and
took her place at the table and began to eat, favouring the
left side of her jaw. Her father shot her a penetrating look,
nodded, presumably with approval at her unbruised appearance, and turned to Lucas.

'The hermit has had his first night in the folly now. I'll
not disturb him for a few days, let him settle in.'

She had not intended joining in the conversation, but
this was startling enough to make her forget that. 'You
have found a hermit, Father?'

He did not appear to notice that she had stopped calling
him *Papa*. Somehow the affectionate diminutive was impossible to use for a man who had raised his hand to her.

'I put it about at my clubs that I was looking for one
and he turned up, don't know how he heard about it, although the fellow is a gentleman of sorts. He seems ideal.
Educated fellow, for all that he looks as though he hasn't
had a haircut or a shave for six months. Says he's a poet
or some such nonsense. Wants to write in peace and quiet.
Told him he can do what he pleases as long as he wears
the costume and looks the part. I'll not send warning that
we'll be about when we do go, so I'll catch him unawares,
see how he performs.'

'Are you going to the Home Farm this morning, Father?'
Lucas looked up from his correspondence.

'Yes.' The earl lifted a bundle of papers. 'These are the

plans for the new Model Farm that Hardwick sent over from Wimpole Hall in Cambridgeshire. Their new buildings are excellent, we'll see how they'd do for our site.'

They left together soon afterwards. Caroline looked out across the sweep of the South Lawn, over the invisible line of the ha-ha to the shoulder of Trinity Hill. Just visible above it was the tower of an apparently ancient chapel which had, in reality, only just been completed.

She finished her cup of tea and pushed back her chair without waiting for the footman to help her. She needed exercise and fresh air and the *faux* hermitage was one place where her father was not this morning. An unkempt poetry-writing hermit might not tempt her to linger long, but at least he would give her walk a destination.

The slope of Trinity Hill was gentle, but for someone who had been shut up inside with no exercise for days it was enough to bring a glow of perspiration to her face and an ache to her legs. Caroline reached the point where she could look down on the lake and on the hermitage, apparently deserted in its shady grove of trees.

She was not at all certain she wanted to converse with a professional hermit, for he must be a strange creature, but curiosity drew her down the slope to the clearing. The door to the chapel stood open and in front, on the other side of the path, a rough trestle table had been created by balancing a slab of wood on two tree stumps. A log was set in front of it as a seat and the table was laid with a pitcher, a pewter plate and a horn beaker, the remains of the hermit's breakfast, she supposed. As she watched, a robin flew down and pecked hopefully around in pursuit of crumbs.

Treading with care, Caroline approached the chapel and glanced at the open door. No movement within, but she did not feel she had the right to pry by entering.

Then the sound of a twig snapping brought her round to face the path up from the little lake, the robin flew away in whir of wings and a tall robed figure walked into the clearing.

The man stopped when he saw her and stared, just as she was doing, she supposed. What did one say to a recluse, even an ornamental one? He was certainly not her idea of a hermit, which was a white-bearded, stooped figure supported by a staff. This man was big, with a mass of thick black curling hair that fell across his brow and shadowed his eyes and a beard that, although not long, covered his lower face completely. It made him look older than he probably was, for he moved like a young, fit man and there was no grey showing in the black hair that brushed the folded-back hood of his brown robe.

His hair was wet, catching the sunlight that filtered through the tree canopy, and droplets of water hung in his beard like improbable diamonds. He must have been bathing in the lake, she realised. In one hand he held a battered leather satchel, perhaps containing soap and a towel.

'Good morning,' Caroline ventured, wondering if a clean hermit was a contradiction in terms.

He inclined his head, but said nothing. Nor did he move any closer.

'Has my father forbidden you to speak? I am Lady Caroline Holm. I hope the kitchen sent you food or do you go down to collect it yourself? You must let us know if there is anything you need.'

His silence was unnerving, but not as unsettling as the feeling of familiarity that was growing as they stood there separated by ten feet of leaf litter and sparse turf. Then, maddeningly, he inclined his head again.

'Which of my questions is that an answer to?' she demanded.

The thicket of beard moved as though he was smiling, but with his eyes in shadow she could not be certain. Of course, if he had been forbidden to speak then it had been quite illogical of her to follow on with more questions.

'Are you required to keep silent?'

The man cleared his throat. 'No, my lady.' He spoke quietly, but the deep voice was quite clear in the still, warm air. It had an attractive lilt to it. 'I have food, I thank you.'

'You are not English, are you? Your accent is unfamiliar.'

'It is a Welsh accent, my lady.'

'Oh.' Then that sense of knowing him was completely illusory. How strange. It must be her need for someone to talk to, to confide in. To plan with, if she could trust them. But all her friends were in London, or away at country houses or at the seaside and she had hardly had a conversation for weeks, except with her maid. 'You are comfortable here?'

In response the hermit gestured to the open door of the chapel. He did not move and when she took a step towards the building he sat down at his makeshift table as though to reassure her that it was safe to enter, that he would not follow.

Inside all pretence of a religious building disappeared. There was a single whitewashed room with a bed made up with coarse sheets, blankets and a worn patchwork quilt. A table and chair stood in the middle of the space and a chipped stone sink was propped up on empty crates that served as makeshift shelves. A wide fireplace with logs stacked beside it was set into what must be the base of the tower, which would disguise the chimney, and a rag rug on the stone floor provided the only touch of decoration or comfort.

Bleak, but weather-tight and warm enough during the

summer. She only hoped her father did not expect the man to stay here in all seasons. There was a small pile of books on the table, some paper and an inkwell and pen. Tools for a poet, she supposed, resisting the temptation to see what he was reading—or writing.

When she left the folly he stood up again and she sensed he was smiling. 'It seems rather comfortless,' she observed. 'Are you certain there is nothing that you need?'

'I am a hermit, my lady. I am supposed to live the simple life.'

'You are *acting* the hermit,' she corrected. 'There is no need for you to endure such a Spartan existence in reality.'

'His lordship requires authenticity and he employs me.' He shrugged. 'When he brings visitors to view the scene nothing must jar.'

He was certainly conscientious. Caroline knew she would have been tempted to smuggle in some comforts if she was in his place. 'What is your name?'

There was a long pause and she wondered if she had disconcerted him. Then he said, 'Petrus.'

'That means Peter, doesn't it? Peter the Hermit. Why does that sound familiar?' Caroline wrestled with the elusive memory. 'Of course—Peter the Hermit, the First Crusade.'

Now she was certain he was taken aback. *Bother that impenetrable beard.* 'You are well read, my lady. It is simply coincidence, not a deliberate choice.'

'I will leave you in peace, Petrus, you will want to get dry...' Caroline could feel herself blushing. She most certainly could not discuss a strange man's washing arrangements. To add to her discomfort her imagination conjured up the vision of that tall, broad-shouldered figure naked in the lake, the water streaming off his chest as he stood up, the thick black hair tossed back from his face.

'Oh!' Before she was aware of moving, of turning to leave before her treacherous mind conjured up any more shocking images, her foot caught in something. She had a split second to realise it was a tree root as she went flying to land in a sprawling, inelegant heap. 'Ouch!'

'What hurts?' Petrus knelt beside her, then caught her by the shoulders as she tried to lever herself up.

'My left wrist.' Caroline managed to sit. 'The leaf mould is soft, but I put out my hand and I... I hurt it a while ago. No, it is all right—'

His fingers were circling her wrist, gentle and firm and all-enveloping. With the other hand he pushed back her sleeve to expose her forearm. There was silence as she went still in his grasp, watching the bent head as he studied the pattern of fading bruises that still encircled her arm. The sprain where her father had jerked her towards him, held her as she fell, was still a little sore.

'Who did that?' Petrus still did not look up and the lilting voice was steady, but she could feel the shock and the anger coursing through him even though she could not see his face.

'It was an accident. I fell and my...someone caught my arm to steady me.'

'No, they did not.' He rebutted her lie quite calmly. 'These are not the marks of someone catching you, but of someone holding you forcibly, as though they intended to hurt you. Who was it? Your brother or your father?'

'Lucas would never—I mean no one wants to hurt me.'

'So it was your father.' He stood and held out his hand so she could take it with her uninjured right.

There did not seem to be any point in arguing with him. Caroline allowed him to pull her to her feet. 'It is none of your business,' she said as she found herself standing with her nose virtually pressed against the rough cloth of his robe.

'And I am merely an employee,' the hermit observed. 'Of course, a husband is permitted by law to beat his wife with a rod no thicker than his thumb and a father may chastise his children. But you are not a child.' His voice became harder, angry.

'No. I am not.' *We are both adults.*

The fingers wrapped around hers were strong and still slightly cool from the lake water. Standing so close, she could smell damp wool from his robe and the sharp tannin scent of crushed bracken and leaf mould and something indefinable that must be the scent of his skin. A little shiver of recognition, as elusive as a breath of wind, stirred her and he let go of her hand and stepped back.

'I am sorry, my lady. It is not my business, as you say. But is there no one to take your side, for you to confide in? Who looks after you?'

'Why, no one! I am twenty-three, Petrus the Hermit, and I have people to look after, not the other way around. Or do you think all women are feeble little things who need keeping in cotton wool?'

'No, I do not. Nor do I think they are fair game for any man who feels he has a right to bully and abuse those who cannot fight back, for whatever reason.' He walked away from her towards the chapel, then stopped and half-turned in the doorway. 'You should go, my lady. You should not be here alone with me.'

The sense of recognition was almost *déjà vu* now. Something about the way he stood there, one hand on the door, the way the broad shoulders filled the frame, the utterly relaxed pose that hinted at an ability to move instantly if the need arose... Caroline gave herself a brisk mental shake. She had never met a bearded Welshman before, her mind was playing tricks on her. The only tall, black-haired, broad-shouldered man she knew was miles away in London, probably nursing a hangover or totting up his gambling winnings. Or just getting up from the bed of some sophisticated and beautiful woman.

Petrus lifted his head, no longer relaxed. 'Someone is coming. Two horses.'

Without a word Caroline turned and plunged down the narrow path that led through the bushes to the lake. It must be her father and Lucas, but she would be safe down here, the path was too steep and narrow for riders to follow.

She reached the shelter of an ancient oak tree and moved behind the massive trunk, round to where honeysuckle had created a tangled screen. Looking up, she could see the area in front of the chapel door where Petrus stood waiting.

The horses moved into the space, large hunters, ridden with no thought that they might be intimidating to a man on foot. Petrus stood his ground, then bowed, his hands inside the wide sleeves of his habit, the gesture somehow utterly lacking in servility and with a hint of the exotic about it.

'You have made yourself at home, I see.' Her father's voice carried clearly. 'What are you up to?'

'Eating my breakfast, bathing in the lake, contemplating a rhyme for *bruise*, my lord.' Petrus's voice was respectful and yet lilting through it was a thread of laughter, of mockery that had a dangerous edge to it.

Bruise. He had been angry when he saw her arm, angry when he realised who had inflicted the fading brownish-purple fingermarks that circled it like a malevolent bracelet. She should have been wary, on her guard approaching a complete stranger like that, and yet she had felt safe, even when he had touched her, even when the savage note had marred the liquid music of his accent.

Her father appeared to have noticed nothing amiss with the hermit's tone, but then he would never believe that an employee would dare to mock him, let alone threaten him. What was the status of a professional hermit anyway? Was he a servant or did he have a professional standing akin to an artist or architect called in to provide a service? she wondered, smiling a little at her own whimsy.

'Very good, carry on as you are.' No, her father had heard nothing amiss and his self-centred imagination had not picked up on the oddity of Petrus's remark about bruises. 'I have house guests arriving in three days' time. I will send word of when I want you to be here, but the first evening I think you should be seen at a distance, wandering across the hillside. It will intrigue the company before dinner, make a topic for conversation. You will receive detailed instructions.'

House guests? Who? And why hasn't Father told me? Now she had to get back to the house without being seen and wait until he deigned to inform her. She could hardly ask straight out or she would betray where she had been. When she looked back her father and Lucas had ridden on and the little clearing was empty.

It would be quickest to return to the chapel, cut down through the slope above the kitchen gardens and enter the house from there. She would then appear to have been inspecting the vegetable and flower crops if anyone noticed her slightly muddied boots.

Caroline crossed the clearing silently. The chapel door was still open and she could hear the hermit moving about inside. As she tiptoed past he spoke, one loud, angry swear word that made her gasp. Then something hit the door and fell to the ground. For an appalled moment she thought the brown huddle was an animal, then a fold flopped over and she saw it was his robe.

Which meant the chapel contained one angry, damp, naked hermit. She picked up her skirts and fled.

Chapter Five

'Woodruffe will be visiting in three days,' her father announced at dinner. 'Thought I would make a house party of it so Calderbeck's coming and Turnbull—they are sound on landscape design—and Lucas has invited some friends.'

'Yes, Father.' Caroline's heart sank. She had always thought it an exaggerated phrase, but it perfectly described the unpleasant lurch in her chest at the thought of her unwelcome suitor's presence in the house. 'Who have you invited, Lucas?'

'Frampton, the Willings brothers and Perry Ratcliff.' Lucas hardly looked up from his attempts to carve a tough chicken.

'Seven, then. An all-male party?' She tried to sound interested and positive.

'Yes.' Her father helped himself from the dish of buttered peas.

'I had best ask Aunt Gertrude to stay.' Caroline chased a sliver of beef around her plate. For once the idea of her aunt's fierce chaperonage was welcome.

'I don't want my sister's Friday face around the place for a week. What do you need a chaperon for when you're in your own home with your father and brother? I've no time for this missish nonsense.'

I need it for protection with Edgar Parfit prowling the corridors at night and a houseful of men I hardly know, she thought, but held her tongue.

'You complain that you don't know Woodruffe well enough to wed him, so this will give you plenty of opportunity. I'll have old Humbersleigh over to draw up the settlements while he's here and tell that useless parson to sort out the licence.'

'But, Father, what about my bride clothes?' Best to pretend that she had given in.

That brought his head up and his attention full on her. Caroline put up her chin and fought the instinct to cringe back in her chair.

'You've spent weeks in London doing nothing but shop. If you don't have enough gowns now you can buy them when you're wed and Woodruffe can pay for them. Hah!' Obviously pleased with the thought of fobbing off expense on her prospective son-in-law, her father returned to his roast.

Protesting to him was not going to work, not with two hundred acres of Woodruffe's land almost within his grasp. Caroline reached for the potatoes and bit into one with sudden determination. She would have to give Woodruffe a distaste for her, make him realise she would not stand to be dominated by him. Being missish and meek had not helped his first wife, he had simply bullied and beaten poor Miranda into submission. No, she would have to be bold and brassy, stand up to him, then he would think her too much trouble to wed. And if that failed, then her desperate plan to flee was the only alternative.

She bit down on her sore tooth without thinking and winced, reminded of what her father's temper could do if he discovered her scheming. But first she had to worry about preparing for a house party of seven with only two days to do it in.

'That's a fine prospect, Knighton, I must say.' Lord Calderbeck shaded his eyes as he looked out from the terrace across the garden to the slopes of Trinity Hill. 'I like what you've done with that tower—it has an air of age and mystery about it, makes a man want to take a walk across the park and explore.'

'That's my latest project.' The earl pulled his pocket watch out of his waistcoat and peered at the time. The shadows were lengthening as the summer evening drew in, but the sun still illuminated the far hillside. Caroline scanned the treeline, realising what her father was waiting for. She had been so busy over the past two days that she had hardly spared the hermit a thought. Certainly, all that afternoon, preoccupied as she had been with greeting the guests and avoiding Lord Woodruffe, she had quite forgotten him.

'Who the devil is that?' young Marcus Frampton demanded, pointing.

'It looks like a monk!' Mr Turnbull, an author of lurid Gothic tales, clapped his hands in delight. 'That's wonderful, Knighton, you have found yourself a monk.'

'A hermit, actually. The building you can glimpse is a chapel and there he lives in solitude.' Her father was beaming now, more than satisfied with the effect of his creation on his friends.

Caroline picked up the telescope that was lying on the bench and trained it on the distant figure. Petrus was walking slowly, using a long staff to good effect, for it showed the fall of his full sleeves. As she sharpened the focus he turned to face the house and flung his arms wide in a gesture that might have been a blessing. Or perhaps a curse.

'Do let me help you, Lady Caroline. That is too heavy for dainty female hands.' A large body pressed against her and one hand came around her waist as the other clasped her fingers on to the telescope, pressing hard so the metal ridges bit into her skin.

'Oh!' Caroline gave an exaggerated start of alarm and stepped back. It had the unfortunate effect of pressing her closer into Lord Woodruffe's belly, but it also brought the narrow heel of her evening slipper down hard on his toes. He staggered, pulling her with him, and she lifted her other foot clear off the ground so her entire weight was on the one heel. When he let go of her hand she allowed her arm to fall so that the end of the telescope swung back in an arc to hit him squarely in the falls of his breeches.

The sound Woodruffe made was gratifyingly like a pig seeing the approach of the butcher. He bent double, his hands clutching his groin as the other men turned to see what all the noise was about.

'Oh, Lord Woodruffe, I am so sorry, but you pulled me quite off balance. Are you badly hurt? Perhaps our housekeeper has a salve you could rub in.'

Seeing where Woodruffe was clutching himself the two Willings brothers snorted with laughter. Even Lucas was struggling to suppress a grin. Caroline fluttered about, full of innocent concern, and her father glowered at the interruption to his discussion about stone quarries with Lord Calderbeck. 'What the devil?'

'I trod on Lord Woodruffe's toes, Father. I am so sorry.'

'Then why in blazes is he clutching his…er…?' The fact that he was addressing his daughter appeared to dawn on the earl and he stopped mid-sentence. 'Brace up, man, and stop whimpering!'

Woodruffe straightened, shot Caroline a malevolent look that made her shudder and limped back into the house.

It was a good start. Now she had to balance her behaviour on the knife edge between giving Woodruffe a disgust of her and betraying what she was doing.

The telescope had rolled across the terrace and she went to pick it up. It was a good instrument and there was a dent in its brass casing now. Caroline raised it to her eye to check that the lenses were not damaged, scanning round as she fiddled with the focus screw. Yes, it was working perfectly, thank goodness.

The trees on the far hill came into sharp definition and there, strolling back to his chapel, was the hermit. *He probably thinks no one is looking at him now he's finished his performance,* she thought with a smile as the tall figure turned and walked up towards the path into the trees. Again that sense of recognition swept over her and this time, without the beard and the accent to distract her, she placed him.

Lord Edenbridge. The image swooped and blurred as her hands shook. *Gabriel Stone. Petrus, the Latin for stone or rock. How could I not have realised?*

'I say, do take care, Lady Caroline, you almost dropped the telescope again.' Mr Turnbull took it from her lax grip.

'Thank you, Mr Turnbull. So foolish of me, but staring through it made me suddenly light-headed.'

Somehow she chattered on, made conversation as the party drifted back into the drawing room. *Gabriel Stone. Here. Why?* It had to be something to do with her. He had no reason to be taking employment of any kind, let alone something as peculiar and uncomfortable as fulfilling an eccentric man's expensive fantasies about landscape features. But what did he want?

'Dinner is served, my lord,' their butler announced, making her jump.

Caroline got a grip on herself. Dangerous peers of the realm might be lurking in the shrubbery—literally and mysteriously—but she had a dinner party to deal with. 'We are a most unbalanced group, are we not?' she said with an attempt at a gay laugh. 'Lord Calderbeck, may I claim your arm? The rest of you gentlemen must escort yourselves in, I fear.'

She had set out the place cards with strict attention to precedence. Marcus Fawcett, Viscount Frampton, sat on her left hand as she occupied the hostess's chair at the foot of the table with Lord Calderbeck on her other side. Woodruffe, a baron, was left watching her from his position midway down the table. She turned and began to flirt lightly with the viscount. The stare turned to a glare and young Lord Frampton sat up straighter, his expression faintly smug.

Just as long as I do not have to deal with him as well! Caroline accepted a slice of beef with a smile and asked the viscount about his horses. From experience, he could be relied upon to bore on for hours once started on that theme, which had the dual benefits of distracting his mind from flirtation and also allowing her time to think about a certain earl.

Why on earth hadn't she recognised Gabriel immediately? That beard and the curling mane of hair, she supposed. And the fact that when they had met before she had been too embarrassed to study his face closely. It was that rangy body with its easy movement that had always attracted her and that was what she had recognised through the telescope.

'Spavined? How distressing,' she responded automatically to Frampton's ramblings about one of his matched bays, then closed her ears to an account of just what the farrier had advised doing about it and what his head groom had thought.

But what was Gabriel Stone doing here with his Welsh accent and his poetry? She would wager her entire allowance for a year that the man had never so much as rhymed a couplet in his life. Surely he hadn't come with a view to collecting on her shocking IOU after all? No marriage had been announced, no betrothal announced, so the terms of the bargain were not met in any case.

They had parted with angry words, on her part at least, but if Gabriel had wanted to make his peace with her he was going to preposterous extremes to do so. Besides, he had not revealed his identity when they met at the hermitage and he had made no attempt to contact her since.

'And what do you think of your father's hermit, eh, Lady Caroline?' Lord Calderbeck's voice was loud enough to draw the attention of all the diners.

'I…I haven't…I mean I don't…' She was blushing, she knew she was. And stammering and generally behaving in a most suspicious manner. 'I have not had the opportunity to view the man at close quarters,' she managed. 'I have been rather occupied. But I consider the impression he creates from a distance to be most picturesque. My father has such a good eye for a landscape effect.'

That at least earned her an approving look from the far end of the table. Perhaps her father's violent anger with her had been forgotten for now, although she could not delude herself that the truce would hold once she defied him again over Lord Woodruffe. And she would defy him, she was even more certain of that now as she watched her suitor eating his way through the mound of food on his plate without the slightest sign of appreciation or discrimination. His eyes, when they met hers, held promises of retribution that banished the image of a portly, middle-aged buffoon, replacing them with threats of domination and pain.

Gabriel dumped the bucket he had carried down to the stream to deal with his after-dinner washing up and closed the door of his cell. It was cool now that the sun was down and the mossy grove seemed to stay damp however high the daytime temperature. He had performed his first charade for his employer, seen the glint as the sinking sun had caught the lens of at least one telescope, and there was small risk the house party guests would leave after dinner to inspect him. It was safe to relax.

The fire was still alight after his culinary efforts earlier and he tossed on some wood, more for the cheerful flicker of light than for the warmth. For a man who had never had to so much as make himself a cup of tea before he was quite pleased with his cookery, even if all he was doing was converting the food sent over from the big house kitchens. He had heated soup without scalding it, he had chopped up what he assumed were the leftovers from yesterday's roast along with onions and a carrot, fried the result with beef dripping and consumed the savoury mess along with a hunk of bread that was only slightly stale, washed down with a mug of the thin ale that had been provided in a firkin.

Not what he was used to, he thought as he stretched out his legs in front of the fire, but he was getting accustomed to it and the constant fresh air was sharpening his appetite, even for his own cooking. It was certainly easier to adapt to the food than it was to the long skirts of his robe. How the devil did women cope with the encumbrance? To say nothing of the fact that it was decidedly draughty around the nether regions.

The chilling effect of cold air had probably been an advantage to monks fighting the temptations of the flesh in their quest for celibacy. Not that cold draughts had been necessary the other day when he had found himself with Lady Caroline in his arms. It had been anger that had heated his blood then, fury that anyone could manhandle a woman, let alone her own father.

He had expected to discover that she had been bullied, but not that she was suffering actual physical harm. Bullying he had expected to be able to deal with by giving her moral support and by finding something on Woodruffe that would persuade the man to drop his pretensions to Caroline's hand. His dubious sexual proclivities were well enough known for that to be ineffectual as a pressure point—Gabriel must find something else. It might amount to blackmail, but he had no qualms about that in this case. And probably Woodruffe would prefer it to facing him down the barrel of one of Manton's duelling pistols, which was Gabriel's fall-back plan. It wouldn't be difficult to work up some kind of quarrel with a man as objectionable as Edgar Parfit.

But if Caroline was being mistreated then the whole business became more serious, for if her father blamed her for Woodruffe's withdrawal then she could suffer more than bruised wrists.

Gabriel lifted the bottle of brandy from behind the log pile, poured himself two fingers into a horn beaker and sipped while the heat of the spirits settled the faint nausea that came with some ruthless self-examination. He had shaken his head over Caroline's lack of foresight beyond her aim of retrieving her brother's estate, now he wondered if he had been equally thoughtless.

He had landed himself in this situation on a sudden impulse when Alex Tempest had reported overhearing Knighton at White's talking about his advertisement in

The Times. He had been brooding on what to do about his unease over Caroline's welfare and Alex's gossip seemed like the answer on a plate, so he'd snatched at it.

Pretend to be a hermit—there would hardly be competition for the post—combine an amusing small adventure with the opportunity to soothe his nagging conscience over Caroline, get himself out of his London rut for a while. It had all seemed like the perfect answer.

Perhaps if things had not fallen into place so easily he might have reconsidered the masquerade and found some other way of discovering how Caroline was faring. But the necessary delay while his 'agent', otherwise known as Corbridge his valet, had negotiated on his behalf, and he ostensibly travelled from Wales, had given him time to grow an impressive beard and for his untrimmed hair to develop an unfashionable shagginess. He had to shave twice a day to maintain an acceptable appearance for a gentleman and the resulting thicket of neglected growth was enough, he was confident, to hide his identity from a self-obsessed man who had only seen him closely in a poorly lit gaming hell.

The Welsh accent that he had learned to mimic when he had stayed with his Great-Aunt Gwendoline near Caernarvon as a boy had come back easily. Alex had been so amused and impressed by his disguise that they had even tried the imposture out on Alex's wife, Tess, although with Gabriel in ordinary clothes and not his monkish robe. Lady Weybourn had carried on almost five minutes of polite social chit-chat in Green Park with Mr Petrus Owen, the gentleman from Wales, before her husband's poorly suppressed laughter had made her suspicious.

It was a shock to find Caroline at the chapel when he'd returned from his morning dip in the lake and he'd been surprised, too, that she had failed to recognise him. With the painful discipline of self-examination that he had imposed on himself recently Gabriel pondered whether his reaction to that lack of recognition was hurt pride. They had, after all, discussed becoming lovers—one would expect a woman under the circumstances to have looked closely at the man she was proposing such a bargain with.

'Coxcomb,' he muttered to himself. Caroline had been in turn embarrassed, mortified, shy, angry and afraid during both of their encounters. It would have been a miracle if she had recognised him in the street, let alone hiding behind all those whiskers. *Which cover all my best features*, Gabriel thought with a grimace as he tugged at the offending growth.

He needed to talk to her again, reveal his true identity and discover the truth about her situation. That might be easier said than done, because catching her alone so that any startled reaction was not observed was not going to be easy. He found that it was not just the fire and the brandy that was warming him. The thought of Caroline Holm was…stimulating. *In much the same way as a hair shirt, no doubt,* Gabriel told himself as he reached for a book and moved the candles closer. She was likely to cause him nothing but trouble, anxiety and hard work, all things that he normally avoided like the plague.

He had become unused to worrying about anyone else's welfare. His employees were easy enough—you paid them properly, made your expectations clear and dealt fairly— and mistresses were much the same. His brothers more or less looked after themselves now they were adults and, except for the occasional request for money, seemed quite happy with the state of affairs.

But Caroline was alone and courageous. She had been hurt, was probably still at risk, and he could no more stand by and see a woman injured than he could fly. And she had blue eyes like speedwell in sunlight and soft, soft skin under his fingers. That thought was almost worse for his peace of mind than fighting old nightmares, but he could not walk away and leave her, not if he wanted to live with his conscience afterwards. Gabriel removed a bookmark and applied himself to an analysis of the post-war European political situation.

Chapter Six

Gabriel, staying firmly in the role of Petrus Owen, poet and hermit, had bathed, broken his fast and tidied his humble residence. He was contemplating a visit to the kitchen door of Knighton Park in the hope of discovering if the mistress of the house came down to give her orders to Cook or sent for her, when the sound of approaching riders brought him to the threshold of the chapel.

He picked up the large book that he had selected, thinking it looked like an appropriate text for a hermit to be studying, shut the door on the domestic interior and took up a position looking out over the wooded dell down to the lake.

The horses filled the clearing behind him, hooves tramping on the leaf mould, bits jingling, breathing heavy after what must have been a gallop up the long slope on the other side of the crest. There were at least half a dozen of them, perhaps more, but the riders fell silent as they saw him and he could not be certain.

Gabriel waited, counting up to twenty in his head in Welsh to make certain his accent was firmly in place. The sound of movement subsided, leaving only the occasional snort and stamped hoof.

When he turned he made the movement slow, scanned the clearing until he saw Lord Knighton, then bowed, straightened and waited, his gaze on his employer's face. The man was pleased, he could see that. Pleased to find his hermit in the right place, pleased with his bit of theatre and pleased, too, by the admiring murmurs from his guests.

There were nine mounted men facing him. Seven guests in addition to Knighton and his son and, on the edge of the group, Caroline on a neat bay hack, her habit a deeper shade of the blue of her eyes, a pert low-crowned hat on her head. He let his gaze pass over her, frustrated by the veil that hid her expression from him.

'So this is your hermit, eh, Knighton!' Woodruffe, of course, was always ready to state the obvious, probably because it saved thinking. 'What are you doing, fellow?'

Gabriel turned by a few degrees, met Woodruffe's stare and bowed again. 'Meditating.' He let the silence hang heavy and saw the two youngest men, the Willings brothers, if he was not mistaken, shift uneasily in their saddles. He had spoken as though to an equal and they were uncertain, he guessed, how to react to that. 'I was pondering upon the transience of glory and the fall of pride.'

Woodruffe nodded, as though he understood some great truth. 'Good show.'

Gabriel managed not to roll his eyes and waited.

'You are a poet?' That was Calderbeck. No fool, the old man, and someone who had known him distantly since Gabriel's childhood. This was no time to be complacent.

'A bard.' He deliberately thickened his accent.

'So you sing?' That was Frampton, who had lost two hundred guineas to him only a month ago. Gabriel bowed assent. To deny an ability to sing would undermine his Welsh credentials if they held to that stereotype.

'You will come down to the house and perform your work for my guests, in that case,' Knighton ordered.

'When it is ready, my lord, with pleasure.'

'You have nothing but what you are working on now?' Calderbeck demanded, bridling at Gabriel's indifferent tone.

'Nothing that is of the spirit of this place.'

'Well, perform something else,' Knighton said impatiently. 'Tonight, nine o'clock.'

'And bring your harp to the party,' Frampton added, making the younger men guffaw with laughter.

'I sing unaccompanied,' Gabriel said. *Hell and damnation.* Could he recall any of the Welsh tunes his great-aunt and her housekeeper had taught him as a child? He could sing well enough, but he had not been prepared for this.

'No doubt your hermit is wary of performing to an audience after so much time alone, Father. Or perhaps he fears his voice is not all he boasts of.' The words, spoken indifferently, brought the men round to stare at the speaker as though they had forgotten there was a woman with them.

'We do not want a poor performance. Not with such distinguished guests,' said Lady Caroline as she rode forward into the clearing. She put back her veil as though to study him more closely and her expression, as she stared down at Gabriel, was suited to a lady who has found the chimneysweep's boy on her new Oriental hearth rug. He risked a quick assessing glance. Her face was unmarked and she seemed to be managing her horse without any difficulty. He let out a breath he had not realised he'd been holding.

'Why not have him come up to the house later this afternoon, Father? Blackstone can show him the salon and let him practise his voice a little.' She shrugged. 'Or not, as you choose. I merely thought it might save us an evening of strange discords if I were to hear what he can do.'

Gabriel kept his eyes lowered, respectfully not staring, it must have seemed, when in fact he was having difficulty keeping the surprise off his face. Where had the Lady Caroline he knew vanished to? This bored, haughty creature was surely not the blushing, passionate, brave woman who had made him that outrageous offer, who had come to visit her father's hermit to assure herself of his welfare?

'A good idea, Caroline.' Gabriel looked up and saw that Knighton was nodding approval. He had no qualms, it seemed, about exposing his daughter to the close proximity of his hermit. Presumably he had every faith in her chaperon. The earl gestured abruptly at him. 'Come to the kitchen door at three. We'll all be outside, no one for you to disturb.'

Except your daughter, but apparently she does not count. 'My lord.' He was finding it mildly amusing to discover the amount of meaning—and insolence—one could convey with an apparently subservient bow. He must see if his own and other servants possessed the same skill.

Gabriel stood at the edge of the clearing and watched the riders make their way along the twisting track that skirted the contour of the hill before descending to the far side of the lake.

'Grottos…'

The word floated back on the still air. Another of Lord Knighton's landscape follies in planning. Gabriel wondered what he would want to ornament his grottos. Water nymphs, perhaps, or tritons.

He watched until the last of the horses, the bay hack with its blue-clad rider, vanished into the trees, ignored and unpartnered. Woodruffe took a complacent approach to his courting, Gabriel thought as he sat down on the log seat. Or perhaps the matter had been agreed and he was behaving as neglectfully as a fiancé as he would as a husband. From what he knew of the man, neglect would be infinitely better for Caroline than his attentions.

The summons to the house solved the problem of gaining an interview with her. If he had not known better he would have thought she had arranged matters in order to speak with him in private, but apparently this confounded beard was enough to hide from even the most perceptive young lady. He tugged at it and thought longingly of his razors before he began to dredge through his memory for Welsh songs, poems or even sermons.

'You are very clean for a hermit.' Mrs Gleason, the cook, eyed Gabriel up and down as he stood in the doorway of her immaculate kitchen looking as meek as he knew how. Subtly mocking Lord Knighton was one thing, but cooks were the empresses of their domains and even their employers treated them with respect if they knew what was good for them.

'I wash in the lake every day, Mrs Gleason.'

'And what's your name then?' That was Molly, the kitchen maid, all freckles and crooked teeth and a big grin that showed them both off.

'Petrus Owen, Miss Molly.'

That triggered the giggles again. 'Ooh, *Mis*s Molly!'

'You'll be Miss Out On Your Ear, my girl, if you don't finish those potatoes,' Cook snapped. 'And you, you big Welsh lummox, stop lurking about like something out of those novels Lady Caroline's maid is always reading, go on through to the end of the passage and knock on Mr Blackstone's door. You give me the cold grues, standing there in that Popish outfit.'

'Yes, Mrs Gleason.' He winked at Molly as he passed and was out of the door before her giggles erupted again.

The butler answered the knock on his door after a good

minute. From the waft of violet pastilles on his breath Gabriel deduced he had been having an after-luncheon snooze to recover from the onerous duty of finishing off the leftover wine.

'Oh, it's you. His lordship said to take you up to the Blue Salon.' He glowered at Gabriel, apparently found nothing obvious that he could object to, considering his employer was misguided enough to employ such a man, and stalked off along the passageway to the foot of the servants' stairs.

'Bring that with you.' He gestured in passing to one of the hard wooden hall chairs. 'I'll not have you sitting on the good upholstery. That robe or whatever it is looks as though it would shed.'

Where Mrs Gleason's distrust merely amused him, the butler's attitude filled him with a strong desire to apply one booted foot to his chubby buttocks. Gabriel picked up the chair by the back rail and hefted it into the salon without replying.

Blackstone waved a hand towards the piano. 'Lady Caroline said you might need to play it.' His expression showed strong doubt that the silent hermit was capable of such a feat.

Gabriel, without acknowledging he had heard, shifted the piano stool, dumped down the chair, sat and ran his hands up and down the keyboard in a series of perfectly accurate scales. He rarely played the piano, but he could recall enough of his lessons to manage that, at least.

'Ha! Don't touch anything else. I will tell her ladyship you are here.'

It was almost silent when Blackstone's footsteps died away. There was the draught from the open door on his cheek, the sound of birdsong through the window and, distantly, the lowing of cattle in the meadow beyond the ha-ha. It was curiously soothing, this bucolic peace. If he was not careful he would find himself seduced—

'What on earth are you *doing*?'

Gabriel brought his hands down on the keys in a jangling discord and swung round and to his feet. 'Lady Caroline.'

'Lord Edenbridge.'

She knows me. 'Not so loud.' He reached her side in three long strides and pushed the door half-closed. 'Where the blazes is your chaperon?'

'Unnecessary, according to my father.' She was tight-lipped and pale and he felt his temper rising.

'Your maid, then?'

'Upstairs immersed in a pile of fine mending and a lurid novel I deliberately left just by the mending basket. Never mind that, we are alone for a few minutes at least, so tell me, what are you doing here? And like this?' Her sweeping gesture encompassed his beard, hair, robe and the scuffed toes of his oldest pair of boots showing beneath the frayed hem. 'I do not know whether to laugh or run and hide in a cupboard.'

'From me?'

'No, of course not from you,' Caroline said with a laugh that wavered dangerously before she closed her lips tightly upon it. 'From my father when he discovers this imposture.'

'What imposture? He cannot seriously delude himself that I am a genuine Welsh hermit. He assumes I am a gentleman or scholar fallen on hard times, but if I am an earl eccentric enough to wish to seclude myself in a chapel and write poetry for a few weeks then that makes me no more peculiar than the earl prepared to employ me.'

'But that is not why you are here, is it?' She had retreated to the far side of the piano and from there was studying his face with an expression somewhere between bemusement and alarm. 'I wish I knew what you were thinking. That beard is extraordinarily effective in concealing both your features and your expression.'

'I am glad to hear it. But how did you realise, if you did not recognise me close up that first day?'

'I was watching from the terrace with the guests that evening. There was something about you that was nagging at the back of my mind and then, when I saw you moving, without the distraction of the beard and Welsh accent, I realised.' She blushed for some reason.

'I came because I was worried about you. Your note saying you were leaving London was written in a hand that shook and you mentioned your father's displeasure. I know what kind of man Woodruffe is and I feared you were under intolerable pressure to marry him. If you are, then I could…discourage him.'

'You were worried? Why should you be? I am no responsibility of yours.'

Gabriel gave a half-shrug. Honour? He supposed it must be that. And he liked Caroline, which in itself was a puzzle. He was unused to liking women for themselves, not as sexual partners, or flirts. Perhaps associating with the wives of his close friends, three brave, intelligent women, was changing his perspective. It was unsettling the way he felt so protective of Caroline. *As though she was a sister*, he thought, then discarded the idea. It felt strangely wrong.

'I am not used to associating with well-bred virgins, but it seems that an encounter with you was enough to lay bare the few gentlemanly instincts I do possess,' he said, unwilling to express his half-understood feelings. 'I was concerned, as I say, but what I did not expect was to find that you had been physically mistreated. I cannot walk away from that.'

'I told you, it was an accident.'

'That is not true, we both know it, Caroline. Women tell those lies to shield the men who mistreat them.' *Mama's voice as she explained away another bruise. So careless, she had been, so clumsy.* His father had hit his own wife and he found the sight of a bruise on a woman intolerable. And now he was an adult he could do something about it. He felt his voice begin to rise and regained control with an effort. 'Your loyalty is misplaced.'

She made a little gesture of rejection, whether of his persistence or of the violence, he could not tell. Nor did he realise he had moved until he found himself beside her, her hand in his. He lifted it and pushed back the sleeve, feeling her skin under his fingertips, satin-smooth, rather cool. 'The bruises are almost gone. Do you have new ones?'

She should make him let go of her hand. Caroline did not stir, letting the warmth from the long, sure, fingers soak into her skin. *Calloused horseman's hands, perhaps swordsman's hands*, she thought. *Strong.* 'No, there are no new ones. My father is content that I am allowing Lord Woodruffe to court me.'

'Is he? Courting you, that is.'

'No, not really. He is behaving as though he already owns me and has no need to exert himself to win my approval. He expects my father to deliver me at the altar steps as a neatly wrapped parcel complete with dowry, in return for his acres that adjoin our land. One daughter disposed of, Lucas's inheritance expanded—all with minimal fuss and bother.' Her aunt would warn her sharply about the bitter tone. So unladylike, so undutiful.

Gabriel was tracing the veins in her wrist with his fingertip. She should free herself, she was not *that* careless of proper behaviour. *But why should I? I want his hands*

*on me, I like the strength and the gentleness and the anger
on my behalf that is in this man.*

'What is the solution, then?' he asked. 'I could shave
off this confounded beard, reappear as myself and chal-
lenge Woodruffe to a duel.'

Was he being whimsical? 'You will do no such thing!
On what pretext? What if you kill him? And think of the
scandal in any case.'

His fingers still circled her wrist, they were close
enough to kiss, close enough for her to breathe in the now
familiar scent of him. Gabriel's lips parted, she caught her
breath. 'You do not worry that he might kill me?'

She gave an unladylike snort of disbelief, shattering the
fragile moment, and saw the laughter lines crease at the
corners of his dark eyes.

'I am flattered by your confidence, Caroline. But to be
serious, I agree that duels are a last resort because of your
reputation. Is there no one you would wish to marry? No
suitor ready to carry you off across the border?'

He had released her wrist and she concentrated on not
closing the fingers of the other hand around it to trap the
sensations that still teased the skin. 'No. There are suitors,
yes. But anyone I would wish to marry? No. Certainly no
one ready to carry me off at the risk of scandal and my
father disowning me.'

'Then we will have to think of another solution.' Without leaving her side Gabriel let his fingers stray over the
keyboard, a ripple of notes, the beginning of a tune she
did not know. 'I have only just arrived and begun to think
around the problem. There is time yet, do not despair.'

'I am not despairing,' she said stoutly. 'If the worst
comes to the worst I will simply run away—once I have
thought of a way to support myself respectably until Anthony comes of age and I can live with him.'

Gabriel raised an eyebrow, his expression dubious. 'He is what? Sixteen? Five years to hide and support yourself is a long time.'

'I know. But I will think of something.' She shrugged. 'I must. Other women support themselves.'

His quizzical look was plain to read. *Most of them do it on their backs.* 'I was considering blackmail.' Gabriel completed his one-handed tune with a flourish. 'Something that would suggest powerfully to Woodruffe that he would do better to leave you alone. Catching the man cheating at cards would be useful.'

'It would. I cannot believe we are discussing blackmail, elopements and duels.' She watched him as he stood so close, head bent, studying the black-and-white keys as though they were all that was important here.

Gabriel glanced up towards the door. 'Someone is coming.' He crossed the room to the rug in the centre. 'I think it would be better if I recite rather than sing, my lady,' he said clearly, the Welsh lilt back to colour his voice.

Blackstone looked round the door, then came in, nose almost twitching with curiosity. 'May I bring your ladyship refreshments?'

'Yes, please, Blackstone. Some lemonade and macaroons. Bring two glasses and plates.'

When he had gone, his face stiff with disapproval, Caroline stayed where she was. 'Why not sing?'

'Because I cannot remember sufficient songs,' he confessed. 'But I can recite Welsh poetry long enough to send an entire house party to sleep. It is a hot day and this evening will be warm. A stage set of sorts on the terrace will give maximum drama and keep your father happy.'

'But why are you doing this? You hardly know me,' she began. 'Why are you helping me?' *It isn't as though you desire me.*

'Hush, my lady. *Mawredd gyminedd, a weli di hyn? Yd lysg fy nghalon fel etewyn*—' He broke off as a footman came in with a tray, placed it on a side table and left on well-trained, silent feet.

The man must have incredible hearing. 'How did you—?'

Gabriel shook his head at her in silent warning. 'That is from a warrior's lament, my lady, many hundreds of years old.'

Blackstone entered, glanced at the lemonade jug as though checking on the footman and went out again.

'"My heart is burning like a brand of flame",' Gabriel translated incongruously as she poured lemonade. 'What time should I make my appearance this evening? "I praised their wealth…"'

'Ten o'clock.' Caroline made herself think of practicalities, not the rich, dark voice weaving ancient magic. 'Have a biscuit.' There were few things more prosaic than biscuits. 'Tell me why.'

'You know perfectly well I cannot just abandon you now I know you are being ill-treated and that your father is forcing Woodruffe on you,' Gabriel said, waving away the macaroons. 'And, if I am to help, this performance consolidates my position here and it gives me the opportunity to get something on Woodruffe that I can use to apply pressure.'

'Blackmail?' Gabriel spoke of it as though *putting pressure* on someone was a normal business practice.

'You don't handle men like him with kid gloves. Or at all, if you can help it,' Gabriel added with a smile that made her think of sharp teeth and dangerous shadows. 'You must set the scene. Flambeaux, a brazier, a pile of furs if you have them, a horseshoe of chairs with the open end to the steps to the terrace.' Gabriel finally took a biscuit and bit into it. 'We want drama and every possible cliché.

You don't have any mead on the premises, have you? Pity, it fits the whole Welsh mystical mood so well,' he added softly as she shook her head, bemused. 'Honeyed wine would do and some soporific if you have anything like that. I'd like to send Woodruffe to bed for a very sound sleep and be able to search his room. If we can solve this by simple pressure on his weak spots, then so much the better. A love letter from the wife of a senior cabinet minister, a handbook on cheating at whist with annotations in his hand or a diary entry on a wartime career as a French agent would be handy.'

'There is laudanum,' Caroline suggested, trying not to think of Lord Woodruffe in an illicit and amorous encounter. Or any amorous encounter, come to that. Of *course* it was normal to be discussing drugging guests with a Welsh bard over lemonade on a summer's afternoon, contemplating blackmail. She was not going to give way to hysterics and the strong desire to run to her room and put her head under the pillow for the rest of the day.

'I recall the exact dose Dr Latimor prescribed when my father had a broken ankle. He and Woodruffe are of a similar build, so it ought to knock him out safely, provided I can manage to serve it to him.'

'Excellent.' Gabriel put down his glass and took her hand in both of his, lifted it and this time just touched the back of her fingers with his lips. 'Courage, my lady. We will get you out of this one way or another.' Then he turned to the terrace door and was gone in a swirl of brown robes.

Chapter Seven

The servants, used to their master's whims, responded well to Caroline's requirements for the after-dinner entertainment. The gardeners produced braziers and flambeaux, set around a semicircle of the most throne-like chairs she had been able to glean from remote corners of the house. A large stool had been heaped with sheepskins with an ancient wolf pelt at the foot and set in the centre, where the steps from the terrace led down to the lawn. Footmen collected armfuls of cloaks against any evening chill and Blackstone was concocting the nearest mixture he could invent that resembled mead.

'I regret we do not have sufficient drinking horns for all the guests,' he apologised to Caroline, who assured him that goblets would do. Slipping laudanum into a drinking horn would be decidedly tricky, she thought, touching the carefully measured dose in the little phial in her pocket. Much as she disliked the man she wanted to do Woodruffe no harm and she had rechecked the doctor's notes and her own measurements.

The guests, well fed and glowing with plentiful wine, came out as she was casting a final look over the stage set. They had forgone their port and she set Blackstone circu-

lating with the honeyed wine as soon as they were all settled. The candles were extinguished in the house behind
them, leaving them in the summer night beneath a clear
sky with the afterglow of sunset to keep the stars at bay.

The men continued to talk, but gradually the atmosphere seemed to reach them and the volume dropped,
conversation became sporadic. In the house the clocks
chimed ten and Caroline, eyes straining, made out a flicker
of movement approaching across the lawn. She nudged
William, the footman with the most impressive bass voice.

'The bard approaches!'

She thought she knew what to expect. This was all
smoke and mirrors, a performance, and yet as the tall figure came up the steps and into the firelight she caught her
breath, seized with an almost superstitious awe. Robed and
hooded in black and holding a long staff, Gabriel had become a figure from the remote past, a mystical creature
of magic and power, both spiritual and physical. This was
not a grey-bearded Merlin, stooped and ancient, this was
a virile man in his prime, as likely to draw a sword as a
magic wand.

Around her there were sharp intakes of breath, the
sounds of men straightening themselves in their chairs—
or leaning away as though faced with a threat. Gabriel
stood, head bowed for a moment, then threw back his hood
and sat down on the heaped animal skins with the air of
a tribal chieftain taking his place on a throne. He held up
his hand as if for silence, although save for the crackle of
the fires and the hooting of an owl in the Home Wood,
there had been no sound.

'Marwnad Cynddylan Dyhedd deon diechyr...'

The words dropped into the night air, soft as the owl's
wingbeat. Only one person there understood their meaning

and yet, shivering, Caroline thought they all knew this was a lament, an ancient warrior's song of glory, loss, death.

The rich, dark voice strengthened, deepened and Caroline lost herself in the sound, lost herself in the enchantment the enthroned figure was weaving. She had no idea how long Gabriel spoke for. When the liquid Welsh stopped it took them all a moment to realise it. Caroline released an unsteady breath and heard around her the others doing the same. One or two of the guests shook their heads as though rousing from a dream. No one applauded, but the very silence was filled with appreciation.

She rose, took the wine jug from the nearest footman and began to circulate, topping up the goblets in the men's hands. They hardly seemed to notice her. Woodruffe certainly did not as she tipped the laudanum from the phial in the palm of her hand into his wine.

She resumed her seat and the spell was spun again.

'Mawredd gyminedd, mawr ysgafael, Yrhag Caer Lwyt- goed, neus dug Morfael...'

The sky was entirely black now, except for a dusting of early stars, and the braziers glowed sullen red.

"'I shall mourn until I enter the fastness of the earth,"' Gabriel said in English.

She thought his right hand moved and then there was a burst of flame as the nearest fire blazed up, making those nearest it recoil, dazzling the dark-adjusted eyes of all of them. From the far end where the staff had gathered there was a scream of alarm. When, blinking, Caroline could see properly again the dais was empty and the robed figure had vanished.

'My dear Knighton!' The men clustered around her father, full of congratulations. 'Magnificent! The atmosphere, the voice, the drama!' That was Lord Calderbeck, uncharacteristically animated. The others echoed him, only Woodruffe hung back, his hand on the back of his chair.

Caroline kept an eye on him as she directed the servants to clear the terrace of its chairs and props, watched him follow listlessly as the other guests trooped back into the drawing room.

'Damn good show, Knighton,' he roused himself to say. 'If you'll forgive me, I'm for my bed. Don't feel quite the thing, you know...'

The others barely spared him a glance. Caroline, assessing the heavy eyes and barely stifled yawns, hurried to his side in a display of feminine concern. 'Are you unwell, Lord Woodruffe? Should we send for a doctor?'

'No, no. Just a trifle weary for some reason. The night air, I have no doubt.' He smiled at her, a knowing smirk that had her fighting the urge to step back. 'You're a good girl to make a fuss of me. Make a wonderful wife for some lucky man, eh?' His chuckle was lost in another jaw-cracking yawn and he wandered off towards the door, leaving Caroline to struggle with the expression on her own face.

'Send a footman to keep an eye on Lord Woodruffe,' she said to Blackstone. 'We wouldn't want any accidents on the stairs.'

Now what? Is Gabriel watching from the darkness, waiting for us to go to bed, or is he already in the house, perhaps in Woodruffe's room? But her part was done. The men drifted towards the card tables and Caroline took herself to bed, still half-lost in the swirling mists of ancient legend.

Her maid was agog with the excitements of the evening. 'Ooh, my lady, when there was that great flame and he vanished I almost fainted with the terror of it. Witchcraft it was.'

'I'm sorry you were frightened, Jenny.' Caroline unhooked her earrings and sat at the dressing table for the maid to unpin her hair. 'It was only the kind of tricks they play on stage.'

'I wasn't really scared, my lady—it was lovely, like a novel. I've got shivers up and down my spine just thinking about it.'

'Well, I have shivers, too. Go and close the doors on to the balcony, please, before the moths get in.'

It seemed to take for ever to get ready for bed and even longer to send Jenny, still bubbling with excitement, on her way. Caroline left the little oil lamp by her bed burning while she lay back, knowing she was not going to be able to sleep, not for a long while.

Part of her was braced for the shouts that would mark Gabriel's discovery, but there was only the distant sound of men's voices from the drawing room, the occasional burst of laughter and, out in the park, the sharp bark of a vixen.

The voices had stilled by the time the sound of fingernails on the glass of the balcony door brought her upright in bed, one hand clapped over her mouth to stifle the shriek of alarm. They carried on their light tapping as she scrambled up and pulled on her wrapper. When she warily pushed back the curtains she almost did shriek in earnest at the sight of a dark figure on the narrow space between door and balustrade.

'Oh, it is you!'

Gabriel in breeches, boots and a dark coat slid into the room and jerked the curtains back again. 'Who did you expect?'

'Not you outside dressed like that,' she said irrationally, then gasped. 'How long have you been out there?'

'Long enough to be almost sent over the edge by your

maid closing the doors. And what did you expect me to be wearing? I can hardly climb the wisteria in a robe.' Her agitation finally seemed to register. 'Yes, I was out there all the time you were preparing for bed, and, yes, the curtains were tightly drawn and even if they had not been, I have no need to lurk outside maidens' bedchambers like a Peeping Tom, hoping for a glimpse of bare ankle.'

'Because you find it all too easy to be inside bedchambers, I suppose.' Gabriel gave a low hum of agreement. 'I do wish you were not constantly putting me to the blush,' she snapped, cross with herself. 'I was surprised, that was all. I thought you would have been inside the house long ago.'

'When everyone was still up and about and I had no idea which room was Woodruffe's?'

He spoke softly and she came close. To whisper back, she told herself. 'It is in the other wing. You'll need to cross the head of the stairs and go straight ahead, take the first right. His is the first door up the little flight of steps.'

'Stairs, across, right, steps. First door. Got it. Did you manage to drug him?'

'I gave him a light dose of laudanum, enough to make him sleepy. I didn't dare use more,' she confessed. 'I suppose murder is a rather extreme solution to the problem,' she added, then had to bite her lip to keep back the totally inappropriate giggles. *I am becoming hysterical with nerves*, she thought and then lost all desire to laugh when she saw the expression on Gabriel's face.

'It is,' he said grimly.

Something in his expression… 'I didn't mean it.' Her voice quavered.

Gabriel pulled her into his arms, her face against his coat. 'I know you did not.'

'That beard looks ridiculous with those clothes,' she

muttered, saying the first thing that came into her head. 'It is tickling my ear.'

'It is driving me insane,' he confessed, his voice a low rumble. 'I wish I could shave it off.'

'Why? Does it itch?' Caroline leaned back a little to examine it at close quarters.

'That, and I suspect that you will not like it when I do this.'

The kiss took her totally by surprise. It seemed to take Gabriel by surprise, too, judging from the sound he made as he gathered her in to the curve of his arm. The beard was soft, but wiry, she discovered, though not as soft as the dark springing hair on his head as she slid her fingers into it, curved them around his head.

My second kiss ever. And it was very different from that first, brief meeting of lips. *It must be the beard,* she thought, trying to stay rational and controlled. Gabriel smelled of cold air and lake water and, she supposed, of man. His mouth on hers was decidedly more active than it had been that first time. More assertive. More... *Oh!* His tongue found hers, then explored the tender inside of her mouth, then his teeth were nipping lightly at her lower lip and she found she was pressed against him, very conscious of his body.

Gabriel stepped back until he held her by the shoulders at arm's length. 'Damn. I had no intention of doing that.'

Her lower lip quivered and she bit it. Gabriel's gaze shifted to her mouth. 'It wasn't *that* bad.'

'I never said it was.' He smiled at her ruefully. 'The *damn* was for me. I apologise for both my presumption and the scratchy whiskers.'

'They are quite soft, actually.' She controlled the urge to pet them and gave herself a little shake. This was merely the release of tension, nothing more. Gabriel certainly did not appear much stirred by the experience and he should know. 'You'll need a lamp, you can take the little oil one from beside my bed.' She watched Gabriel check the wick. 'I think I will come with you to keep watch outside the door.'

'And if anyone comes? How are you going to explain what you are doing at this hour, flitting about a house full of men?'

'Um… Overcome by desire for Woodruffe? My father would approve of that.'

'Your father would have you married to him by special licence ten minutes after he manages to locate a bishop to provide one if he thought you had committed that sort of indiscretion in front of witnesses.'

'I suppose you are right. I could say I heard a sound like breaking glass so I went to investigate?'

'Without calling for help?'

'I am just a poor air-headed female.' She widened her eyes at Gabriel and the corner of his mouth kicked up. 'It never occurred to me it might be anything other than the wind on an unlatched casement that I ought to close.'

'You are not air-headed, Caroline. You are a positive menace. But come if you must.'

She followed him out the door, resisting the temptation to clutch at his coat tails. The house was as silent as it ever was, alive with the creaks and groans of its old timbers, the whistle of the wind in the chimneys, the tap of the branches of the elm on the east parlour side. Gabriel moved, soft-footed as a housebreaker, drifting down the corridors, across the stairhead with a glance down at the hooded chair by the front door where the footman on duty was asleep, a lamp turned down low beside him.

At Woodruffe's door Gabriel put his ear to the panels. 'He's asleep,' he murmured in Caroline's ear as he eased the door open and slid through the gap. Then she was alone on the landing with only the shivery sensation of his warm breath on her cheek to tell her that this was not some fevered dream.

Woodruffe was sprawled snoring across the bed, still in his shirt. Gabriel averted his gaze from the white hairy legs, the slack-mouthed face, and scanned the rest of the bedchamber.

Imagining this man in bed with Caroline did nothing for his concentration. He had been fighting the urge to kiss her, to toss her on to the nearest flat surface—piano, *chaise*, bed, hearthrug—and plunder that innocence until they were both exhausted. So far at least he had managed to behave like the gentleman he was supposed to be and not the rake he actually was, and keep his hands off her body.

Knight-errantry was supposed to bring its own rewards, not acute frustration, he thought bitterly as he studied Woodruffe's belongings. He should have thrown Caroline out the moment he found her in his drawing room, now he could not help himself trying to right her wrongs, not now he knew she had been hurt, not knowing what he did about Woodruffe. He was a man now, not a desperate child, and he had the power to thwart both men who threatened her. But once he had done something about this he was going to take himself off to Paris and plunge into mindless, hedonistic pleasure because virtue was, most certainly, overvalued.

A dressing case sat on the table, the lid pushed up by the paper that had been jammed inside it. Gabriel set the lamp down so the light was shielded from the sleeper and lifted out the contents. Bills, most of them third or fourth demands, a letter from Woodruffe's steward and a bulky, folded, piece of parchment that weighed heavy in his hand.

Gabriel opened it, wincing as the stiff folds crackled like gunshot. The weight was explained by the red seal that swung free at the bottom. A marriage licence and, by the size of it, a special licence at that. He did not risk unfolding the thing, knowing it would be the size of the table top, but set it aside and checked the rest of the box.

The collection of prints secreted at the bottom were certainly obscene. Gabriel was no prude, but he found he was handling these with the tips of his fingers as though the smut would rub off. Woodruffe had an unpleasant predilection for images of helpless women tied up, or in chains—and none of them appeared to be enjoying the experience. Certainly not the whips and canes the leering men in the prints were wielding.

He packed it all away, then took the lamp and searched the drawers in the dresser, the clothes press and finally, as Woodruffe snored on, the books on his bedside table.

Feeling he was in need of a bath, Gabriel eased his way out of the door and closed it silently behind him.

'Did you find anything?' Caroline whispered.

Too much. He studied her in the simple white nightgown that reached to her bare toes, her hair in a plait over one shoulder. She looked worryingly like the innocent victims in Woodruffe's pornographic prints. The thought of the man laying his sweaty hands on her, let alone anything else, almost made Gabriel shudder.

'Not here, back to your bedchamber.'

Once they were inside, the door locked, he picked up her robe from the foot of the bed and handed it to her. 'Put that on.'

'I am not cold. Tell me what you found.'

'Put it on. Please.' He sat down in one of the armchairs and studied the toe of his boot while he sought for some control.

'Oh, very well.' She shrugged into it and came to perch on the edge of the stool opposite. 'What did you find?'

Gabriel resisted the urge to lean over to tighten the sash and pull the edges of her robe together. 'Nothing actually illegal.' He was certainly not going to describe those prints to her. He recrossed his legs and contemplated the other toe. 'How eager is your father to get his hands on that land of Woodruffe's? Is it valuable?'

'No, just pasture. Not even good rich water meadow. I don't think it is worth much.'

'Woodruffe is in debt, by the look of it. You come with a good dowry, I assume? More than that land is worth on the open market?'

'Goodness, yes. Father might regard daughters as an irrelevance in the greater scheme of things, but he would be mortified to have it known my dowry was anything but generous. The value of the land is irrelevant, it is the en-largement of the estate that matters to my father.'

'Damn. I'd hoped that there might be a let-out there. In that case you need to know that the two of them must be quite determined on this match. Woodruffe has a special licence in his possession.'

'A *special* licence? That means he can marry without delay, wherever he wants, doesn't it?'

'It does.'

'I can keep saying no.' A thread of uncertainty ran through the statement.

Gabriel looked up, then leaned forward and caught her hand, pushed back the sleeve. The bruises had quite gone now. 'They have a clean slate to begin again. If your father hit you once, he will do it again if you anger him. And Woodruffe…' How the devil did one explain such tenden-cies to an innocent? 'Woodruffe is aroused by violence. Your resistance will only encourage him.'

Caroline met his eyes and shuddered. 'I don't think I want to know what you mean by that or how you discovered it.' She squared her shoulders and pulled her hand free from his lax grip. 'I will have to run away then. I've been hoping against hope that I wouldn't have to, but at least Anthony is at school much of the time and old enough to go to friends in the holidays. He is in no danger of anything but neglect from our father.

'I don't suppose you are any good at safe breaking? Mama's own jewellery is locked up in the study along with the things my godmother left me. I don't want to sell it, but I will need to part with some of it to live on until I find work.'

'I can pick a lock. Some locks,' Gabriel qualified. He hadn't needed to since his childhood. 'It all depends on how good it is.'

'You really are unscrupulous, aren't you?' Caroline's expression had turned from anxious but determined to something close to judgemental. 'Not that I am criticising, you understand.'

It sounded like that to him and, amazingly, her words hurt. 'You are not?' he enquired, unable to prevent the hint of ice in the question. What the devil was the matter with him if one young woman's opinion had the power to pierce his armour and wound? He was becoming vulnerable and he had never felt so before. Not mentally, at least.

'I know you are only trying to help me and I am very grateful, but subterfuge over who you are in order to become the hermit, searching Woodruffe's things with a view to blackmail and now lock-picking...'

She was right, this was over the thin line and into illegality, even if the jewellery was Caroline's. He should walk away. Now.

Chapter Eight

Walk away, for her own good. For mine. I have never become emotionally involved with a woman before and that is what this is.

Women wanted a man's thoughts, his secrets, his soul. His mother had uncovered her husband's soul and what she found had blighted her entire marriage, had driven her to the drug bottle and to her death. Gabriel had done what he had promised her, but taking responsibility for another person was like a heavy chain around the neck. His brothers had needed his protection and he had given them that at the cost of pain and loneliness and, almost, his freedom, if not his life. But a woman would want emotion.

Emotion is dangerous. Someone is going to get hurt. Stop now before this has gone beyond the point of no return and find some other way to help her. Gabriel found it was easier to decide to walk away than to do it. He sighed inwardly at his own unfamiliar indecision and tried to work things through logically.

Caroline was learning caution fast, it seemed. At first, seized with the desperate need to retrieve those deeds, she had almost innocently offered herself in order to save her brother's land and future. Now she was regarding the man who had been a stranger, perhaps almost an unreal figure, with speculation. There were questions in the clear blue gaze, questions and doubts that had not been there before he had kissed her.

'You think I should not do these things and ignore a lady in distress in order to preserve my own moral purity?' he asked when she did not speak. *And when did you ever have morals, let alone pure ones? Get down off your high horse, Edenbridge.* 'And now we are in deep you wonder just who you are involved with? You knew I was a sinner, not a saint, when you first came to me. I might break the law here and there, but are you telling me that your father and Woodruffe do not deserve to be thwarted?'

'No. No, of course not.' He could see the thoughts chasing each other, the anxiety and the doubt, the desire to snatch at help and the growing awareness that she was getting into very dangerous waters with a man she did not know. 'And I was the one who suggested you pick the lock,' Caroline added, obviously striving to be fair.

'Look, you can stay here, pretend none of this ever happened, marry Woodruffe.' Her shudder was an adequate answer to that suggestion. 'Or you can stay here, but refuse to marry him.' She shook her head. And he did not miss the betraying way one hand went to her cheek, cradling it. So the swine had hit her in the face as well as bruising her arms. Gabriel thought longingly of having Knighton at his mercy at the card tables again, a sure and legal way to ruin the man. But hell, the thought of killing him was tempting. Far more tempting. *Murder solves nothing*, he reminded himself. But it was so easy to do, the human frame was so vulnerable. He saw his father's broken body at his feet, all that power and vigour rendered impotent in a moment.

Gabriel clenched his fists until the nails bit into his palms and breathed deeply until the swirling memories were back under control. 'Or you can flee, with my help or without it. I assume as you have put it off this long that there is no one you can run to?'

How had he got himself into this? One step at a time, of course. He had let himself care, allowed himself to feel responsible for someone for the first time since his father's death, and now he had no more choice but to help Caroline than if he had found her drowning.

'There is no one.' Gabriel saw the conscious effort she was making to gather her courage and cope. 'I can go without your help, or with it, as you say. I had thought to find some cheap lodgings while I looked for work, but I really have no idea how to go about that. The risks to me are far greater if I try it alone—' She caught the involuntary twist of his lips and smiled, although it was not with much warmth. 'I have realised that you have no desire to take me up on my foolish IOU, so that makes me feel even safer.'

'I kissed you. Twice.' Where was this scrupulous urge to point out all the facts coming from? And he wanted to do far more than kiss her. He forced himself to plan how he was going to get her away, what he was going to do when he had.

Caroline shrugged. 'Men do tend to try to kiss women, I have observed. It doesn't mean anything.'

So his kisses were to be dismissed, were they? Gabriel got a grip on what remained of his sense of humour after this evening's events and waited for her to work her way through to a decision before he told her the results of his rapid planning.

'I will be safer with you, whether or not we can retrieve my jewels. But,' she added as he drew breath to suggest that, if she had made up her mind, they should get on with things, 'it has decided disadvantages for you.'

'It has?' Perhaps she was not so innocent after all.

'I am asking you to commit a criminal act, even if they are my own jewels, because the safe is not mine. And I will be putting you to considerable inconvenience and, I rather fear, expense. At least until I can sell or pawn some jewellery and pay you back.'

'This much entertainment is cheap at the price,' he drawled, hoping to lighten her mood, or at least make her cross enough to carry her through the night. Cost, if she only realised it, was the least of their problems.

'We will get to London and I will take you to one of the wives of my best friends. They are all married to women of…' he groped for the words to encompass the three and compromised with '…independent thought. It will not disconcert them in the slightest to harbour a runaway and we can rely absolutely on their discretion. Pack what you will need for about four days in your smallest valise. Then we will take the jewellery and be on our way. The fewer trips back and forth inside this house tonight, the better.'

'Oh, yes, thank you, that would be wonderful. The thought of some female support is, I must confess, very welcome.'

Gabriel braced himself for a long wait and then a tussle over a bulging valise and a hatbox or two. Caroline surprised him by removing a few items from drawers and bringing an oilskin bag and a hairbrush from her dressing room. Finally she lifted the lid of the window seat, rummaged inside and produced a large purse that clinked. 'I have been hoarding my pin money,' she explained when she saw his attention on the bag.

It all fitted into a small case. She scooped up the trinkets from the dressing table and swept them in on top, then draped a woollen pelisse over her arm. 'That is all I need.'

'You would make a good wife for a soldier,' Gabriel commented.

'I have been planning this for days,' Caroline countered. 'I hoped I would not have to do it, but now I do not think I have a choice.' He saw her cast a lingering look around her bedchamber which probably represented sanctuary and privacy, certainly comfort, but she did not hesitate. His respect for her increased another notch.

The night had begun to feel like a dream. Her surroundings were familiar, yet her behaviour was not. Things that she took for granted suddenly loomed terrifying and strange—the grotesque carvings on the newel posts, the suits of armour in the Long Gallery, the grinding sound the long-case clock in the hallway made as it readied itself to strike, all were exaggerated.

The man beside her was a stranger, too. He was not the softly spoken Welsh hermit, nor the dishevelled rake she had caught on his way to bed that first morning. Neither was he the elegant, if careless, nobleman who occasionally spared social events an hour or two of his time. This man was a creature of the dark, moving through the shadows like a cat, prepared to break the law to help her and quite confident about his ability to do so. This was the man who had kissed her with careless expertise, leaving her wanting more, even as she shocked herself with that wanting.

What would his friends be like? At least they were all married, although the idea of the women of *independent thought* was rather more alarming than the prospect of meeting three more rakish gentlemen. What if the wives all despised or disliked her? Or worse, pitied her.

She was worrying so hard that she almost walked past the study. 'In here,' she breathed.

The door was unlocked and well oiled. Once inside Gabriel drew the curtains tightly closed before he turned up the wick of the lamp. 'Where is the safe?' With light on him she could see the tension in his body, the alertness. He looked ready to fight.

'Here.' She lifted down a landscape in a gilt frame to reveal a small door set flush into the wall.

'I can force this easily enough.'

'It is iron painted to look like wood,' she warned.

'Damn.' Gabriel produced the two hairpins that she had seen him lift from her dressing table. 'Hold the light to shine on the lock.' He straightened the first pin, slid it into the keyhole and began to manipulate it.

Ten minutes passed. Caroline shifted the lamp to the other hand and propped her arm against the wall to ease the ache. Gabriel's eyes were narrowed, his lips compressed. He had two pins, bent at odd angles, in the lock now.

'It must be fifteen years since I tried this,' he muttered.

'If it is too difficult—' she began. The clock made its grinding noise and they both froze, then relaxed as it chimed three.

Gabriel closed his eyes as something went *click*. 'Got it.'

It was almost an anticlimax to have the door swing open to reveal nothing more than some folded documents, a bag of coin and a stack of jewellery boxes. In the almost Gothic atmosphere of flickering lamplight and tension the least the safe should have contained was a skull and a vial of poison. Caroline did not feel this was the moment to be sharing such fancies with Gabriel.

She sorted out her own jewels from the family gems, which were to be passed down to the eldest son for his wife, and nodded to Gabriel. He closed the door, manipulated the picks until, much faster this time, the lock clicked home, and then lifted the picture back into place.

'What do we do now?' she asked as she stuffed the valuables deep into her valise.

'We go to the hermitage until I can make arrangements.

Is it possible to get out of the house without leaving a trace? I'd like to delay pursuit as long as possible.'

'The side entrance to the garden. There's a trick to jiggling the lock.'

Gabriel cracked open the door. 'Hell.' He pushed her back into the study. 'Someone is coming.'

'There's nothing beyond this room. It must be my father.'

Gabriel cast a swift look around, then fell to his knees, dragging her with him as he blew out the lamp. 'Under the desk.'

It was a double-depth partners' desk, designed for two men to face each other as they worked. The kneehole might give them both enough space to remain hidden, provided no one sat down and extended their legs. Crushed under there against Gabriel, the valise jammed under her raised knees, Caroline held her breath until coloured dots began to swirl in the blackness.

As the door opened she drew in a shallow breath. Surely her heartbeat must be audible? Beside her Gabriel was utterly still, then she felt his finger begin a slow movement against the back of her hand. *I am here*, it seemed to say. *Don't be afraid.*

She closed her fingers around his, holding on as the tension grew. Her father put down his lamp and began to sort through the papers on the desk above them, muttering irritably as if he could not locate what he wanted.

Her body was hot and cold. Cold with fear, hot where it touched Gabriel's. Beneath the broadcloth she could feel his strength, the muscles tensed for action, the total control. His confidence seeped into her, allowing her to relax just a little, to breathe more easily, and as the panic ebbed something else flowed in to replace it, an aching physical awareness, the need for Gabriel's arms around her, his mouth on hers. She lowered her head until her parted lips touched the back of his hand and then she stilled, breathing in the smell of his skin, letting the taste of him seep into her mouth. His fingers tensed in hers.

Finally her father gave a grunt of satisfaction and moved towards the door. The light vanished and the sound of his footsteps dwindled away. Gabriel backed out of the tight space, pulled out the valise and finally Caroline, unresisting and shivering, into his arms. His kiss was hard, almost angry, over in a second, a wordless acknowledgement of their narrow escape.

'Hurry.' He let her lead the way to the garden door and watched the passageway behind them as she lifted the handle, wiggled it up and down and then pressed on the door panels. The lock opened with a scrape, then, as she pulled it closed behind them, it dropped back into place.

The tall hedges that led from the house to the ha-ha made deep shadows and Gabriel set a fast pace, the sharp scent of the yew drifting back as he brushed the edges.

He vaulted down from the lawn into the ditch and she sat on the edge, then jumped into his upheld hands, gripping his shoulders to steady herself. His mouth sought hers again, with fierce and fleeting heat, then he set her on her feet and turned to climb the gentle slope of the other bank.

Panting with fear and relief and desire, Caroline gathered up her skirts and followed across the pasture, hurrying in the wake of Gabriel's long stride.

As they reached mid-slope Gabriel stopped, turned and looked back at the house. 'No lights. We're clear away for now.'

She tried not to puff. She should be flattered, she supposed, that he had assumed she could keep up, that she would not need treating as though she was some fragile little flower who required cosseting. She was going to need all the strength she had to make good her escape, however much help she had. She would not think about those kisses. Not yet.

'Are you all right?' He might have read her mind, or perhaps her breathing was not as controlled as she had thought. It was impossible to read his face by starlight.

'I…I don't know,' she said as he caught her hand and began to stride on up the hill. *Know what?*

When they reached the chapel Gabriel slammed the door, caught her to him and locked his mouth on hers. When he finally lifted his head he seemed as breathless as she was. 'Yes?'

'Yes.' *This. Now. We're safe, we're alive and we did it together.*

His lips captured hers again, his hands moved over her clothes, things fell away, cool air touched her skin. *Bare skin.* Gabriel was still fully dressed.

Caroline scrabbled between their bodies, found buttons, pulled and tugged and now he was helping her. His shirt was gone, her breasts were crushed against his bare chest and he was still except for his hands caressing down over her shoulders, his thumb tracing her spine, his breath hot on her neck.

She wriggled, not knowing what she wanted, only knowing that she needed him.

'Shh.' Gabriel's voice was a breath in her ear, a shiver that followed his fingers on her backbone. He set her slightly away from him and she protested, then stilled as the space gave room for the crisp hair on his chest to tease her breasts, for him to slide one hand up between their bodies to capture a nipple between thumb and forefinger, his palm cupping the breast as he rolled the sensitive nub until she was gasping, her forehead dropped on his shoulder for support, her hands clutching at his upper arms.

He moved, pulling her with him, and she was sprawled in his lap as he sat on the edge of the bed, one hand still tormenting her breast, his mouth on the other nipple, sucking and licking as the waves of sensation rippled through her, down to her belly, down between her legs. There was pressure, a building, aching pressure down there and she arched up, needing something to ease it, to end it, to make it last for ever.

As though he understood, Gabriel's hand slid from under her and he touched her *there* where she needed him. His fingers slipped into the swollen, wet, intimate folds as she bowed up to him, he bit gently on the nipple he was sucking and a shudder of some electric, terrifying sensation ran through her, then he slipped one finger, two, into her and she heard her own voice in an incoherent cry as the pleasure swept her away. Impossible to withstand, terrifying, wonderful.

He moved. She found herself alone on the narrow bed and whimpered, reaching blindly for him, for his heat, then Gabriel's weight was over her.

'Caroline.'

'Yes,' she panted. 'Gabriel. Please.'

He kissed her again, his lips travelling softly over her jaw, down her neck...

She smiled to herself, wrapped in the warmth of the pleasure he was giving her. She ran her fingers through his hair and gasped as his tongue met her breast again.

'Are you finally claiming my IOU?' she murmured, trailing her fingers down the solid muscles of his back.

He stilled.

Under her splayed fingers she could feel the shift of muscle, the tension that shivered under his skin. Then he rolled off her, down the floor and sat, back to the bed, his head on his raised knees.

'Gabriel?'

'I am sorry, Caroline. That should not have happened.'

Not? The pleasure still rippled through her, wonderful, transforming, but something inside her shrivelled like a rosebud in the frost. 'I want you. I am a grown woman, I can make my own decisions.' *I will not feel shame.* 'And you want me.' Which was the truth.

He stood up. Tall, beautiful, arrogantly male, half-naked. She wanted him to come back so she could touch him, explore that loose-limbed body, but she was too proud, too hurt, to ask.

'That was a mistake. The result of shared danger, suspense and too-close proximity.' Gabriel scooped up his shirt from the floor and pulled it over his head, his back turned to her. 'I have never… *Damn it*, I do not sleep with virgins. I should never have taken that idiotic IOU.'

He gathered up her scattered clothing, heaped it on a chair close by her, still without looking, and went to the fire.

'I do not regard it,' she said. She dragged on her clothes, fingers fumbling with laces and hooks.

'You are good to forgive it. Now it is better forgotten.'

What was there to say to that? *But that was the start of something wonderful? Please come back to me?* Presumably he thought verbal cold water worked as well as the real thing for quenching desire.

The silence seemed to fill the room like fog. Someone had to find a way through it. Be practical.

'Gabriel, where is there to hide here? The first thing Father is going to do is search all the buildings on the estate.'

He took a breath as though she had jerked him back from far away, but his voice was perfectly normal when he spoke. 'When I arrived here I looked for a cache for the things I brought with me that would have revealed my identity.' He had stopped frowning, no doubt because he could now stop thinking about what had just happened. 'You might say I've discovered a priest's hole. It is certainly large enough to hide you in.'

He bent over the hearth, raked the embers into a heap at the back and ducked under the piece of timber that had been nailed across the opening to make a shelf. 'Come and see.'

There was just room to stand beside him on the hot stone. Gabriel took the candle, put his foot into a crack in the masonry and began to climb. She saw the light dim as he seemed to thrust the candle into the wall, then with a heave he vanished, too. 'Can you follow me?' His head emerged, apparently out of solid stone.

'I'll try.' Caroline tucked up her skirts and got her toe into the first foothold.

It was a scramble, but with Gabriel's strong arm to haul on she found herself level with a hole that opened into a small chamber. 'What is this?' It smelled, not unpleasantly, of wood smoke.

'They built the tower as a hollow sham. Then your father wanted the place made habitable and told the builders to make a hearth. They created a shaft inside the tower with the chimney poking out below the crenulations, roofed over the top and sealed the opening at ground level. They could have filled in the tower completely, but that would have wasted stone and taken time, so they simply put in this intermediate level, I assume for support.

'I worked out what they had done, moved a stone or two to see if there was a possible hiding place and found this space. You can't see it from below and I doubt your father even realises it is here. I only found it because I was expecting makeshift construction—the whole place is no more than a stage set.'

Caroline looked around. There was a pair of valises stacked in the corner and when she lifted the candle she could see the roof high above her head. 'There's room to lie down and sleep.'

'I'll bring you up blankets.'

'Not yet. We have to talk.'

'In the morning.' Gabriel backed out of the hole and vanished. She heard him moving around below, then he reappeared with two blankets and her valise, went down again and brought up a jug. 'Drinking water.'

'I am coming down for a minute.' Caroline clambered down, which was considerably less easy than climbing up. 'I'll be back shortly,' she said as she went outside and headed for the edge of the clearing. There was a nice non-brambly clump of bushes just there, she recalled, and there were limits to how long she could be expected to sit in a tower trying not to think about running water. Although that was less uncomfortable than thinking about facing the man who had just brought her that shattering pleasure and almost relieved her of her maidenhood.

When she came back Gabriel was remaking the fire at the front edge of the hearth. 'I'll light it when you are up and keep it in all night, I've checked and the draw on the chimney is so good the smoke hardly gets into the chamber at all. When your father turns up I want the hearth to look as normal as possible.'

'You think of everything.' She paused beside him, laid her hand on his arm. 'Thank you so much. No one else would help me like this.'

'You have nothing to thank me for. I have nothing to lose by it and I was bored.'

She tried to disregard the cynicism which she suspected masked a very real anger over their almost-lovemaking. 'But if he discovers you helped me, my father might call you out.' Under her fingers she could feel the strength of his forearm, a swordsman's arm.

'And I would refuse to fight a man old enough to be my father, a perfectly honourable course.'

'Lucas, then!'

'I'd put him on his back with a neat rapier hole in his shoulder. Much less dangerous to his health than pistols.'

'You are exasperatingly calm about all this.' Caroline sat down on the simple wooden chair, her legs refusing to tolerate any more.

'I'm sorry.' Gabriel hitched one hip on the table and folded his arms. He had an edge to him that was new to her, the sense that he was operating at a different level of concentration and awareness than anyone else. Perhaps this was what made him the successful gambler that he was. Or perhaps that was what a frustrating, almost sexual encounter did to a man.

'Would you rather we had high drama?' he asked. 'I find that sort of thing distracting. Tomorrow I will send a letter and arrange a rendezvous. The hermit will vanish and your father has no means of finding him because every step of the process in London was under false names. My eminently sensible and well-connected friends will put their heads together with us and we will decide on how you can vanish and begin a new life.'

'I have been incredibly lucky, haven't I? And hopelessly naive.' The awareness swept through her along with the weariness. 'I was so worried about Anthony's lands that I came up with a quite shocking solution and I did not deserve your forbearance. And now you rescue me again at the risk of scandal.'

'Scandal does not concern me.'

'Why not?' She was almost asleep where she sat now, drowsy with reaction and a strange mixture of tension and relief. And awareness. The room seemed to be full of man… This man who now knew her body intimately, while she knew him not at all.

'There's a Scottish proverb I have always held by. *They say! What say they? Let them say.* I concern myself with the good opinion of those I respect, everyone else can go to the devil. And you, my lady, are asleep where you sit. Bed for you.'

That seemed such a good idea. He was pulling her to her feet and his arms were around her and he smelt of warmth and yew trees, smoke and man, and something musky. Mingled, it made a very excellent scent. 'Bottle it,' Caroline murmured, holding on to as much of Gabriel as she could get her arms around. Yes, bed was a wonderful idea. Bed with Gabriel.

'Asleep and dreaming,' he murmured in her ear. 'Come on, one foot in front of the other, and duck…and this foot up and there you go.'

A large hand was under her backside and she was heaved unceremoniously up and into the secret chamber. Her searching fingers found rough wool and Caroline had enough strength to roll on to one blanket and pull the other over her. Then she fell asleep.

Chapter Nine

Caroline woke to the scent of wood smoke mingling with coffee and bacon. A faint red glow marked the entrance to the chamber and she realised that Gabriel must have stirred up the fire and was making breakfast. She stretched, blushing as she remembered last night.

She crawled to the entrance and called down, 'Gabriel?' before she could think about being shy.

His voice echoed up the chimney. 'Stay there and I'll scout around.'

'But I need—'

'Stay!'

He was back within moments. 'Someone is coming. Keep back, keep silent.'

All thoughts of coffee, of embarrassment, of a convenient bush or of warm water vanished. Caroline retreated into the corner with the valises, pulling the blankets with her, and heard what had alerted Gabriel, the hoofbeats of horses moving fast.

'My lord?' That was Gabriel, his voice carrying from outside. He must have left the door open.

'My daughter. Have you seen her?'

'Lady Caroline? Not since last night, my lord. Is something amiss?' Gabriel had remembered his Welsh accent.

'Of course there's something damn well amiss, you idiot! She is missing.' That was Woodruffe.

'Search the place.' Her father again. There was the sound of booted feet on the stone flags.

'My lord, I protest!'

'You are in my employ and this is my property. I'll search what and where I please.' Her father was in the room now, his angry voice carrying clearly up the chimney. Caroline froze into immobility as the scraping of furniture being dragged over the flagged floor drowned out the sound of voices.

There's virtually nothing to search once they've overturned the bed. A loud thud suggested they had just done that.

'The chimney.'

'But the fire, my lord. It's alight.' That was one of the grooms.

'Step round it and look up, you dolt. Take the lantern.'

'I can see the sky, my lord,' the man said after a moment. A flicker of light hit the wall opposite the opening, but from below she knew the entrance was invisible. 'There's no one up there, that's for sure. And there's no ladder or rope or anything.'

'All right, come out, take that path there. You, go down that ride. Look for tracks.'

'My lord, I may be in your employ, but that does not mean I have to accept accusations of assisting in—what? A kidnap? Abduction? Elopement?' Gabriel had found just the right note of angered innocence.

'You, and every man in this place, will accept what I say,' her father snapped. 'And you spent time with her. Enough time for her to wind you round her finger.'

'And why should Lady Caroline do that, my lord?'

'Mind your own business and keep your place, damn you.'

Her nails were digging into her palms at the threat in her father's voice. She had seen him use his whip once on a hedger who had answered back. If he struck Gabriel she had no idea what the reaction would be. Murder, probably.

She had moved to the opening when Gabriel, sounding like an affronted Welsh solicitor's clerk, said, 'Then I must reconsider my employment here.'

Caroline stuffed her knuckles into her mouth to stifle the sudden urge to laugh. He was a loss to the stage, her father's hermit.

'Don't be a fool. Who else will pay you for sitting on a stump writing poetry? Stay here and keep watch. If you see anything, send to the house. If you can lay hands on her, lock her in the chapel.'

There was the sound of horses moving off, of shouts becoming fainter.

'Stay put a little longer,' Gabriel said quietly from below. 'I'll climb the hill and locate them all.'

It seemed like an hour before he came back, but she supposed, counting her own pounding pulse in the darkness, that it was only a few minutes.

'You can come down now.' When she arrived in front of him, rumpled and dusty and sneezing from the soot, he checked from the door again. 'You're safe to go out for a few minutes now, I'll heat you some water.'

When she returned Gabriel was busy at the fireside. 'Here, have some coffee. I have seen them all at a good distance. The guests are out with your father on horseback. There were three grooms, also mounted, they've gone down towards the lake away from here. I could see

people searching on foot, but they're nearer the house. I
think you can wash and we can safely have breakfast, then
I'll go to the village and leave a letter at the posting house.'

Caroline sat down with more of a bump than she had
intended. 'Don't go yet.' Her voice wavered and she took
a moment to steady it. 'The post boy doesn't get to the inn
until past ten.'

Gabriel put a mug on the table beside her and hunkered
down to look into her face. 'Are you about to cry?' He
sounded less than happy at the thought.

'No, of course not.' She wished she felt as confident of
that as she sounded. 'I am just rather…shaken, I suppose.'

'Is this about last night?' He jerked his head towards
the bed. 'Do you want to go back home?'

'No!'

'I wouldn't let you if you did.' Gabriel got to his feet
with a swish of brown robes. 'I would assume you'd lost
your wits. Look, last night must have been…fraught. You
are tired. You are anxious and uncertain and you have no
idea what is going to happen to you. And you have lost
control of the situation to me. That's a combination cal-
culated to make you weepy or angry or stupidly docile.
Any one of those would be perfectly natural, but we have
no time for any of them.'

'I can certainly manage anger,' she said and sat up
straight to glare at him. 'Do you talk to every lady of
your acquaintance like this? That must explain your reputation as a lover.'

'Sarcasm does not become you. And, no, I do not usually talk to a lady like that.' Gabriel smiled. The slow,
reminiscent curl of his lips made something shift inside
her, distracted her for a moment, dismayed her as she recognised both desire and jealousy in the jumble of emotions. 'I am speaking to you frankly as I would to a man

because we do not have the luxury of soft words and end-
less discussion here.'

Gabriel had not treated her as another man last night.
He must have seen the kindling light of indignation in
her eyes because he threw up his hands, palm out in the
fencer's sign of surrender. 'Wash and eat your breakfast
while I write the letter outside where I can keep an eye
on things, then back up the chimney with you and I'll go
to the village.'

Irritation with the entire male sex got her through bacon
and eggs. Caroline cleaned the plate and mug in the bucket
of warm water by the fire and put them away, leaving the
remains of Gabriel's own breakfast where they lay. He
could do his own washing up and besides, it emphasised to
anyone who looked in that there was only one person there.

She scrambled up the chimney by herself, still determined to show him that she was not some weak and
clinging female, subject to weeping. Show him that those
moments in his bed had meant nothing. It was only as she
rolled herself into the blanket and tried to catch up on her
sleep that she realised he had probably been deliberately
provoking her into just this spirit of militant determination. 'Wretch,' she muttered, despite the tinge of admiration for his tactics.

The day passed somehow. She slept, woke to find Gabriel had returned from the village and came down to eat,
then retreated back to her cave. Life was beginning to take
on an unreal, dreamlike quality. Perhaps she would spend
for ever in this safe, smoky little chamber, venturing out
at night like some woodland creature. Behind the unreality was the awareness that Gabriel was there, standing
between her and whatever lurked in the darkness beyond
the fire.

She worried about Anthony and how she would be able to write to him now. Would she find some way to see him when he was at school? How would she know if he was ill or unhappy? She had done the best she could for him, but she fretted that it was not enough. Her only consolation was that if she was married to Woodruffe she would not be with her brother either.

There was another visitation, this time by some of the guests, although they did not enter the chapel. The lurch of fear at the sound of their shouts shattered her dreaming state and she lay, gripping the edge of the blanket, as tense as a leveret hearing the fox stalking towards it through the grass.

When they had gone Gabriel stayed outside and she supposed he was presenting an innocent face to anyone who might be secretly observing. Eventually, stupefied by a mixture of boredom and anxiety, Caroline slept again.

She woke at the sound of someone inside the chimney, grabbed the water jug and raised it to throw as the pale oval of a face, eerily lit, rose above the edge of the opening.

'It's me,' Gabriel said, sharply.

'You frightened the life out of me. What happened to your beard?'

'Shaved it off. The relief is immense.' He boosted himself into the tiny room and pulled a candle and flint from his pocket. When he struck a light she could see that he was in breeches and shirtsleeves, his hair tied back.

'Oh.' Caroline grounded the jug and sat down again in her nest of blankets. 'But if anyone sees you they will guess something is wrong.'

'Petrus the Hermit has evaporated. We are about to leave.'

'Already?'

'It is almost dawn. The letter will have reached London by the evening post and one of my friends will be on his way with some sort of vehicle by now. I wrote to the two of them who are in London at the moment.'

'You are sure someone will come? What if they were engaged yesterday evening?'

'The letter had my seal with a certain mark we all use beside it. Our servants know to deliver messages immediately if they see that. Cris de Feaux once left a royal *levée* to bail Alex out of gaol when his footman smuggled that in to him.'

'The Marquess of Avenmore? But no one leaves a *levée* before the king. What did he do?'

'Fainted dramatically. Full length—which you have to agree is considerable—in front of the princesses. They had a lovely time fussing over him.'

'I have never spoken to him, but the Marquess of Avenmore looks so chilly and correct. I can't believe he would do such a thing.'

'Neither did anyone else. Therefore it could only have been genuine, so he got away with it. Cris has got away with a lot behind that façade of perfection.'

'And he would drive through the night for me?'

'No, for me. Although that's not to say he wouldn't rescue you if he knew you needed it. It might be Cris who comes or it might be Alex Tempest, who is Viscount Weybourn. The third of my closest friends, Grant Rivers, the Earl of Allundale, is at home in Northumberland. Come to think of it, Cris is probably still engrossed with the smuggler's widow, his new wife, so my money would be on Alex.'

Smuggler's widow? No, do not ask, just be thankful for rescue, although it was a shock to discover that three noblemen whom she had always assumed were upstanding members of society were, apparently, as ramshackle as Gabriel.

'There's hot water below and tea. You come down and get ready, I'll keep watch.' Gabriel vanished down the chimney, then called up, 'Hand down the valises first.'

An all-over wash in a bucket in front of the embers of the fire was bliss. Caroline had not realised how sticky and sooty she had become until she was clean again. She put on the fresh underwear she had packed, braided her hair tightly out of the way and found Gabriel outside checking over the clearing in the gathering light.

'Just making certain it all looks normal out here. I'll build the fire up, so there will be smoke from the chimney for a time, and we'll leave the interior as though I was coming back. It might just win us an advantage if they come by and assume I'm down at the lake or communing with nature in the woods.'

'Do you often commune with nature?' Caroline found she was feeling a trifle tipsy. The sense of unreality had returned.

Gabriel gave a snort of amusement. 'I wouldn't know how.'

No, she supposed he spent far too much time in smoky gaming hells. *When he isn't entertaining ladies in their luxurious silk-hung bedchambers.* 'This Spartan life must have been uncomfortable for you, in that case.' It came out more tartly than she had intended and she saw the sidelong look he sent her.

'I am capable of roughing it,' Gabriel said mildly. 'I do occasionally set foot outside, you know, but I am not used to spending so much time simply existing in one spot in the countryside.' He slung a leather satchel over his shoulder and picked up the valises. 'It is curiously restful. At least, it might be if I wasn't trying to remember my Welsh accent and using far too much energy keeping my temper with your father. Ready?'

'Ready.' She managed a smile as she fell into step beside him. What on earth was she doing? She was running away from home with a man she barely knew other than as a hardened gambler and a skilful deceiver. Just by leaving Knighton Park she had compromised herself and, after just one night alone with a man, had almost ruined herself. Not that Gabriel appeared to have been very affected by those hectic moments on his bed, Caroline thought ruefully, all too aware of the rangy body moving easily beside her, the wicked gypsy-dark looks of the man she was trusting with her life.

I might as well be hanged for a sheep as a lamb. If I am ruined it is a pity not to do it properly, not that he shows any interest in actually making love to me. He must be right and it was simply reaction, heat of the moment.

She stumbled over a tree root and Gabriel caught her arm, steadied her and then walked on, apparently as untroubled by the contact as he had been untouched by nearly making love to her last night.

Caroline resisted the urge to rub her arm where those long fingers had curled and held her, tried to ignore the shiver of heat that ran to her fingertips. *He doesn't want me.* He touched her with a careless efficiency that somehow underlined how unimportant those moments of contact were to him and was now acting like a totally impersonal escort through the woods.

She would do better to stop entertaining immodest thoughts about the Earl of Edenbridge and think instead about what she was going to do when she reached London. She had no money, no references and no skills to market. She doubted whether she'd even make a halfway competent housemaid. It was one thing knowing how a household should be run, another to have the knack of polishing metalwork, getting stains out of carpets or black-leading grates. She could speak French competently, Italian a little, play the piano and add up accounts, so she supposed she might be employable as a governess in a not-very-demanding household. But who would entrust their children to an unknown young woman with no recommendations?

Perhaps Gabriel was a forger as well as a lock-picking, play-acting, potential blackmailer… Her thoughts came to a crashing stop as she walked into his exceedingly solid back. *'Ough!'*

He had stopped behind a large oak by the opening into the lane that led to the turnpike road. 'All clear.' He turned towards the highway.

'The village is that way.' Caroline pointed to the footpath that led away across the meadows.

'I said in the note to meet us at the junction where the gibbet is. With any luck no one will see the carriage and they certainly would if it were to drive into the village to collect us. If we keep to the wheel ruts we will avoid leaving tracks in the dewy grass.'

Caroline hitched up her skirts, jumped the shallow ditch and followed. 'They gibbeted Black Sam Baggins the highwayman there last year and they haven't taken the remains down yet. It's disgusting.'

'All the more reason for no one to suspect you'd be hanging around there—if you'll pardon the expression—waiting for a passing vehicle.'

When they reached the sinister black gallows with the dangling iron cage Gabriel contemplated the revolting object while Caroline studiously counted how many varieties of wild flower she could see in the opposite hedge.

'There's not a lot left of him,' Gabriel remarked.

'Some of the local people stole his clothes very early on, before he began to…you know. And now the superstitious ones have been taking bits as they drop off—finger and toe bones and so forth. They grind them up and put them in medicines. Apparently fragments of highwaymen aren't as efficacious as murderers, but we haven't had any of those for many years, thank goodness.'

'What on earth are deceased highwayman's toes supposed to cure?' Gabriel sounded more intrigued than disgusted. 'There's a fallen tree over there you can sit on while we wait. It looks dry, it is shielded from the road and you won't have to contemplate the remains of Black Sam.'

Caroline sat down. 'I think the bones are a cure for toothache and sore throats.'

'I'd rather have the sore throat. You stay here.' Gabriel melted away into the undergrowth.

By straining her eyes she could just make him out, still and watchful, his attention on the road. For a man who said he spent little time communing with nature, he certainly knew how to take advantage of it when he needed to. His russet greatcoat with its modest double cape and the conker-brown leather of his boots merged into the mottled foliage of the hedgerow and his dark head was hidden in the shade as the sun at last began to penetrate the trees.

As she stared she was able to make out one ungloved hand resting on the low bough of a young oak, then the sunlight sparked a glint of light off something metallic and she realised he was holding a pistol. If her father came, or Lucas, would he fire? Would she want him to? Of course not. But he wouldn't, she told herself. He would threaten, that was all. Gabriel wasn't reckless, nor really a criminal. He simply had a rather broader view of acceptable behaviour for an earl than she was used to.

There was the thud of hooves, felt through the soles of her boots before she heard it, then the jingle of a harness and an elegant carriage, glossy black and driven by a team of fine bays, appeared around the corner and drew up opposite her. The horses sidled and snorted, sensing perhaps the horrid thing hanging from the gibbet, and the coachman soothed them with a murmured word.

They stilled and for a moment nothing moved. Then Gabriel stepped out into the road, the hand that had held the pistol empty at his side. 'Good morning to you, Thomas.'

The coachman touched the brim of his hat. 'Good morning, my lord.'

The door on the far side from Caroline swung open and a man got out. 'This is a damnably early hour for anything but a duel, Gabe,' he remarked, his voice a pleasant drawl. 'Have you any idea what time I had to get out of my bed?'

'Did you bother to go to it?' Gabriel enquired. Caroline caught a glimpse of him across the backs of the horses as he strode forward and took the other man by the shoulders in a brief, fierce embrace.

'Oh, yes,' his friend said with a chuckle as he returned the gesture with a buffet to Gabriel's arm. 'My lady wife expects me to act in a husbandly manner these days.' Despite the laughter in his voice it was obvious to Caroline that this was one husband who was not bored with his marital bed.

'And how is Lady Weybourn?' Gabriel led his friend around the carriage.

'Blooming, now the queasiness has left her. But why the devil am I summoned to this particularly gruesome spot at the crack of dawn?'

'To rescue a lady in distress. Caroline, come and meet Alex Tempest.'

She emerged from her hiding place and walked towards

them, smiling slightly at the contrast between Gabriel's wild looks and the careless way he wore his plain and practical clothing and the elegant gentleman with the quizzical brows and the fashionable crop.

'Oh, well done, Gabe,' Viscount Weybourn said as she emerged. 'And about time, too.'

Chapter Ten

'No,' Gabriel said. 'No, no, and absolutely no. You have the wrong end of the stick, Alex.' Caroline was staring at him as though he was talking complete nonsense. Alex was within a whisker of a smirk. And of receiving a right hook to the chin.

'Lady Caroline, may I present Alex Tempest, Viscount Weybourn. Alex, Lady Caroline Holm, the daughter of Lord Knighton. Lady Caroline finds it necessary to leave her home clandestinely. Alone.'

'Alone?' Alex's infuriatingly expressive eyebrows rose. 'Then this is not an elo—'

'Absolutely not.' Caroline, thankfully, was still looking mystified. Gabriel contemplated kicking Alex on the ankle, then settled for saying, 'I am merely helping Lady Caroline remove herself from her father's house.'

'Where to?'

'London to start with. What happens after that is still to be decided.'

'Urgent, I gather?' Alex offered Caroline his arm and began to walk back to the carriage. 'I believe we have danced together at Almack's before now, Lady Caroline.'

'Just Caroline, please. And, yes, I recall that with pleasure, Lord Weybourn.'

'Before we begin a delightful reminiscence of every time the pair of you have met socially, could we get on our way, do you think?' Gabriel retrieved the bags and handed them up to the coachman. 'There is a certain urgency.'

'Why? An infuriated father with a shotgun on your trail?' Alex helped Caroline into a forward-facing seat and sat down beside her, leaving Gabriel to sit with his back to the horses. He lounged back into a corner and propped his boots up on the other end of the bench, enjoying Alex's wince at the insult to the plush upholstery.

'That and the prospect of a trip to the altar with Woodruffe.'

'Lord Woodruffe? Edgar Parfit?' Alex's eyes narrowed. 'No, really, Caroline, you don't want to go marrying him. A sad dog, that one.'

'No, of course I don't, which is why I am leaving home and Lord Edenbridge is helping me.'

'Your father is not open to reason on the subject?'

'No.'

There was a tremor in her voice and Gabriel glared at Alex, even as he saw the other man's face harden as he heard it, too. He knew about Woodruffe's proclivities, too, it appeared.

'Nothing for it but to take a bolt to town, I see,' Alex said easily. 'You've nothing to worry about now. Gabe's a scape-gallows, but I am thoroughly reliable and exceedingly respectable.'

'If you are respectable it is only because of Tess's influence.'

'The love of a good woman,' Alex said smugly.

Was that why Alex was so eager to assume this was an elopement—he was in love and therefore Gabriel's actions must stem from the same source? He liked Caroline. Very much, he realised as he watched her making the effort to be calm and pleasant with Alex. He admired her. He desired her physically, which was hardly a surprise to him. And he would fight anyone who tried to hurt her. But then any gentleman with a shred of honour was duty-bound to protect a lady. The uncomfortable feeling of possessiveness was simply because this was the lady whose safety had fallen to him to defend.

'Now, are you hungry, Caroline?' Alex said. 'We have a breakfast hamper under Gabriel's seat. Dig it out, there's a good fellow.'

'Food that someone else has cooked?' Gabriel swung his feet down and bent to explore the wicker basket. He was hungry. That was probably why he was brooding on his emotional state, of all things. 'Heaven.'

'Do I deduce that you have been fending for yourself?' Alex caught the packet of bacon-filled rolls that Gabriel tossed at him. 'That I should like to see.'

'Lord Edenbridge has been acting as a hermit, part of my father's landscaped park.' Caroline took the roll Alex passed to her and a napkin that Gabriel unearthed from the hamper. 'The kitchen sent him down supplies, but he has been cooking for himself in the hermitage.'

'One snigger from you, Tempest, and you will regret it,' Gabriel warned.

'Dressed how?' Alex demanded, filling beakers from a flask of cold tea. 'Not in robes, surely?'

'Oh, yes, with an enormous beard and a beautiful Welsh accent.' Caroline was recovering her spirits along with the food, Gabriel was glad to see. 'He was very convincing.'

'Of course I saw the beard.' Alex chuckled. 'He was able to fool even Tess with such a disguise. But why—?' Under Gabriel's fulminating stare Alex snapped his mouth shut, but there was more speculation than amusement in the sharp hazel gaze that met his.

'Later,' Gabriel said. 'I am only going to explain this once and I have no doubt there will be an audience awaiting us. Where are we going?'

'Half Moon Street. My house. I sent a note to Cris and told him I would fetch you, but you are right, it is certain we'll find him there with Tamsyn when we arrive.'

'The Marquess of Avenmore? I have never met him, but I know his reputation. He is not going to approve of me, is he?' Caroline sounded anxious again.

'Cris is a pussy cat since his smuggler's widow got her hands on him,' Gabriel said, contemplating the choice between a raised pork pie or a slice of cheese flan and deciding on both.

'He'll fillet you if he hears you describing Tamsyn in those terms.' Alex poured Caroline some more tea and settled to explaining that the new marchioness was a perfectly respectable lady who had committed the minor indiscretion of a first marriage to the leader of a gang of smugglers.

She was relaxing now, even laughing at Alex's irreverent remarks. He had an indecent amount of charm when he chose to exert it. Before his marriage he had been wary of directing it at unmarried ladies and since his marriage he was probably in danger of grievous bodily harm from his adoring wife if he flirted, but Gabriel could tell he could not resist trying to put Caroline at her ease.

He should be glad of it. The last thing they wanted on their hands was a frightened woman, too nervous to make a decision about her own future. On the other hand, his idiocy last night had probably given her plenty to think about. Thank heavens he'd the self-control to stop. But what had he been thinking about? *With my damn boots on, too.* He could only account for it as the release of tension after the dangers of the night.

'What are you glowering about?' Alex enquired.

'Is anything wrong, Gabriel?'

The last thing he needed was anxious sympathy and a pair of worried blue eyes gazing at him, to feel this strange pang under his breastbone because she was looking weary and that lovely blonde hair was bedraggled, with just one lock coming loose to her collar. He wanted to kiss the shadows under those periwinkle eyes...

'Tired, that's all. If Alex would only be quiet for five minutes together, I'd go to sleep.' He stretched his legs out along the seat again, tipped his hat over his eyes and prepared to feign slumber. It came immediately, taking him by surprise, whirling him down into soft darkness and strange dreams, soothed by a soft, unfamiliar chuckle. *I've never heard her laugh, not like that...* Gabriel slept.

'We have arrived. Do you have a veil?'

Alex's words, the first in over an hour, jerked Caroline out of the trance state she had entered as the effects of food, warmth and safety took effect. She had been watching Gabriel as he slept, his long body loose and beautiful in its unconsidered sprawl. He should have seemed vulnerable, but she had seen the sudden tensing of his hands as they had slowed for a turnpike, then the instant relaxation as the familiar bustle of the gate registered with his sleeping brain. In a crisis he would have been awake and dangerous in seconds.

'A veil? No, I am sorry.' Of course, the viscount would not want his neighbours recognising the crumpled and unchaperoned female stumbling out of his carriage. This was a fashionable street and at least a few residents would know her by sight.

'No need to worry, Tess made me bring one.' Alex produced a handful of black gauze from his pocket and she swathed it over head and face as Gabriel sat up, got his feet on the floor and his hat straight.

'What time is it?'

'Gone twelve. Later than I'd planned, but Caroline would not let me spring the horses, said it would wake you up.'

Alex got out as the front door opened and Caroline made a business of ordering her skirts, grateful that the veil obscured her blush at the look Gabriel sent her. No doubt he was as surprised over her concern as Alex had been.

'Have you got them safe?' A lady was in the hall, flushed from Alex's enthusiastic kiss. Caroline's immediate impression was of softness—soft brown hair, soft curves on a slender frame, soft voice. 'Oh, yes, there you are, Gabriel, and this must be— Oh!' Caroline pushed back the folds of her veil. 'But you are Lady Caroline Holm, I recognise you, although we have never met.' She turned to the open door behind her. 'Cris, Tamsyn, they are here safe.'

The tall, intimidating figure of the Marquess of Avenmore appeared in the doorway and, in front of him, a young woman who said, 'But I've seen you before. In the corridor at Lady Ancaster's soirée, with Gabriel.'

'At Lady Ancaster's…' That must have been when Gabriel had just kissed her, had told her that he had never meant to act on the IOU for her virtue, had dismissed her, leaving her feeling naive and gauche and unwanted. This young woman had come up behind Gabriel. Had she overheard what Caroline had said? *A promise is a promise, but if you do not want me—*

It could have meant anything, she told herself desper-

ately. *If you do not want me to dance with you next week.
If you do not want me to give you one of the kittens…*

'Kittens,' she said out loud, wondering if she was about
to faint.

'For goodness sake, the poor dear is on the point of collapse.' It was the brunette again. 'Make room, all of you,
and let her come into the drawing room.'

Hands propelled her through the door before she had
the opportunity to make her curtsy to the marquess, which
suddenly seemed important. She found herself seated on a
chaise in front of a small fire that was comforting, despite
the warmth of the day.

'Tea is coming. Now put up your feet and we will send
these men out.' The brunette made vague flapping ges-
tures as though shooing chickens and the three large males
obediently took themselves off, leaving the room sooth-
ingly quiet.

'Now do not feel you have to explain anything just yet,'
the lady from the soirée said. 'If you have been with Gabriel for several days you probably just want to lie down
with a cold compress on your head and sip camomile tea.
That man manages to be utterly exhausting, even when
he is simply standing still.'

'It is because he looks as though he is thinking wicked
thoughts all the time,' the soft-voiced one said. 'Really *very*
wicked thoughts, even when he has a perfectly straight
face. And I get intrigued and wonder about them and how
wicked they are…and then I catch his eye and I am convinced he knows I am imagining such things so I blush and
he smiles and then—' She laughed. 'And here I am, very
happily married, passionately in love with my husband,
pregnant, and the very last thing I want is to be doing anything even mildly naughty with Gabriel Stone. I'm Tess,

by the way. Teresa Tempest, which is a ridiculous name.
And this is Tamsyn de Feaux.'

'Lady Weybourn, Lady Avenmore.' Caroline dragged
her tumbling thoughts back from contemplating Gabriel
and wickedness and tried to remember her manners. 'I am
Caroline Holm, Lord Knighton's daughter.'

'And you are very welcome to my house,' Tess said
warmly. 'Gabriel's note simply said you needed rescuing.
May we ask what from?'

'Edgar Parfit, Lord Woodruffe. And, I suppose, from
my father.'

'He wants you to marry that slug? Well then, certainly
you must be rescued!' Tess turned to Tamsyn. 'Have you
met him? He's a nasty, unhealthy, pale colour with fat
hands and thick lips and a beastly habit of ogling any female who is not well protected. Even when you are, he
tries to stand too close, or brush against you by *accident*.
I stood on his toes with my new French heels the other
evening—quite by accident, of course. He had tried to
pinch my *derrière*. And he must need money because he
is wildly extravagant.'

'Fortunately I haven't been out in London society long
enough to have encountered him.' Tamsyn regarded Caroline, head on one side. Caroline made an effort to sit up
straighter and not look as feeble as she felt, just at this
moment. This woman, the smuggler's widow, looked as
though she would take a musket to Lord Woodruffe if pro-
voked, not run away. 'I suppose that just refusing to marry
him didn't work?'

'No.' Caroline took a deep breath. 'You will probably
think I am exaggerating the problem. I had better tell you
everything.' *Not about my IOU, bartering my virginity for
the deeds, but everything else. They need to understand.*

* * *

There was silence when she finished, then Tamsyn, her faint Devon accent heightened by emotion. said, 'Your father is somewhat obsessional, is he not? And in the grip of a strong compulsion to gamble. I can understand how dangerous that can be. My cousin Franklin, Lord Chelford, got himself in over his head with gambling debts, then moneylenders, and ended with vandalism, murder and an attempt to frame me for the crime.'

'And he almost managed to murder you,' Tess said with a shudder. 'It is all a secret, of course. People think he went slightly insane and died after an unfortunate encounter with a Bow Street Runner.

'Anyway, we understand that people do act in these extreme ways and that you aren't exaggerating in the slightest. Besides anything else, if your father is going to use force, then nothing else matters. And Gabriel is just the person to help, he was wonderful with Tamsyn's problem.'

'Once he stopped lecturing Cris on how unsuitable I was for a marquess,' Tamsyn said with a grimace. 'He was quite right, of course, but it did not endear him to me at the time!'

'There are four of them, close friends.' Caroline tried to pick her way through the relationships. 'Gabriel, your husbands and someone else? Gabriel did tell me, but I'm afraid I have forgotten.'

'Grant Rivers, Earl of Allundale. He and his wife Kate live up in Northumberland with their two children. I wish they would come down to London for a while, but Kate is shy of society. So, you have five of us on hand to help, although if you need to flee the area, I am sure Grant and Kate would give you sanctuary.'

'I can't just run away and hide for ever. I do not have any money, just a little jewellery, so I must earn my living somehow. I suppose I could become a nursery governess, or a companion to a reclusive old lady, if you wouldn't mind providing me with references? I am very reliable, despite appearances.'

And horribly afraid, and ridiculously homesick, despite everything. And Anthony. Could I have looked after him any better by staying?

'It would not be as bad as marriage to the Egregious Edgar, but a pretty grim existence nevertheless,' Tess said. 'I almost ended up like that, only in my case it was that or become a nun.'

A nun? 'I can see that marriage to Lord Weybourn was preferable,' Caroline said, finding her spirits rising as she finished her second cup of tea. She still could see no easy way out of her problems, but at least she felt confident her new friends would not desert her. She need not feel afraid now and married to Woodruffe she would have been just as cut off from Anthony.

There was a tap on the door and a maid came in. 'The bath is ready, my lady. And Miss Perkins is brushing and pressing your gowns, ma'am,' she added with a bob of a curtsy to Caroline.

'A bath would be heaven,' Caroline said as the door closed behind the maid. 'I have spent a day and a night up a chimney.'

'I would have thought that Gabriel would look after a lady better than that,' Tamsyn said with a chuckle. 'On the other hand, he is the only man I know who would think of hiding someone in such a place, so, on balance, it was probably for the best.'

'Are you ready to get out now, ma'am? Or should I top up the hot water?'

'Oh, top it up, please. I'll lie here for a while longer.'

Caroline slid under the scented water once more, rubbing at her scalp until she was convinced that every last piece of grit, soot and dead spider was out of it.

'I'll be back in a while then, ma'am.' The maid heaped towels on a chair and went out.

After ten minutes the water began to cool and there was no sign of the maid. Or of a bell pull. Caroline climbed out and wrapped herself in a large bath sheet, towelled her hair and began to explore. She tried one door and found herself in a large bedchamber, the dressing table littered with perfume sprays, hair brushes and ribbons. She rather suspected that this was Tess's own room.

She could hardly rummage in the clothes presses for a robe. Caroline tied her damp hair up into a turban with a small towel and cracked open the door on to the corridor. Still no sign of the maid, so she ventured out, her bare toes curling into the deep pile of the carpet runner over the polished boards. What had happened to the girl?

The door opposite her opened, she took a hasty step backwards, trod on the trailing edge of the towel and sat down with a thud as one of the Roman emperors appeared on the threshold.

'Caroline? What the devil are you doing?' Not a Roman emperor, just Gabriel, swathed as she was in linen.

'Looking for the maid.' She scrabbled at the fabric, too embarrassed to look down and see just how much of her wet body was exposed. Even if there was no bare flesh, then damp linen was surely clinging to every curve. She tried to hold Gabriel's gaze to stop it moving down below her face. 'She vanished and I've no robe.'

'Nor have I and Alex's valet is nowhere to be seen.' He grinned, but behind the amusement was something she had never seen in his face before, the thing that had been piquing her feminine pride ever since her first reckless

proposal to him. There was heat in his eyes, and awareness, and he was not the rake who had made the agreement,
not the man who had kissed her at the soirée. And he was
most certainly not the hermit who had been focused on
knight-errantry and rescuing her from her father's ploys.

This Gabriel was looking at her as a man looks at a
woman he wants, with all his attention, and she had no idea
whether she was terrified or thrilled. It had meant something to him, after all. *He is remembering what nearly happened in the chapel, he desires me.* The blood was singing
in her veins and her breath was coming in short gasps and
the sight of his naked shoulders and arms was enough to
make her want to drag him back into the dressing room
and— He stepped back and closed the door sharply just
before she, too, heard the hurrying footsteps.

'Oh, miss, I'm ever so sorry, I was bringing your robe
from the laundry and then Prue knocked a pile of my
lady's lace on to the floor, so I bent to pick it up before
it got soiled and tripped up his lordship's valet who was
bringing Lord Edenbridge's robe and...'

'Not a problem. Just shut the door.' Caroline got to her
feet, careless of dignity. Those eyes, dark and intense and
locked with hers. She looked down at herself and was
faintly surprised not to see steam rising.

'Yes, miss. Sorry, miss.'

Caroline put on the robe and let the maid deal with her
hair, then dressed, scolding herself all the while.

*Focus. This is not about Gabriel. This is about making
a new life for myself, about staying safe. About not ending
up starving in the gutter or in some brothel. The man is a
rake and whatever he wants, even if it is me again for five
minutes, it will not last. So stop daydreaming. And anyway, he doesn't really want* me, *he's just a typical man.
That night we were so wound up it is a miracle we didn't*

combust from tension and just now I was sprawled at his feet, nearly naked. He would have reacted like that whoever it was.

'Her ladyship says, she can send up luncheon on a tray, or you are very welcome to come down. Whatever you wish, miss.'

'I'll go down.' Caroline put her shoulders back, her chin up and made for the stairs. This was the start of her new life as an independent woman and she was going to take control, with the help of her new friends and allies.

Chapter Eleven

'What is this? A Board of Inquiry, or a jury?' Gabriel entered the drawing room to find a semicircle of his friends facing him. 'I deny everything, on principle.'

The habit of self-protection, of hiding his feelings and his vulnerabilities, came back to help him. Then it had been a shelter from his father's savage temper, the act that had allowed him to be strong enough to protect his brothers, the locked door behind which he could trap his own fear and vulnerability, his own guilt that somehow he could have prevented his mother's suicide.

It had become his gambler's mask and now he was using it to conceal emotions from his closest friends. He did not understand what he was feeling himself and, if he was not careful, he was going to entangle an innocent woman, a woman who had to be protected from all the darkness in his soul, just as she must be protected from Woodruffe's cruelty.

'We are concerned, that is all.' Cris de Feaux sat back and crossed his legs, the gleam on his Hessians a reproach to every other pair of boots in the room.

'For both of you,' Tess said, a crease of worry between her finely drawn brown brows.

'You must admit, this affair is not going to be easy to carry off without scandal,' Alex said. 'Sherry?'

'Loathe the stuff. Scandal is out of the question. We need to get Caroline out of this with as little gossip as possible.' He slouched in the one remaining armchair, the one facing the jury, and concentrated on keeping the tension out of his expression. 'Woodruffe must not find out where she is, let alone her father. The man beat her.'

'Bastard,' Tamsyn said, with feeling. 'Men like that need a good flogging themselves.'

Caroline's slender shoulders as she sat there on the floor draped in that bath sheet, the pale, soft skin. The delicate bones under his hands on the narrow bed... He could not get the image out of his head. And that swine had struck her. He was going to pay for that.

'But I do not see how we can avoid scandal,' Tess said. 'Caroline is of age, of course, and that helps. But you can't marry her under a false name and even though you can obviously protect her physically, you can't hide her. This is not a novel with secret wives hidden in some tower in the forest. Knighton and Woodruffe will raise every kind of storm. Lady Caroline will never be received at Court.'

'Or, given your reputation already, Gabe, anywhere else,' Alex commented.

'Marriage?' Gabriel stared at them, jolted right out of his normal control. 'Are you mad? Whatever gave you the idea I want to *marry* the chit?' *Damnation, this was what came of brooding about* feelings, *I let my guard down and overreact.*

'The fact that you eloped with her?' Cris said.

'Lord Edenbridge did not elope with me. He helped me escape.' The voice from the doorway was cool and polite and, Gabriel could tell after days spent in her company, the speaker was furious.

The other men got to their feet and Gabriel followed, more slowly. Caroline was standing behind him, her hair in ringlets on top of her head, her creased gown restored to order, her expression completely unreadable.

'I have no intention of marrying Lord Edenbridge and he has no desire to marry me, which is an agreeable co-incidence, is it not?'

She passed him, close enough to touch, close enough for him to have reached out and twitched a pin or two out of that provoking coiffure to see her hair tumble free. Gabriel kept his hands by his side and worked on restoring his expression to one of amused calm.

'I am very grateful to you, my lord,' she said earnestly, stopping just in front of him. 'But if you call me a chit again I will have you kidnapped and force-fed sherry for a week.'

'You were eavesdropping,' he drawled, still fighting the tumbling curls fantasy. 'No one ever hears good of themselves by listening at doors.'

'A fortnight,' Caroline amended with a sweet smile.

Cris gave a crack of laughter. 'Please, take my chair, Lady Caroline.'

'Thank you, Lord Avenmore.'

She sat with perfect decorum, while Gabriel's memory provided a series of images of anything but ladylike behaviour—Caroline scrambling up the chimney, Caroline in a tangle of wet towels, Caroline standing on his hearth rug making him an outrageous proposition. Caroline under him in the split second before he got control of himself. He knew which version he preferred. He lowered his lids and sent her the smouldering look that was guaranteed to send innocent young debutantes fleeing to their mamas like a flock of panicking chickens. The one that should send her to safety from a man who was thoroughly unsuited for matrimony.

She looked down her nose at him, perfectly composed, then turned towards Tess. 'I do not expect ever to regain the place in society I once had,' she explained. 'I am hoping for something respectable, but retired, like a companion's post. I might pass muster as a nursery governess, I suppose. Or I could keep house, I have done that for my father for years.'

'You would need references,' Tamsyn pointed out. 'Although we could supply those.'

'You are ridiculously young to be a housekeeper,' Gabriel said, sharply enough for the others to turn and look at him.

'It is the most respectable option,' Tamsyn pointed out with annoying reasonableness. 'And the safest. Housekeepers have some status in the establishment so they are less at the mercy of predatory males in the household than governesses are and companions are very likely to become general dogsbodies.'

'Even so.' Gabriel waved a hand to encompass Caroline's face, hairstyle, figure. 'She looks far too young.' *And vulnerable. And tempting.* And she should be kept away from men like him. Men who had no model of a decent marriage, men whose very blood was tainted. *Blood.* The picture swirled back from behind the locked door. His father's broken body, the blood on the marble. His father dead, the death itself the scandal of the area because Gabriel had failed in his duty to those who depended on him.

'A cap, a pair of spectacles with plain glass and a severe manner,' suggested Tess, her head on one side, eyes narrowed, as she studied Caroline. 'Add a sensible wardrobe, a chatelaine... There is nothing like a bunch of keys rattling at the waist to give an impression of gravitas. I made Alex an admirable housekeeper.'

Her husband snorted. 'I would be interested to see the slightest evidence of gravitas, my lady.'

'I still do not like it,' Gabriel said, attempting to ignore their exchange of adoring looks. What the devil was he doing? He had brought Caroline here so his friends could help her and they were. It was not as though he had any brilliant ideas himself. They would help protect her from Woodruffe and her father and they would protect her from him, the man who wanted to taste that innocence at the same time as he wanted to guard it.

All three women sent him exasperated looks, Alex regarded the ceiling and pursed his lips in a silent whistle and Cris observed, 'If you do not marry Lady Caroline, her options are very limited.'

'Lord Edenbridge's wishes in the matter are irrelevant,' Caroline said, very pink in the face. 'I have no intention of marrying *him*. Grateful as I am to him for rescuing me, he is not, I am sure you would agree, suitable husband material.'

'I never suggested that I was,' Gabriel retorted. *But if I was, would I be courting you, Caroline? Would I want that smile and those lips, that loyalty and that passion, for myself? Oh, yes.*

'Luncheon is served, my lady.'

'I'm sure we'll all be in a much better frame of mind for planning when we have eaten,' Tess said, getting to her feet and leading the way to the dining room.

'How did you meet?' Cris enquired once they were all seated with food in front of them.

'My father lost an estate in Hertfordshire to Lord Edenbridge. It should have gone to my younger brother. I explained the situation and Lord Edenbridge kindly agreed to keep Springbourne in trust for Anthony until he is of age.'

The words *He did what?* hung unspoken in the air.

'Remarkably generous of you, Gabriel,' Cris eventually remarked.

'Remarkably unlike you,' Alex added.

'I am not in the business of robbing innocent striplings of their inheritance simply because their parent is a fool,' Gabriel retorted. 'I would never have accepted the stake if I had known. Lady Caroline saved me from an unwitting blunder.'

'It was brave of you to approach someone with such a wild reputation as Gabriel, Caroline,' Tamsyn said. 'That would have been at Lady Ancaster's soirée, I imagine.'

'No, I went to his house before then,' Caroline admitted calmly.

Surely she was not going to tell them about that outrageous offer? His conscience, unused to scrutiny in the harsh light of day, was still tender on that subject.

'I explained the circumstances frankly and Lord Edenbridge was very…accommodating.'

'I am still not clear when Gabriel realised you had a further problem, or quite what he was doing in Hertfordshire,' Cris said as he buttered a roll. 'From a fleeting allusion he made when he was down in Devon, I gather you had met some time in June, yet here we are in early August.'

'We had some limited correspondence about the estate,' Gabriel said, choosing his words with care. 'I suspected something was wrong and when I discovered that Lord Knighton was looking for a hermit for his park I thought it would be amusing to see if I could fool him and check on Lady Caroline's well-being at the same time.'

'A hermit?' For once he had the satisfaction of seeing

Cris's jaw drop. He made a quick recovery. 'Hence the appalling length of your hair, I assume,' he drawled.

'It went beautifully with the beard,' Caroline remarked demurely. 'Lord Edenbridge grew a most impressive one and spoke with a Welsh accent.'

'Yes, and please do not do it again.' Alex gave an exaggerated shudder. 'My dear fellow, one must make every effort to assist a lady, but really, there are limits.'

'I doubt you could produce a beard that would cover your features in under a month, Tempest,' Gabriel retorted.

'I'd advise a severe and fashionable crop as well,' Cris said. 'Just in case Knighton comes storming up to town and recognises his missing hermit. I'll get my valet to cut it for you.'

'The things I do for you, Lady Caroline,' Gabriel said, trying to recall the last time he had had a haircut that might have been thought *severe and fashionable*.

'I am exceedingly grateful, my lord.' She dimpled prettily at him across the table, looking so much like some airheaded miss, and so unlike the young woman he had come to know, that he almost choked on his ale.

'I have an idea,' Tess said suddenly. 'We'll go down and talk to Mrs Sanders, our housekeeper. She'll soon transform you into a convincing candidate.'

'She transforms me into a nervous jelly,' Alex admitted. 'Fearsome woman.'

'And Tamsyn and I will write you references, and I'll get in touch with Kate in Northumberland and ask her for one as well, and then you'll be ready to approach the domestic agencies. Unless we can come up with someone who needs a housekeeper before then.'

Needs a housekeeper... Really, his brain must have been atrophied by the country air. Why on earth had he not thought of it before? 'There is no need for references, although the training might be a good thing.' Gabriel put down his knife and fork and swept a glance around the table. 'May I present to you the new housekeeper of Springbourne?'

'Oh, how clever of you, Gabriel!' Caroline beamed at him across the table, all dignity forgotten, and he caught the swift exchange of glances between the other women at her use of his name. 'Why didn't I think of that? I'll be safe there until Anthony comes of age in five years' time. Father thinks it is yours, so he will have no reason to go anywhere near it. Then, when Anthony can legally control it, I can continue living with him.'

'Are there staff there now?' Tess asked.

'Just a few, I think, more for security than anything else,' she said, suddenly serious. 'They certainly do not know me by sight.'

'I sent my man of business down to report,' Gabriel said. 'He found a tenant at the Home Farm who had only been there a year and who seemed competent enough. The house is virtually shut up, as Caroline says, with an elderly housekeeper and a trio of indoor servants. He suggested I pension off the housekeeper, who is anxious to go and live with her sister in Worthing, and keep the other staff. I haven't had time to reply to him yet.'

'It is the perfect solution.' Caroline was glowing at him again, which was good for his self-esteem, but fatal for his detachment. Gabriel thought about scratchy beards, porridge and Edgar Parfit and shifted in his seat when all of those failed to stop most of his blood supply heading southwards. It was lust, simply lust, that he felt and the sooner she was away, the better.

'I will be working for my brother, so I can draw a wage and living expenses from the estate with a good conscience and I will make certain it is in perfect order for him when he can finally claim it.'

'What will you tell him?' Tamsyn asked. 'Does he know your father has lost the estate?'

'No. I thought it best not to say anything unless Father told Anthony, in case he reacted in a way that betrayed the secret. But I am sure my father has simply put it out of his mind. Water under the bridge.' She bit her lip. 'Anthony will be wondering why I haven't written, I always do every week while he is at school. Normally he'd be home now, but he is staying with a friend in Buckinghamshire. I miss him.' She smiled bleakly. 'I wonder when I will see him again.'

'We will discuss the details now if you have finished your luncheon.' Gabriel stood. 'I'll find my notes. There is no need to trouble the rest of you. We can use your breakfast room, I suppose, Tess?' There was a limit to how long he was prepared to stay the focus of his friends' fascinated scrutiny, or to endure Caroline looking at him in public as though he was her hero again. The sooner they had this sorted out and she was in safe seclusion in the country, the better.

'I'll come now, if you will excuse me?' She stood up, smiling at the others, and he wondered just how well that smile would stay fixed if she knew the lascivious thoughts that would not get themselves out of his head, the urge to seize her and snarl *Mine!* at every man who looked at her.

He picked up his portfolio from the luggage in the hall and led the way to the little breakfast room. Caroline sat on the sofa, folded her hands neatly in her lap and appeared ready to give him her full attention, much as if he was addressing a public meeting.

Nettled, Gabriel sat at his ease in the chair opposite her, fished out the correspondence from his agent and ran a finger down it. 'I'll get him to pension off the old house-keeper and tell the staff I will send them a new one.

'Now, money. Wilkins is already managing the staff salaries. I'll have him add you to the list, but pay you a year in advance, and I'll authorise you to draw on an account for everything you need for the household and for yourself.'

'Will he not be surprised at the payment in advance?' She yawned, hastily hiding it behind her hand.

'He'll assume you are one of my light-skirts that I am paying off,' Gabriel said with deliberate crudity as he studied the papers again. He had no idea what was motivating him, which was worrying in itself. Perhaps he wanted to prove to himself that he was the same old rakehell he had always, so comfortably, been. Or perhaps he simply wanted to provoke some reaction, even if it was only a delightful blush.

There was no response. He looked up, anticipating one of Caroline's frosty stares, which were stimulating in their own way, and found that she was asleep, slumped sideways on to the sofa cushions. The piled curls were already surrendering to the forces of gravity, the pins sliding free from the glossy, newly washed hair, and her mouth was very slightly open, the parted pink lips wreaking havoc with his pulse rate. When he got silently to his feet and bent over her he saw the dark curl of lashes on her cheek, the soft vulnerability of her skin, the shadows of worry and exhaustion beneath her eyes.

Gabriel thought about lifting her feet on to the sofa, of loosening her bodice, her stays, so she could be more comfortable… *No.* But he leaned down, touched her cheek with the back of his fingers, watched as she smiled in her sleep at his touch and felt something turn over in his chest. Innocence and trust were enough to touch even the most cynical of hearts, it seemed.

He went out into the hall, closing the door softly behind him and met Tess. 'Caroline is asleep.'

'I am not surprised, she must be exhausted. I don't suppose it occurred to you to allow for a little feminine weakness in planning your adventure?'

'If I had, she'd be back in her father's hands by now. Or I'd have shot him. She's tougher than she looks, is Caroline Holm.'

Tess shook her head at him. 'Idiot man. She is brave and stoical and she will obviously do anything for her little brother.' Her penetrating stare had him wanting to shift uncomfortably. He resisted the weakness and smiled back, his lazy wolf smile. Tess's glare hardened. 'She is not strong, Gabriel, simply courageous. Do not try her too hard. I was brought up in a nunnery, in cold rooms, on plain food and hard work. Tamsyn has been acting as an estate manager for years, out in all weathers on that harsh Devon coast. But Caroline is like Kate, a lady—and raised as one.' She moved as though to leave him, then added, 'And don't you dare ruin her.'

'You believe I haven't already?' The way she was sniping at him, he would not be surprised if she had not guessed at the temptation that racked him.

'Do you honestly think I would have you in this house if I suspected you would do that? Friend of Alex's or not, your sorry carcase wouldn't cross the threshold, believe me.'

The dangerous silence that followed that remark hung between them for a full half-minute, then Tess laughed. 'It is such fun to tease you.'

He laughed, too, as he followed her back to the drawing room, telling himself that he had absolutely nothing to worry about. Caroline would be safely, respectably, hidden and his life could return to normal, mercifully free of female interference. Perfect. He wondered why he did not feel happier about it.

Cris strolled in. 'If you've nothing better to do, my valet will cut your hair now.'

Gabriel hauled himself to his feet and went upstairs to his fate.

Chapter Twelve

'It is a very extravagant carriage for a housekeeper.' Caroline stood on the front steps of Tess's house and studied the chaise and four that stood at the kerb while the footmen loaded on her new trunk. 'Will it not cause gossip if I do not travel on the stage?'

'You are a very superior housekeeper and I am a top-lofty employer who would not dream of his upper servants being seen on the common coach.' Gabriel said. He seemed distant somehow, with his fashionable cropped hair, and he was more smartly dressed than she had ever seen him. He had a cool detachment that she guessed was the manner he adopted when he was playing cards. It certainly succeeded in hiding his feelings from her.

Not that they had been very apparent for the past four days in any case. While she had remained secluded in Half Moon Street he had communicated by politely formal notes, recounting his agent's progress in despatching the elderly Mrs Buckley to her retirement and setting up funds for Caroline to draw on. Yesterday evening the man himself had arrived, fresh from the country, bringing the account books for Caroline to go through with him.

Tess's housekeeper had chosen her new wardrobe of

respectable plain gowns and caps and Dollands in Bond Street had sent two pairs of spectacles with plain lenses. She had gone, heavily veiled, to the domestic agency to interview for her own maid who would be picked up from there on the way so there was nothing to connect her with the Weybourns' house. The address of Reddish's Hotel in Jermyn Street had completely satisfied the agency.

'You look the part and we have left no kind of trail anywhere.' Gabriel seemed relaxed, standing on the step beside her, but she could tell he was watching the street.

'And you look different,' she said without thinking.

'It is the hair.' He glanced down at her, a formal stranger.

'No, it is more than that. You look positively respect…' *Oh, goodness, that was not tactful.* 'I mean…'

'Respectable,' he agreed with a shrug. 'Wrestling with your brother's estate has prompted an unusual desire to be about the business of my own properties. I have the haircut so I thought I would further unnerve my various solicitors, bankers and agents by looking like the sort of earl they normally have to deal with. My brother Louis is in town, so I'll drag him round, too. Hopefully he won't decide that estate management is the last thing he wants to do and bolt on me.'

'That will be pleasant, being with your brother.' The footmen were still struggling to secure the trunk to the chaise. 'Is he very like you?'

Gabriel gave a snort of amusement. 'Hardly. Louis is a serious soul with my head for figures, which you need to be a good card player, but I doubt he's ever played more than whist for sixpenny stakes. He's a cautious lawyer to the bone, although where he inherited that from, I have no idea. When he's finished his final year at university I hope he will take control of the estates for me. He could go to the Inns of Court and eat his dinners, qualify fully, but I think he wants to get down to work.'

'He is not your only brother, is he?'

'He is the youngest. Ben's in the army and George is a vicar. I haven't seen them for over a year, I suppose. We're not a close family and they don't seem to have wanted money recently. Not so much they needed to turn up to ask for it in person, anyway. Oh, for goodness sake! Haven't you two the slightest idea of how to tie a rope?' He strode across to the chaise and snatched the rope from the flustered footmen, flicking it into place and tying off the ends with a complex, rapid knot.

How sad that he was not close to his brothers, Caroline thought. She adored Anthony and even Lucas was good company when he wasn't pandering to their father's latest whims. A soldier, a vicar, a lawyer and a gambler. In most families the gambler would be the youngest son, not the oldest. Gabriel was intelligent, decisive, gallant and...*isolated,* she thought. Despite his friends, despite his title and rank, he seemed to be a wolf walking in the wild, fierce and independent and alone.

'Ready,' Gabriel said, and opened the chaise door for her. 'You have everything you need?'

'I will miss you.' The words were unconsidered, true. Unwise.

Gabriel's expression had been neutral, now it became even more shuttered. 'You should be glad to see the back of me.'

'You gave up a valuable estate for me. You understood that I was in trouble, so you rescued me. You have made a future possible for both Anthony and for me. It all took time and money and effort and risk. I am very grateful.'

'I am easily bored, it was a diversion,' Gabriel said with a shrug. 'Do not have any delusions, Caroline. I take what

I want for as long as it is amusing and no longer. You have my lawyer's address for any correspondence.' He closed the door and walked away as the others appeared on the steps.

'Gabriel?' Tess called, then shrugged and came to where Caroline still stood on the step of the chaise. 'Men! Now, take care and don't forget to write. Let us know if there is anything that you need.'

'You have been so very kind, thank you.' *Of course* her lip was trembling and her vision was blurred. Tess and Tamsyn had become friends in these past few days and it was a wrench to leave them. Nothing to do with insensitive, amoral, hard-hearted men. Nothing. She had been a distraction for a while, now he no longer wanted her. She was no longer *amusing*. Fair enough. She did not want him. Not at all.

Caroline blew her nose briskly as the chaise rattled away over the cobbles and into Piccadilly. By the time it drew up in front of Wellings and Arbuthott, Suppliers of Domestic Staff to the Nobility, her new spectacles were firmly in place, her face composed and her spine straight. She had been snubbed, but that was her own fault for attempting to get close to a rake. The lesson was learned and she wouldn't make that mistake again if she ever saw Gabriel Stone in the future, which was reassuringly unlikely.

'There is a young gentleman to see you, my lord.'

Gabriel turned with relief from Louis's lecture on the desirable length for agricultural leases. He was never certain whether his youngest brother was naturally earnest or whether it was a shield he erected when they were together. For the thousandth time he wondered if Louis was actually afraid of him, then dismissed the thought. He was unconscious that night when their father…died. He could remember nothing of it, surely?

He realised that Hampshire was waiting for him to collect his thoughts. 'No card?'

'He is too young a gentleman to have one, I believe, my lord.' Hampshire cleared his throat. 'He is very much on his dignity and, if I may be so bold, I would advise caution. I sense repressed emotion about him. Some instability.'

'I'll stay. It sounds as though you might need a lawyer,' Louis said with rather too much enthusiasm.

'Show him in, Hampshire. And you,' he added as the butler closed the door, 'you remember that you aren't a lawyer yet and keep quiet.'

'Breach of promise, do you think?' Louis speculated, for once acting his age. 'You wouldn't gamble with a stripling, so that's all I can think of. So, outraged younger brother come to defend his spurned sister. George says it is about time you—'

'Louis. Shut up if you value your allowance.'

'Mr Holm, my lord.'

Oh, Satan's toenails. Her baby brother. 'Mr Holm. I am Edenbridge. This is my brother, Mr Louis Stone. How may I assist you?'

The young man standing in front of him was obviously Caroline's brother, with his blue eyes and blond hair and handsome, open countenance. Anthony swallowed once, hard, but made a very proper bow. 'My lord. Mr Stone. I have come about a property.'

'I see.' No mention of Caroline yet. 'Will you sit down, Mr Holm? A glass of brandy, perhaps?'

He could see in the boy's expression the desire to appear a man of the world warring with the knowledge that he was not going to be able to drink strong spirits at five in the afternoon and carry on a discussion at the same time.

'Thank you, no, my lord,' he said, winning points with Gabriel. He sat down, crossed his gangling legs with a fair assumption of ease, and then looked anxious when Gabriel sat, too, but remained silent. 'Er… Springbourne, my lord.'

'Call me Edenbridge. I won a Hertfordshire estate called Springbourne from your father some time ago.'

'I need to buy it back. I can't pay you now, of course, but if you tell me how much, then I will start to make repayments just as soon as I am able. You will expect interest and I realise it will take some time…'

'What is your allowance?' Gabriel enquired.

'Twenty-five pounds a quarter.'

'And you are how old?'

'Sixteen, sir. My lor… Edenbridge.'

'Louis, how much is Springbourne worth?' His brother whipped open a file and produced a neat summary paper. Gabriel handed it to Anthony. 'At compound interest of even a modest four percent, can you work out how long it would take you to pay it back?'

'Yes.' For a moment his chin wobbled, then he got it under control. Gabriel had a vivid recollection of Caroline firming her own jaw before launching into an explanation of why she had come to him that first morning. 'I can see it is impossible. But that was my future, you see. I had to try. However, I quite understand. I will not trouble you further, my lord. Good day.'

He was on his feet, but Gabriel did not move. 'Sit down. You give up very easily, Mr Holm. How did you find out that your father had lost the estate to me?'

The boy sat. 'He told me two days ago when I said I wanted to spend some of the summer there.'

'I imagine he was not conciliatory.'

'No.' Anthony tightened his lips and, for a moment, his shoulders hunched.

The bastard hit him, Gabriel realised with a surge of anger. Boys expected to be beaten for misdemeanours, but not for enquiring about property they thought would be theirs. And not thrashed. Involuntarily his hand reached for Louis, then he jerked it back.

'He's not in a good temper at the moment because of my sis…I mean… Oh, drat, I shouldn't have said that. You'll forget it?'

'Forget what? Mr Holm, I am not in the habit of gaming for property that has been promised to someone other than the person staking it. I discovered the facts about that estate and it is now being held in trust for you without your father's knowledge. The income will be invested and the whole, less running costs, will revert to you on your twenty-first birthday.'

Suddenly, appallingly, the boy burst into tears. After a moment he dragged a bedraggled handkerchief out of his pocket, blew his nose and peered wetly over the top at Gabriel. 'I'm sorry, sir. But are you serious? You aren't jesting with me?'

'Look at my brother. I'm a frivolous sort, but Louis never jests, certainly not about money, do you, Louis?' He had told his brother the bare outlines of the story, without telling him how he had discovered that the estate was destined for Anthony Holm and certainly without mentioning Caroline.

'Of course not.' Louis, all of three years older than Anthony, sent Gabriel his best lawyerly reproving look, the one Gabriel suspected he practised in front of the mirror. 'You may scrutinise the books at any time, Mr Holm. We realise that you are not able to employ anyone to audit them, but if you nominate someone we can set that against the estate income.'

'I should not advise any son to deceive his father, but in

this case might I suggest that you do not reveal this conversation to Lord Knighton? You had best pretend that Springbourne is lost to you for five years,' Gabriel said.

'Yes. Yes of course. Thank you, my... Edenbridge.' He set his jaw. 'I was going to join the navy. Or I would have done if only I'd known where Ca... Anyway, I won't need to now.'

'Have that brandy.' Gabriel stood up and poured three glasses. Had Caroline written to her brother yet? He waited until Anthony had taken a huge swallow of the spirit, choked, been thumped on the back by Louis and then settled down, rather red-eyed, but happier. 'It is some time since I had the pleasure of speaking to your sister. I trust she is well.'

'Er... Yes. Yes, she is quite safe.' It seemed to occur to him that this was odd phrasing. 'I mean, she is quite *well*. Resting, you know, somewhere...I mean elsewhere. Rather a trying Season, I believe, but she writes to me. I'll tell her you were asking.'

'You do that,' Gabriel said with a smile. *Just never apply for the diplomatic service or any occupation where you have to deviate from the truth, young man. You are the worst liar I have ever come across.*

'Where does your father think you are now?'

'Staying with a school friend in Chelsea. Which I am, actually. I went home a few days ago, Papa told me about Springbourne and then I remembered Percy had invited me to stay with him, so I came down here.'

'You'll need some ready money if you are to enjoy London.' Gabriel opened a drawer and peeled fifty pounds off a roll of banknotes. 'Louis, enter that in the ledger as an advance to Mr Holm. Don't go near women, cards, drinking dens or friendly older men who offer to show you a good time.'

'No, sir! Thank you very much, my… Edenbridge.' Anthony's grin threatened to reach his ears. He got to his feet, only slightly unsteady, and bowed. 'I'll never forget this. Never.'

'Was that wise?' Louis enquired as the door shut behind young Mr Holm. 'He's off the leash in London, goodness knows what he will get up to.'

'Speaking from experience, Louis?'

'Certainly not.'

Gabriel grinned at the offended expression, but it was Anthony who gave him pause. His father had been reminded about Springbourne and that could be dangerous. Might it occur to him that Caroline had gone there? Gabriel doubted Lord Knighton had actually told Caroline about the loss of the estate—in fact, he seemed to recall her saying she had discovered its loss by overhearing him talking about it, so he might think she'd see it as a refuge.

He should write and warn her. Or go and see her? He really ought to inspect the estate after all. It wasn't right to leave it entirely to agents, however reliable.

'I'm going to Hertfordshire, look at this place for myself,' he said abruptly.

'Fine. I'll pack.' Louis got to his feet.

'No need to trouble yourself.' Gabriel said it with regret. It gave him unexpected pleasure that Louis wanted his company, but the last thing he needed was an encounter with Caroline with his little brother looking on. 'I only want to familiarise myself with it. I'll go first thing tomorrow and be back the day after.' A brisk conversation with Caroline, just to put her on her guard, a rapid look at the place and then he would put up at the Red Lion in Hemel Hempstead for the night. All done and dusted.

Gabriel recalled the last glimpse he'd had of her, her bounty of blonde curls wrenched back into submission, her blue eyes wide with hurt behind those ridiculous spectacles, the shock on her face at his snubbing words. It had been for the best, of course. Women became…attached and she had no experience of men like him. She saw him as a rescuer, not as what he was, jaded and amoral and severely tempted to take what he should not.

She needed a nice young man, a countryman, perhaps the son of a local gentry family. She'd be safe with a man like that, someone straightforward who wouldn't hurt her, who wouldn't become bored with innocence and trust as he assuredly would. The ache in his chest at the thought was presumably his damnable new conscience again.

'George and I were wondering,' Louis began.

Words to put fear into any older brother. 'Yes?' Gabriel said warily, half his thoughts still on a suitable husband for Caroline.

'Are you intending to get married? Because, he's a good chap of course, but Ben's in the army, which doesn't seem very safe for the heir, and George really wants to be a bishop.'

'I was not planning on needing an heir in the near future,' Gabriel said, all his concentration jerked back to his brother. It was very unlike Louis to venture into such personal territory. 'What on earth is this about, anyway?'

'We wondered, that's all. You taking an interest in the land now. And your three closest friends marrying. You are getting on, after all.'

'I am twenty-nine,' Gabriel snapped. 'Hardly in my dotage.'

'You ought to think about it,' Louis persisted. 'I've been reading up on marriage settlements and entails and all that recently, so I'm completely on top of the subject for when you need advice.'

'Louis.' His brother raised short-sighted green eyes and

squinted at him. 'Pay attention. I do not require lectures on marriage and the production of heirs from my spotty little brother.' He got up and left the room, followed by Louis's indignant protests.

'I am not spotty!'

'Hampshire, my travelling carriage for eight tomorrow morning. Breakfast for seven and tell Corbridge I'll not be needing him, just an overnight bag.'

'My lord.'

Gabriel took his hat from the hall stand and let himself out of the front door. There was a new hell off Hill Street that was as informal as the stakes were high. It was one place he was quite certain he'd be safe from prosing brothers, well-meaning friends, matchmaking mothers and respectable damsels with big blue eyes and that was where he would be until midnight.

Chapter Thirteen

It had never occurred to her that a housekeeper's life would be a lonely one. In a large household there was a butler, a steward, a cook and a mature lady's maid for the mistress of the house, a little inner circle of upper servants. But here, with no family in residence, the housekeeper reigned in an isolated state.

Caroline set the flower arrangement on a table in the hall and looked out through the open door, down the carriage drive between the high yew hedges that were receiving their first good cut in years and on to the green haze of the Vale of Aylesbury in the August sunlight. Behind the house the beech woods rose like a blanket over the swell of the Chiltern Hills, nestling it into the tiny valley of the Spring Bourne, the seasonal stream that rose from the chalk after heavy rain, then vanished in summer.

This was a lovely spot, the house was charming and soon it would become a home for Anthony and for herself. But meanwhile, although there was a lot to do and even more to be thankful for, the loneliness pressed in on her. *And it has only been three weeks.*

'I've finished the panelling in the dining room, Mrs Crabtree.' Jane, the housemaid, came into the hall carrying a basket of jars of beeswax and polishing cloths. 'It'll take a few more goes to get the shine up proper, though.'

'Once a week and not too much wax, more elbow grease,' Caroline said. That was what was advised in *Mrs Pomfrett's Household Management*, the thick tome that was her night-time reading. 'Too much wax builds up and dulls the shine.'

'Yes, ma'am. I'll lay the table in your room, Mrs Crabtree. Almost time for luncheon.'

That was another thing. Every meal had to be taken alone in the housekeeper's parlour while the cheerful sounds of chatter from the servants' hall echoed down the flagged passageway. She'd been tempted to prop a book up in front of her, but that was a bad example to the maids, so must be resisted. They relied on the training they received here for their next post, perhaps promotion to a bigger household, or cook-housekeeper to a widow or single gentleman. It all left far too much time to be thinking about a certain brown-eyed gentleman.

'There's a rider coming up the drive, Mrs Crabtree.'

'Who can that be?' Caroline squinted against the sunlight, heart pounding. A boyish rider on a chestnut hack with a rather shambling gait. Not a tall man on a fine piece of bloodstock. Of course not.

'Close the front door, alert William that someone is coming. Possibly they are lost and want directions.'

She followed the scurrying maid towards the back of the hall and waited in the shadows while the footman emerged, tugged down his waistcoat and went to open the door.

'Good morning, sir. I regret that none of the family is in residence.'

'Well, I am now.' The light, cheerful voice cracked mid-sentence, betraying the speaker's nerves as well as his age. 'I am Mr Anthony Holm and this is my house.'

William's gulp was audible. 'Perhaps you would come through to the drawing room, sir, and I'll fetch the house-keeper.'

Caroline hardly caught a glimpse of her brother before William had him shut in the front room. She met the foot-man halfway across the hall.

'Mrs Crabtree, ma'am, I didn't know where to put my-self! The poor young gentleman can't know his father's sold the estate to Lord Edenbridge.' That was the story she had told the staff, not wanting to expose her father's folly at gambling it away.

'I'll go and speak to him. Don't bring refreshments until I ring.' She went in and closed the door behind herself. 'Anthony,' she said quietly. 'This is a surprise.'

'Caro!' He spun round from his contemplation of the view from the window, his face a mixture of pleasure, sur-prise and then, when he took in her costume, bafflement. 'What on earth are you doing here dressed like that?'

She hugged him fiercely, shaken by how much his gan-gling frame had grown since the last time she had held him. He was not her little brother any longer. 'Oh, how I have missed you! Sit down and I'll tell you everything—and then you must tell me how you got here.'

She left out the offer to exchange her virginity for the deeds, saying instead that she had explained the situation to Gabriel and he had immediately returned them. When it came to her reasons for fleeing she told him only that Woodruffe had an unsavoury reputation. Even so, Anthony was clearly old enough to guess it was worse than she said.

'The old devil,' he gasped when he heard that their fa-ther had beaten her. His horror became fascination at the story of Gabriel's imposture and he was boy enough to be vastly amused at the thought of an earl disguised as a hermit.

'So here I am, guarding your inheritance and staying safe myself,' Caroline finished.

'He's a great gun, isn't he? Lord Edenbridge, I mean.' Anthony's face glowed with hero worship. 'Father told me, just in passing, about losing Springbourne. I said what I thought, pretty loudly, and got a thrashing for my pains.' He shrugged off her hands when she would have caught him to her for a hug and stuck out his chin pugnaciously. 'I'd got an invitation to stay with Percy—you know, Herrick's younger brother?—near London, so I went there. Father didn't mind.

'Then I called on Lord Edenbridge and he told me he was looking after the estate for me. His youngest brother was there, a bit of a stuffed shirt, I thought.' His blue gaze slid round to her. 'Edenbridge didn't say anything about you.' When she did not comment he shrugged. 'Anyway, he advanced me some money from the estate, so I thought I'd come and have a look. May I stay?'

'Of *course* you may.' She just wanted to hold him and not let go. 'But you must remember that you are here as a guest of Lord Edenbridge and I'll let the staff know you were upset because of the estate being sold, but that the earl has allowed you to visit for a while. And you must call me Mrs Crabtree and treat me like the housekeeper. We can say that I knew you when you were a little boy, which is true and that will explain any familiarity.'

'*Crabtree?*'

'I realised I hadn't thought of a name and when I arrived that was the first thing I saw,' Caroline said defensively. 'I think it sounds suitable for a housekeeper.'

'Gnarled and vinegary,' Anthony teased.

'I'll ring for luncheon. You'll have to eat it in solitary splendour because it wouldn't do for the housekeeper to sit down with you.' As she stood up she glimpsed move-

ment at the end of the drive. 'A carriage is coming. Of all
the bad timing! You had best stay out of sight. I do hope
it isn't Father.'

Anthony leapt to his feet with an oath that had her scolding him.

'Not in front of ladies, you brat! Look, it is a team of
greys.' She relaxed. Her father always drove bays. It was
irrational, of course, this fear. There was not the slightest clue to bring him here, but even so, she kept waking
in the night in a cold sweat of dread, fighting a nightmare
of being dragged back to Knighton Park and Lord Wood-
ruff's grasping hands.

'And very nice, too,' Anthony said with a sigh of envy.
'Real high-steppers. I'll go into the back garden.'

Caroline followed him out, called for William and retreated to the back of the hall again. She had not seen a
single visitor all the time she had been at Springbourne
except tradesmen and local people and now someone had
to turn up hot on Anthony's heels. This was like one of
those farces with everyone diving behind sofas or into cup-
boards as more and more people arrived at inconvenient
or compromising moments. It would make Gabriel laugh,
she thought as William, peering through the glass at the
side of the door, opened it before the caller could knock.

'Good afternoon,' said a very familiar voice. 'I am
Edenbridge.'

'My lord.' William sounded even more flustered than
he had at Anthony's arrival. She could hardly blame him:
she was totally confused herself. And, she realised, very
happy.

'Might I come in?' Gabriel enquired mildly.

'Yes, of course, my lord. I do apologise, my lord, keeping you standing on your own doorstep.' His ears and the
back of his neck were crimson as he took Gabriel's hat

and gloves. 'I'll…er… Should I have luncheon sent up, my lord?'

'Please do. This is the drawing room? Ask the house-keeper if she could join me at her convenience.'

'Yes, my lord. Certainly, my lord.' The footman closed the door and scurried to the back of the hall. 'It's Lord Edenbridge, Mrs Crabtree.'

'Ask Cook to prepare luncheon for three and I will join the gentlemen. Go to Mr Holm and give him my compli-ments and tell him I will be with him as soon as possible.' The staff would think it strange, but now the two of them were here she simply had to talk to them together. But Ga-briel first. And alone.

'Caroline.' He came across the room to her, his hand stretched out, and it took her a second to realise he intended to shake hers, not gather her into his arms.

Of course, you idiot. She smiled and offered her own hand and asked him to be seated with commendable com-posure. His hair had grown out of its strict crop since she had seen him last and his breeches, boots and riding coat were as carelessly thrown on as always, even though he had come in a carriage and not on horseback.

'How are you managing?' he asked, studying her as she sat there looking, she was very aware, like a neat, dowdy housekeeper.

'Very well, thank you, my lord. It is quiet, but there is plenty to keep me occupied. Might I ask what brings you here? Not a problem, I trust. Or perhaps you have become bored and fancied a change of scenery?' That was bitter and she regretted the words as soon as she spoke them. They betrayed how much his parting words had hurt her. She had her pride.

Gabriel did not make the mistake of apologising, which was sensible of him as well as preserving what dignity she had left. 'Your brother Anthony arrived on my doorstep proposing to buy back Springbourne. It was necessary to explain the true circumstances to him. Your father had told him he had lost it and it occurred to me that he had not told *you*. For all Knighton knows you still believe this to be a family property, one where he never visits and somewhere you might think of as a sanctuary. I wanted to warn you and discuss how to mitigate the danger.'

So her night-time fears were not so far-fetched after all if Gabriel shared them. 'Thank you, I appreciate you taking the trouble to come in person.' It sounded stilted, but perhaps she should be making the effort to distance herself with formality. It was too easy to yearn for the closeness that had been between them when Gabriel had been the hermit and she a fugitive.

Caroline kept her gaze on her own hands, folded neatly in her lap, and not on his long, expressive fingers. 'Anthony is here. He arrived very shortly before you did.'

'The little devil! I advanced him some money, but I thought he was staying with a school friend. What is he doing here?'

'Heaving a huge sigh of relief that it is his again, I suspect. He was taken aback to discover that the housekeeper, Mrs Crabtree, knew him very well.'

'I am not surprised, *Mrs Crabtree*. We had better have a council of war, the three of us.'

'That is what I thought. I told him about Woodruffe.'

There was a tap on the door. 'Luncheon is served, Mrs Crabtree.'

'Thank you, William. Please ask Mr Holm to join us in the dining room.'

Anthony came in, looking wary. 'I heard your voice in the hall, Edenbridge. You're wondering what I am doing here, I suppose?'

'You may go where you please.' Gabriel held the chair for Caroline, then took his own place opposite her. 'I am not your guardian.'

'I know, sir, but you gave me money and I let you think I was staying in London.'

'I advanced you your own money. It is of no matter. Let us eat and think how best to handle the situation. I came because I was uneasy that your father might search here for Lady Caroline. We're mired in a tangle of deceptions: I'm pretending to own this place, you are pretending you do not know it is now yours again and that your sister is hiding from her own father and posing as the housekeeper. I just hope you are a good actor, Anthony, because you are going to have to face your father and play the role of the disappointed son well enough to convince him that you are pining for Springbourne. And you're a poor liar, I've noticed.'

'I'm a good actor, though,' Anthony said, reaching for a slice of cold beef. 'I've acted at school and got some pretty enthusiastic reviews. And this is important, really important. It isn't as though it is some little white lie I might forget about. I'll sulk a bit and keep out of Father's way, that's what he'd expect.'

'And what about you, Mrs Crabtree?' He seemed to find the name as amusing as Anthony did.

'I never answer the front door, of course. If my father does come, then I will leave by the back and hide in the woods. He could search for a year and not find me there.'

'I suppose it will have to do.' Gabriel looked unsatisfied, although it did not seem to be impairing his appetite.

Caroline wondered whether to ring and tell Cook to send up the apple pie along with the cheese. She helped herself to the game pie before the two hungry males demolished it. 'It gives me bad dreams, imagining he has found me,' she confessed. 'But I really do not think it is a serious risk. He is very self-centred and I don't believe he thinks much about other people's motives.'

As she spoke the doorbell rang, followed by the thump of the knocker. 'Who now? Really, after weeks of perfect peace the place is like the White Horse Cellar when the mails come in!'

Then there was the sound of William opening the door and the voice of the caller and the footman's agitated protests. Caroline dropped her knife with a clatter on her plate and Anthony jumped to his feet as the door swung open.

'So you *are* here, boy, you impudent whelp.'

Chapter Fourteen

Her father strode into the room, brushing past her as she froze, her back to the door. 'I thought you were too meek when I told you about this place so I decided I had better check that you hadn't sneaked off here. What in Hades do you think you're doing? And who the devil are you?' He moved closer to Gabriel, who stood up with leisurely, dangerous grace. Caroline edged her chair backwards. A few more inches and she could slide from her seat and tiptoe out.

She stood, turned, and came face to face with Lucas.

'Caroline!'

'What?' Her father swung round his face choleric with a mixture of surprise, temper and triumph. 'You are both here? You plotted the whole thing, you disobedient little slut. What is Edenbridge going to do when he finds the pair of you skulking here?'

Gabriel moved to stand between him and Caroline. 'If you use language of that kind to Lady Caroline again I'll floor you, Knighton, even if you are old enough to be my father.'

'Edenbridge.' Her father finally recognised who was standing in front of him. 'What the blazes do you think

you are playing at?' His gaze swung back and forth between the three of them and then fixed back on Gabriel
with dawning recognition. '*You*. You're the hermit. Lucas,
tell me I'm right. It's that cursed Welsh hermit.'

Lucas pushed past Caroline to stand at his father's
shoulder. 'Yes, you are right. Take away that beard and
change the voice and it's the same man. But what is going
on?'

It was a nightmare, and when Gabriel swung round and
cursed Anthony, it seemed to Caroline simply part of it.

'You stupid brat, coming here with your idiotic pleas
for her to go home. You led them here.' He grabbed Anthony by the neckcloth and began to shake him, his face
pressed close to the boy's.

Suddenly Anthony began to fight back. 'I knew I had
to when I found her here! It isn't right, what you are doing,
of course she should come home with me.'

Gabriel made a sound of disgust and pushed him into
his father's arms. 'Have the little prig. He turns up here
whining that he wants just one more look at the place, finds
us and reads us a fine sermon.'

'You were trying to make her come back?' Her father
held Anthony away from him so he could look into his
face.

'Yes, sir. Of course. I was upset about the estate, and I
shouldn't have come here, but Caroline and that man…'

He really can act, she thought. *And Gabriel has saved
him from total disgrace with my father and a beating,
thank Heavens. But what am I going to do?* Lucas had
moved to block the door and it was too far to reach the
window and scramble through, even if Gabriel held back
her father and brother. They were two to his one and if
they attacked him she knew she could never leave him and
run. He might overcome them—he was strong and coura-

geous—but her father always carried a knife in his boot and she knew he'd use it without scruple.

'Good boy,' he said now, pushing Anthony towards Lucas. 'And as for you, my girl, I'll have to sweeten the pot now to get Woodruffe to take you, damn it. Used goods.'

'I will not warn you again, Knighton,' Gabriel said. 'I am marrying Lady Caroline and no one threatens or abuses my fiancée.'

'Marry her? You? Her reputation will be in the dirt after this.'

Marry me?

'Mine is not that wonderful,' Gabriel said with a smile that was guaranteed to infuriate. 'But as I will procure a special licence from my cousin, the Archbishop of Canterbury, that should help. Even better if he'll marry us. I believe he's at Lambeth Palace at the moment, which is convenient.'

Her father expressed an opinion on what the archbishop could do with his crozier. 'I refuse my consent.'

'Lady Caroline is of age,' Gabriel pointed out. He seemed perfectly calm, contemptuous even, her father's rage breaking against him like a wave against a rock, with as much effect.

'You'll not see a penny piece of dowry from me.' Her father was puce with frustrated rage now.

'I do not need your money, Knighton, although that reminds me, you owe me a week's wages for my stint as your hermit.'

'Under false pretences! You inveigle your way into my home, you seduce my daughter—'

Caroline finally found her voice. 'Lord Edenbridge came to help because you were forcing me to marry Lord Woodruffe.'

'Woodruffe will call you out,' her father threatened Gabriel.

'That lump of perverted lard is welcome to do so. I would enjoy puncturing him.'

'And you, Lucas. What kind of brother are you? Why aren't *you* calling him out?'

'I imagine Lord Whiston has more common sense than to make the situation worse than it already is. Besides, I am not prepared to meet the man who is about to become my brother-in-law.'

'Father, it has gone too far to stop. He's an earl, he's perfectly eligible, and she's of age.' Lucas stood his ground, perhaps given strength by the appeal to his reasonableness. 'He's earl, a better match than Woodruffe, after all.'

'Not for the family, he isn't. He won't bring me land.' He switched his attention back to Gabriel. 'What about settlements?'

'I will settle property and investments on Lady Caroline in consultation with lawyers of her choice. It is, Knighton, no longer your affair.'

'You'll be sorry, Edenbridge. And as for you, my girl, you've made your bed, you may lie in it. Don't expect to come crawling home when you discover what kind of man you've married. A Captain Sharp, a charlatan, that is what he is and I will make certain the whole world knows it.' He snapped his fingers at his sons. 'Come on, both of you.'

Anthony trailed behind, rather white around the mouth, but he turned at the last minute to wink at Caroline. She managed a quick smile for him, then turned all her focus on Gabriel as he stood at the window watching the carriage drive away.

'They've gone,' he said finally.

Caroline sat down with a bump in the nearest chair and

said the first thing that came into her head. 'Are you really the Archbishop of Canterbury's cousin?'

'Third, once removed. I won't have any difficulty getting a licence, but I don't think I will ask him to marry us.' He turned and, for the first time in what seemed like a hundred years, smiled. 'Unless you have set your heart on it?'

'Don't jest about this, Gabriel. You do not want to marry me, I know that perfectly well. And I will not marry you.'

'You will not? I am deeply wounded, my lady.' The smile had become thinner.

'Of course I will not. What kind of marriage would it be? You have been put in a position where you have had to do the honourable thing, but I have no wish to take a martyr for a husband.'

Gabriel shrugged, that mocking smile still in place. 'I am an earl, I need a wife, as my so-sensible youngest brother informs me. You are the daughter of an earl and perfectly eligible. There may be a scandal, but I do not care about that.'

'I do.' As soon as the words were out she knew she meant them. The talk, the turned shoulders, the whispers, the cuts… She had seen it happen to other people, now she would be responsible for putting them both in that position. If they had a chance of making a happy marriage she would be very tempted to wed this man. But like this? *Never.*

'Is this the woman who came and offered me her virginity? Who plotted to shock her husband on her wedding night? Is this the woman who broke into her father's safe to purloin her own jewels and ran away from home with a man of dubious reputation? And *now* you quibble about scandal?'

'It is not a quibble and everything has changed. I would have done whatever it took to get this estate back for Anthony—except something that put you in such an invidious position. And I was naive before to think I could escape that marriage by shocking my suitors.

'This is my responsibility to resolve. I will ask Tessa and Tamsyn for references. Perhaps your friends in Northumberland know of someone who needs a housekeeper.' *I do not want to be married to you with a cauldron of anger seething just below that smile that isn't a smile. I do not want to be responsible for you losing your good name because, rogue you may be, you are received everywhere. Now.*

'You would rather be a domestic servant than my countess? What did I do that made you dislike me so much?'

'Nothing.' She found she was wringing her hands and stilled them. *I like you too well, that is the problem.* 'You have done nothing except treat me better than I deserve, be concerned about me, rescue me. You do not have to do this, Gabriel. Let me be and I will vanish.'

'Leaving me with the reputation of a seducer, a man who abducts an earl's daughter and then abandons her? Or worse. If you disappear I have no doubt your father will put it about that I've disposed of you. Once the story of my hermit imposture gets around this will all seem a very dubious plot indeed. Now that really would be a scandal.'

'So I must marry you for the sake of *your* reputation?' He was right, of course, her father's spite would whip up a storm of vicious talk.

'Ironic, isn't it? I cannot force you, Caroline. I may be a scoundrel, but I do draw the line at that. I just want you to see that it is no help at all, you being noble and refusing me.'

'But you hope my sense of honour is at least as well developed as yours.' She rather feared it was.

Gabriel stopped prowling around the room, sat down on the other side of the table and rested his forearms on the cloth. It should have been better because he was no longer looming over her, but his focused, unsmiling gaze was no more comfortable. He looked weary, she thought, seeing the shadows under the dark eyes, the tightness of his mouth.

'I hope that you will see that, unsatisfactory though this is, it is the only way for us both to deal with the situation,' he said with the control of a man hanging on to his patience by a thread. When she did not reply he flung himself back in the chair. 'Surely I have to be better than Woodruffe?'

'Of course you are. But I do not want to be married to anyone. Not my father's choice, not someone who has been trapped into it.' It sounded mulish, but it was the truth. The thought of perhaps fifty years of marriage to a man who resented her, tolerated her, was repellent.

'Waiting for hearts and flowers and a meeting of soulmates?' Gabriel enquired perceptively. 'You've more patience than I have and more romance in your soul than is good for you.'

Caroline gritted her teeth at the mockery. 'Your three friends married for love, did they not? I heard how you tried to stop Tamsyn marrying the marquess because you thought she was unsuitable, but you have accepted it now, because they are made for each other and even you can see it. What are they going to say about you settling for *this*?' She waved her hands to encompass the whole impossible situation.

'You are neither the illegitimate offspring of a bigamous marriage, nor the mother of a child out of wedlock nor the widow of a man who was almost hanged as a smuggler, which between ourselves, describes the brides my friends have taken. You are an eminently suitable match, if one ignores your father, which I devoutly intend to do. My friends have no right to dictate my emotional life—'

'Or lack of it,' Caroline flung back. 'What if we marry and then you fall in love with someone else? Or I do?'

'We do what aristocrats down the ages have always done, we cope with it. An heir and spare is non-negotiable. After that, provided you don't fall for a short redhead there is no problem.'

'How can you be so cold-blooded? You wouldn't be if the situation did arise—you would be shooting my lover at dawn.'

'Why do you think my brother Louis is half a head shorter than his older brothers, has green eyes and sandy hair?'

'No! Did your father know?'

'Of course.' Gabriel's expression was bleak. Then he shrugged. 'So does Louis. He took one look at Lord Belmond and announced it was a relief to finally know who his father was. No one in the family treats him any differently.'

'Poor boy. As if I could do that to a child of mine. If I married you I would be faithful and I would expect you to be faithful, too.'

'The rules require me to be discreet.'

'The vows demand rather more,' she snapped, more shaken by his cynicism than she would have thought possible.

Gabriel shrugged. 'I am a sinner. You knew that from the very first.' There was a knock at the door. 'Come in, damn it!'

'Mrs Crabtree, should we clear now, or bring tea, or what, ma'am?' Jane hesitated on the threshold, the wooden tray clutched to her skinny chest like a shield.

'Tea, in the drawing room please, Jane.'

Gabriel followed her through in silence that persisted while she poured and drank two cups of tea. That did something for the raging thirst that had suddenly gripped her, but not a great deal for the confused misery inside.

He left his own cup untouched, waiting with a controlled patience that frayed at her nerves more than ranting and temper would have done. *I suppose I am used to ranting,* she thought miserably. *No one is ever in any doubt about my father's mood or desires. I cannot read Gabriel's.*

'Is there no other way than marriage?'

'No. Not to escape without a major scandal and ensure your future. It will be a nine-day wonder, but everyone knows how eccentric and difficult your father is, so there will be sympathy for your desire to flee his roof. And I may not be society's darling, but there are not many who hold much of a brief for Woodruffe.' He picked up the cup and drained the cold tea, then smiled at her. 'Caroline, we get on well enough.' He reached out, touched the back of his hand gently to her cheek. 'We will be good in bed, I think, even if we have not had the best of beginnings in that respect. Now what are you blushing about?'

'I am not used to such frankness.'

'This from the woman who tried to barter her virginity for this estate? And I still have that IOU. Your marriage has been announced and I intend to call it in.'

Of course she expected that this would be a full marriage, a man in need of an heir did not propose a union in name only. But surely he did not mean… 'You mean *before* we are married?' *I need time.* 'We have not fixed the date.'

'Five days' time should be perfect. We'll go up to London tomorrow. Then there are three days for you, Tess and Tamsyn to shop for all the things you'll need. I'll sort out the licence and the legal details and find a clergyman. I'm hoping that Cris will let us use his house in St James's Square. That will prevent any hint of the hole-and-corner about the marriage.'

'It certainly will,' Caroline said hollowly. The thought of Crispin de Feaux's cool blue regard simply made her want to curl up into a ball and seek out every hole and corner she could find.

'So, are we agreed?'

There was the sensation of holding her breath, as though she was about to jump into icy water or walk out along a narrow ledge. 'Yes,' Caroline said. There was a guilty relief in surrender that she tried not to analyse too closely.

'Then I think we should summon the staff, who are probably all agog about this morning's incidents and making up the most lurid tales. We will tell them who you are and that we are to be married. There's no disguising the clandestine nature of all of this, so let us hope they are both loyal and idiotically romantic.'

Idiotically romantic, like me. And I am also idiotically loyal, Gabriel Stone. Vows mean something to me.

The staff had been embarrassingly excited to be part of what they obviously saw as a Great Romance. Caroline promised to send them a new housekeeper as soon as possible and spent the afternoon immersed in practical details, which at least had the advantage of keeping her mind distracted.

Gabriel appeared to have employed the time creating a stack of letters which he sent off with the groom to the nearest receiving office. Dinner was formal and polite with only an exchange of the most trivial chitchat. Caroline made her excuses and retired immediately afterwards, frankly retreating from the domestic intimacy of tea in the drawing room.

At least Harriet, the personal maid who had been recruited in London, was sufficiently down to earth to ask questions. 'Will you still be requiring me when you go back to London, ma'am? My lady, I should say.'

Caroline sat at her dressing table as the young woman unpinned her hair before brushing it out. 'I need a lady's maid, Harriet, and you've done very well. But can you manage elaborate hair styles and the care of fine fabrics? I will be a countess and that will mean a considerable social life and the clothes and jewels to go with it.' *Provided we are not completely shunned by decent society.* 'I quite understand if you think it will be too much and I would give you an excellent reference.'

'Oh, no, my lady. I can do it.' Her face broke into a happy smile. 'I might have to learn a few things, but if you tell me when I go wrong, I learn ever so fast, truly I do.'

This is really happening. I have my affianced husband in the house, I have a lady's maid, I have a wedding date. And I very much fear that the man in question is going to come to my door tonight. And then... Will I open it?

Chapter Fifteen

The knock on the door came at midnight. It was nicely judged, Caroline thought as she got up from the chair where she had been curled up with an unread book. Not a demanding thump, not a wary tap, not a secretive scratch. Just a mannerly light knock.

She opened it, and stepped back so that Gabriel could enter. He came in far enough to close the door behind him, then studied her as she stood there in her sensible flannel wrapper, suitable for any night-time emergencies that might call a housekeeper from her lonely bed. It took an effort not to clutch the lapels closed or fold her arms defensively across her well-shrouded bosom.

'I have been thinking. We need a very frank discussion.' He gestured to the ottoman at the foot of the bed and raised an interrogative eyebrow.

'Yes?' Caroline retreated to her chair, tossing Byron, who was less than helpful under the circumstances, to the floor. Gabriel sat down and regarded her from beneath heavy lids. She did not make the mistake of thinking him sleepy.

'You raised any number of objections to this match, as I recall. I am also aware that I have two, shall we say, sticking points, which have become stickier the more I considered them. I am not prepared to make a marriage in name only, but on the other hand I am not prepared to force an unwilling woman. I was wrong to try to pressure you by referring to my own reputation suffering.' He shrugged. 'I thought it might work, but I can't blackmail you, Caroline. Just because we cannot see a way out of this now does not mean there is not some other solution if we think hard enough. But answer me this. If I had asked you to marry me in June, what would you have said?'

The question took her completely off balance. 'Yes,' she said, surprised at herself. 'I would have said yes, I think.'

'Why?'

'Because…' Caroline swallowed and studied her bare toes. 'Because I found—find—you physically attractive. You know that.' She fixed her gaze on the point where Gabriel's robe formed a vee exposing bare skin and a curl of dark hair and tried to stop gibbering. 'I found you intelligent and interesting. And although you were shocking you were also kind to me. Much kinder than my impetuosity deserved. And you did the right thing for Anthony when it meant a significant financial loss and you had no reason to want to help him.'

'So, a mixture of gratitude and sexual attraction.' She could not tell without looking at his face whether he was amused or annoyed.

'And you were much better than the alternatives,' she added frankly and found herself looking at him. That curl. Would it feel silky if she twined her fingers around it?

Now his expression was definitely sardonic. 'Have any of those opinions changed?'

Caroline shook her head.

'So your objections are because you feel my hand has

been forced, not because you object to marriage to me as such?'

'I suppose so. Yes.' Strangely she was beyond embarrassment, driven by an instinct that only the truth would serve them now.

'You are very frank, Caroline. I would expect any sheltered young lady to faint dead away before admitting to physical attraction.'

'I must be honest with you. With myself. Coyness and misunderstandings are not going to help us, are they? If I had not already seen you, found you attractive, then I would never have made the proposal that I did. Which puts my so-called sacrifice for my brother in a different light, I suppose. It would hardly have *been* a sacrifice. Young women have to pretend that we have no idea about physical matters when of course we do. We certainly do not keep our gaze fixed above a man's waist level.' Gabriel's lips twitched. 'I was attracted by the way you moved,' she confessed. 'So it would be hypocritical of me to pretend I am shocked at the prospect of sharing a bed with you. Nervous and shy, yes. Shocked, no. But it would be very wrong to expect you to marry me.'

'I find I am becoming strangely reconciled to the prospect, my lady.'

Caroline realised it was her turn to be taken aback. Gabriel was smiling in a way that brought the blood to her cheeks, which must be why her heart was beating so erratically. 'Are you certain?' she demanded. 'Why?' *And why do I know you are telling me the truth?* Perhaps it was simply desperation or exhaustion and she was delusional, but she trusted Gabriel.

'Possibly because I've never had to work so hard to get a woman into bed as I have today. If it had been anyone else I'd have given up hours ago.' She frowned at his levity and he smiled. 'I am teasing you. Marry me, Caroline. I admire your courage and your sense of honour. I think you're beautiful. And I am driven to distraction by that garment.'

He admires me, thinks I'm beautiful? Can I believe him? 'This?' She plucked at the wrapper which was a discouraging shade of grey.

'Any right-thinking man would want to burn it, which means taking it off first.'

I want him. He apparently wants me again. He is being scrupulous about this. And that put all the onus for a decision on her. Caroline took a deep breath. *I ought to say no. But I am at least an eligible wife for him in rank and I know I will do my best to make the marriage work.* 'Yes.'

'Yes, you will marry me knowing me as you do, having heard me warning you that I will not be the sort of husband you dreamed of?' She nodded. 'Yes to tonight?'

'Yes to both.' She got to her feet and walked past him, turned the key in the lock and then came to stand in front of the ottoman. It gave her the illusion, at least, of being in control.

'You are nervous,' Gabriel said, looking down to where the sagging hem was quivering just above her bare insteps.

'I told you I was and I would wager so were you when you lost your virginity,' she retorted. She had admitted that she desired him and he was probably far too experienced not to have realised it anyway, but instinct told her to hide how he made her feel, hide just how much she wanted *him*, not simply that rangy body. Somehow she had to retain some strength in this relationship.

His hands came to rest lightly either side of her waist, warm even through the flannel, then, when she stayed where she was, he tugged the ends of the sash so the robe fell open to reveal her equally chaste white cotton nightgown.

'As for my virginity, the second time, yes, I was nervous. The first time I was so excited that I wasn't thinking about anything. Not coherently. My father took me to a high-class brothel to be initiated into lovemaking, just as he selected the right tutors for us, bought us the right horses to learn on, sent us to the right teachers for fencing and shooting. Everything had to be perfect for his sons.' She thought his voice took on a bitter edge. Then it was gone. 'After he died I did the same for my brothers.' He slid his hands under the robe to caress the curve of her hips through the cotton. 'You are a very lovely shape. Classical.'

Caroline sorted her breathing out. 'I am appalled at your father. How old were you?'

'Fifteen.' Gabriel pulled her a little closer, leant in to kiss the slight swell of her stomach.

'That's younger than Anthony! And you took your own brothers.'

'We will worry about your baby brother's education later.' Gabriel was on his feet and her wrapper, somehow, was on the floor and so was his robe.

Under it he was naked.

There was silence, broken only by the sound of her breathing, which was not even, and his, which was not either. That was comforting. Slightly. They were standing so close that she could feel her nightgown brushing against his legs, the warmth of his bare flesh. And so close that it was surely safe to drop her gaze.

Or not. Bare chest, dark curling hair that did not conceal his nipples and that arrowed down over a flat, muscled stomach to his navel and...

Caroline had no idea what to do. But talking, especially

when one was nervous, was easy. 'I know about the mechanics of the act, of course. No young lady with access to a library, some knowledge of basic Latin, an enquiring mind and eyes to see men in tight evening breeches need be ignorant, exactly. And there was the night in the hermitage, of course. Only I was not quite prepared for...*that*.'

She made a wildly sweeping gesture and found her hand resting on Gabriel's chest, her fingers in that intriguing hair. 'Oh, it is soft. I wondered.'

'Feel free,' he said. 'Explore. And don't worry about *that*. We'll get to him later. We have time now.' He was amused, but not laughing at her, more inviting her to share a joke. Could lovemaking be *fun* then? He seemed so relaxed with her, as though he truly liked *her*, not just her body.

'Him?' She teased her fingertips into the curls, trailed a pattern into them, brushed his right nipple accidentally and stopped, fascinated as it hardened and puckered. She rolled it gently between her fingertips. 'Yours do that, too?'

'As you see.'

'And *him*?'

'It is definitely male. It has a mind of its own and is inclined to be unruly at the most awkward moments.' Again she was aware that Gabriel's breathing was not quite under control. 'You may carry on exploring, you know.'

Above the waist was safe. That unruly male object could definitely be left for later. Much later. 'You are very warm. And I did not expect your skin to be smooth.' She tried to circle her fingers around his upper arm and realised just how muscled he was. 'So hard underneath. And I can see the muscles. I've got some, I think that is from riding, but mine are smooth.' She traced a finger down the arrow of hair and Gabriel sucked in his breath as she dipped her finger into his navel. 'Am I talking too much?'

'There are absolutely no rules, although you are wearing altogether too much clothing.'

'I am shy. I told you that, too.'

Gabriel pulled her gently forward until her forehead rested on his chest. 'You are beautiful and you are even more beautiful naked in my arms. How long is your hair, Lady Godiva? I have never seen it out of its plait and it will veil your blushes.' His fingers were busy in it as he spoke, then he combed it out over her shoulders until it hung around her. 'We may safely undo some of these buttons now.'

'You are very good at undressing,' Caroline said after a moment as the fiddly buttons yielded, one after another.

'I am handy with corset strings, too. There, almost unveiled.' Her nightgown slipped down, clinging precariously to her hips. Gabriel smoothed her hair down, the palms of his hands brushed her nipples, then stilled as she made a faint, involuntary sound. He bent his head and blew gently on the strands, parting them so he could seek her left nipple with his mouth. His hands held her steady by the waist as she stiffened, then softened into his embrace.

It was bliss, and frightening, and delicious all at once. She could feel every movement of his lips, the tiny nip of his teeth, the soothing stroke of his tongue, not only at her breast but deep in her belly and between her thighs. Before had been wonderful, but so fast she had hardly been aware of anything but the urgency of their desire, the shock of that violent pleasure building. Him leaving her at that crucial moment.

Gabriel moved to the other breast, his hands sliding up to cup her, then down to give the nightgown the one last touch it needed to send it pooling around her feet.

Caroline caught at his shoulders, off balance with desire, confusion, the need to touch him. She found herself swept off her feet and deposited on the bed, wrapped in Gabriel's arms, his leg thrown over her hips, her whole body gathered in against his heat and hardness, all at once both safe and overwhelmed, swept up in the sheer masculine power of him.

Her body remembered, responded with enthusiasm as she burrowed against him, her hands running over the powerful shoulders, down to the narrow waist, the hard swell of his buttocks. She should be ashamed of her eagerness, her upbringing warned her, but she did not care. Everything throbbed and ached and wanted more. 'Tell me what to do,' she managed when he lifted his mouth from hers.

'Whatever you want, or just leave it to me.' His hand slid between her thighs as he spoke and she parted her legs instinctively, then almost arched off the bed with the pleasure of it and the embarrassing discovery that she was wet and aching there and that his fingers were sliding inside and she *liked* it.

They were more than sliding. They were stroking into the folds of flesh that seemed swollen and more sensitive than she could ever have imagined, then he focused his attention on one spot, teasing and caressing and everything, the entire universe, her whole needy, pleasure-filled body, was focused on that single point and the sensation became unbearable and then impossible and suddenly everything fell apart into something that was more than just pleasure.

She was vaguely conscious of being on her back, of a weight over her, of Gabriel's lips on hers again and then... 'Ow!' Indignant at the discomfort that shattered her bliss, she dug her fingernails into his shoulders. She had forgotten it might be painful, and he was very large and she was very new to this.

'I'm sorry.' His voice was husky. Caroline opened her

eyes to find herself almost nose to nose with him, the points of her nipples fretted by the hair on his chest, his hips tight against hers, and realised his body was deep within hers. 'It will get better in a moment, I promise. Trust me.'

She was not so sure, not when the pleasure and the tingling and the heat were ebbing in the face of this male intrusion. Why couldn't he be fast, so she didn't need to think? She could push him away, resist it, or she could trust him, she realised as he began to move again, rocking slowly into her, edging deeper. She closed her eyes, unable to cope with sight as well as touch and sound and the scent of their passion, musky and heady. Gabriel had never let her down yet, she realised as her body began to soften, embrace his hardness, open to him like a flower worshipping to the sun. And the pleasure flooded back, different from before, better than before.

'Come for me, Caroline,' he said and she opened her eyes to meet his, dark and deep and utterly focused on her. She did not understand what he meant, but he slid his hand between them, touched her in that magic place, and she spun out of control, out of herself again. She was conscious of Gabriel surging deeper, of his hoarse cry, of heat deep in her core and then she was lost in the strange bliss their two bodies had created.

Caroline came to herself with her head on Gabriel's chest, knowing exactly where she was, who she was with. *I love him.* She knew that as a certainty, too, and she knew not to say the words. Not yet. *I will show him if he will only give me the chance.*

She raised her head and discovered that Gabriel was asleep. Infinitely slowly she wriggled and slid until she could prop herself up on the pillow next to him and study him. The clever, cynical face was relaxed and off guard.

Vulnerable. He looked younger with the dark lashes on his cheeks, the wayward hair tousled over his brow, the mocking mouth softened and curved into a half-smile. She could imagine him as a wild, eager youth and wondered at the process that had turned him into the self-sufficient man behind the gambler's mask.

She reached down to pull the sheet up over their bodies, left the candles to burn themselves out, then snuggled back against him. *I will be sleeping with this man for the rest of my life now. If I can keep him. If we can make this work.* Her lids drooped and she fell asleep to the beat of his heart beneath her cheek.

Gabriel woke to dawn light and a feeling of bodily well-being. Except for cold feet. There was a definite warm draught stirring the hairs on his chest. He turned his head on the pillow and found Caroline curled up against him, her nose buried just under his collarbone, her hair veiling her face.

He had taken her virginity before marriage, yet he could feel no guilt. *We've done it, there's no way back from this, she cannot change her mind now.*

Her honesty about her physical desires had taken his breath away. Caroline, it seemed, was not good at prevaricating, not with herself and not, apparently, with him. That could be refreshing, it could be perilous. The little white lies and hypocrisies of everyday life kept the wheels of society moving smoothly and they probably kept marriages running smoothly as well, at least on the surface.

The nights, it seemed, would be pleasurable if Caroline's sensual enthusiasm was anything to judge by. Which should mean she would be with child soon and that, surely, would content her. He supposed he would have to modify his life a trifle. Now he was about to take a wife he could hardly act the rackety bachelor every night. He wanted her to be happy, to enjoy being a countess. She deserved that. *Dinner parties*, he thought vaguely. *She'll want escorting around to balls and so forth when the Season starts. Almack's, even.* He grimaced. Alex and Cris would be taking their wives, Caroline could join their parties.

But that aside, his life wouldn't change that much. He'd give her a good allowance, let her loose on the London house to start with. When a child was on the way she could move down to Edenvale and amuse herself with making that over as she wanted. The more she changed it, the happier he would be. There was no need to worry about emotions, about breaking her heart. This had been a marriage of necessity and he had been frank from the start. She was an intelligent woman who could have few illusions about him.

He found he cared that she was happy, an uncomfortable, unwelcome burden. *Keep her at a distance*, his head warned him even as he felt that warm, contented, sensation in his chest. *You'll only let her down sooner or later if she comes to believe this is more than it is.*

Caroline stirred, stretched, and her hand began to move slowly across his stomach. Yes, this was going to work.

'Good morning.' He slid up against the pillows with the result that her hand slipped southwards in a most delightful manner.

'Oh!' To his regret Caroline let go of his enthusiastically awakening wedding tackle and sat up in a swirl of sheets. Her eyes were sultry with sleep, her mouth was swollen with kisses and her cheeks were pink. 'Gabriel.'

'Which is who you were expecting, I trust. Did you sleep well?'

'So well.' She stretched with her arms above her head, presenting him with a ravishing picture of perfect small breasts, the movement of skin and muscle over her rib cage and stomach and a glimpse of her secret triangle of dark-blonde hair.

There was no artifice in the gesture, no calculation. Caroline was waking up, she needed to stretch and she was comfortable enough with him to do so without hesitation or self-consciousness. He was not used to that and it was, 'Delicious,' Gabriel murmured and pounced, rolling her on to her back and leaning on one elbow to look down at her. 'Are you sore?'

That did make her blush. She wriggled experimentally, causing his heart rate to kick up several beats. 'A little.'

He tossed the sheet on to the floor, slid down the bed and worked his way between her legs, pushing her thighs apart with his shoulders.

'Gabriel?'

'Shh. Relax. Go back to sleep if you like.' *As though I would let you.*

'Gabriel!' His name broke in the middle and Caroline gave a faint shriek as he lowered his mouth to her.

He put his hands firmly on either side of her hips to hold her still and licked into the core of her, exploring her secrets, relentlessly gentle and persistent until her gasps of protest turned into sighs and she began to lift her hips to meet his questing lips and tongue. He took her over once, then again, then came up her body to slide into the soft wet heat that was so ready for him. She came for him again, crying his name as she convulsed around him, sending him over the edge, all technique and restraint forgotten.

'Are you still reconciled?' she asked a little later, her eyelashes tickling as she leaned over to kiss his throat.

'Oh, yes, I think so, although I believe we will have to repeat the exercise frequently to make certain.'

She laughed softly as he pulled her tight against his side

and Gabriel relaxed. Caroline was a darling. This marriage business would be no trouble at all, provided he kept it at the level of sex and friendship.

Chapter Sixteen

'Lord Edenbridge. Good morning, my lord.' The Avenmore butler regarded Gabriel with a more kindly eye than he deserved, given that they had arrived on the doorstep of the St James's Square house at the outrageous hour of nine o'clock. 'My lord and lady are at breakfast, but if you would care to wait in the drawing room, I will apprise them of your arrival.'

'We'll join them, Benson. Just send in two more place settings.'

'Yes, my lord.' The butler did not quite roll his eyes, but Gabriel suspected it was a close-run thing. 'Should I announce you? The lady—'

'No need.' He took Caroline's arm and ushered her through to the dining room. 'Good morning.'

'What have you done now?' Cris enquired, folding *The Times* and setting it beside his plate as he got to his feet. 'Good morning, Lady Caroline.'

'Cris!' Tamsyn scolded, getting to her feet, too, and hurrying around the table to hug Caroline. She released her, regarded Gabriel with her head on one side for a moment, grinned and hugged him, too. 'You are going to get married, aren't you? Sit down and have some breakfast and tell us all about it. I'll just ring for— Oh, thank you, Benson.'

Gabriel waited until he had served both himself and Caroline from the buffet. 'Yes. I am almost afraid to ask how you know. Some form of Devon witchcraft, I assume.'

Tamsyn shook her head at him. 'A woman's instinct. I only had to look at the pair of you.'

'What happened?' Cris, with his usual uncanny nose for trouble, knew this was more than a sudden attack of romance.

'My father found me,' Caroline said. She was wary of Cris, he knew, but he could only admire the calm way she gave him back blue-eyed stare for stare. 'And Gabriel was there.'

'So Caroline gallantly saved my honour, and what remains of my good name, by consenting to marry me.' He saw her fingers tighten on the knife and fork as he spoke. *You must get used to it, my dear. Life with me is no romantic bed of roses.*

'You are a fortunate man,' Cris said. 'I felicitate you. Caroline, tell me what we can do to help you. We are entirely at your disposal.'

'I hardly like to ask it, but Gabriel suggested that you might allow us to marry here.' She was perfectly calm, perfectly composed. For a moment Gabriel was lulled into thinking that everything was all right, that Caroline was placidly accepting things as they were, as they had to be. Then he realised that she had learned this calm acceptance as a defence against her father's tempers, his moods, his blows. And now she was using it as a defence against him.

'Gabriel?'

He looked up at the whisper to see Tamsyn's concerned expression, then down to where the fragile coffee cup had cracked in his hand. *Unthinking violence. Hell, what is happening to me?*

'Lord, I'm a clumsy oaf,' he said lightly. 'I'm sorry, Tamsyn. I'll replace it.' He glanced around and found Cris was still talking to Caroline.

'Please, don't worry about it. I bought them in Mr Wedgwood's showroom across the Square only a few days ago. It is no trouble to find another.' She passed him another cup and murmured, 'Gabriel, is everything all right?'

'Yes, of course it is. Unpleasant for Caroline, of course, her father ranting and raving and then finding herself landed with me as a husband. But for myself, I couldn't be happier.'

'No. Of course not.' Her expression was a trifle quizzical. 'As the daughter of an earl she must be considered most eligible, which we know is of paramount importance to you.'

'Are you ever going to forgive me for opposing your match with Cris?' he asked.

'Certainly I will.' Her slanting smile carried promises and threats. 'Provided you make Caroline a good husband.'

'I have every intention of doing so.'

'I am sure you have. But is your definition of a good husband the same as mine, I wonder?'

Gabriel had told himself he was not going to be riled by her, that her wariness of him was more than understandable, so it was a surprise to find himself snapping back. 'As we all know Cris is a paragon of all the virtues, so I doubt anyone else can reach his level of perfection as a husband.'

He deserved a snub for that remark, he knew, not to provoke Tamsyn into laughter. He assumed an expression of mild enquiry, accompanied by one of his better sardonic smiles, as Cris said, 'Now what is amusing you, my love?'

'Gabriel considers that you are a paragon of all the virtues and must be making me an absolutely perfect husband.' Tamsyn was mopping her eyes with her napkin.

'And am I not?' Gabriel had never seen that tender look in the ice-blue eyes before.

'You are coming along very nicely, my lord,' Tamsyn said primly. 'Constant practice is, of course, required.'

'As with everything,' Cris observed. 'I must confess myself deeply flattered by your opinion, Gabriel. On the other hand, if I was certain you would know a virtue when you saw one, I might be more complacent.'

'Gabriel has many virtues,' Caroline said hotly. 'I beg your pardon, Lord Avenmore, but I will not sit by and have him abused.'

'He is teasing me,' Gabriel said, and then, when she still looked unconvinced, added, 'Male friends do, you know.'

'It is true,' Tamsyn put in. 'You must have observed it. The fonder they are of each other, the more objectionable they become. Men are not good at showing their emotions. Look at them—they both look thoroughly uncomfortable now.'

'As Gabriel appears to have finished his breakfast he and I can go and be uncomfortable together and leave you two to the full and frank exchange of your emotional states while you discuss arrangements for the wedding.' Cris got to his feet. 'Bring the coffee pot, Gabe, and we will retreat to the library to lick our wounds.'

'I have known you for years, yet when you look like that I still cannot read you,' Cris observed as they settled into the chairs facing each other on either side of the library fireplace. 'I have no idea whether you are delighted that your hand has been forced or appalled that you have to do the honourable thing.' He took a mouthful of coffee. 'Which is why I never play cards with you except for coppers.'

'I am neither,' Gabriel said. Strange that he did not resent Cris's probing, but then he and his three friends had never had secrets, not about the things that really mattered. Certainly not about the wounds they all carried from long ago. Except the one thing that he never, ever, talked about. 'I am simply content with the arrangement. I should marry because of the title and Caroline is perfectly eligible if one discounts her appalling father. I like and admire her. There is a certain basic mutual attraction.'

'Yes, one can see that.' Cris's lips twitched.

'I believe her reluctance is because she knows my hand is being forced. I made the mistake of attempting moral blackmail when I was desperate for her to agree. However, she is now resigned because I am, apparently, considerably better than the alternatives on offer.'

The twitch became one of his friend's rare grins. 'The more I see of Lady Caroline the more I approve of her.' He filled his cup and watched Gabriel over the rim. 'So why are you merely content, given that you are definitely attracted?'

'You think I will make any kind of a decent husband? Leaving aside this scandal, my reputation is not going to be any help to her. If we're received I'll squire her about, of course, but I'm hoping she'll be happier in the country bringing up the children.'

'This is not really about your reputation, is it?'

'I always thought you were a loss to the legal profession. You should be making some poor soul's life hell on the witness stand, not interrogating me.' Gabriel leaned across to take the coffee pot and stayed silent until he had drunk the fresh cupful. 'But, yes, you are right, of course. Damn it, Cris, I have no idea how to be a decent husband.

I'll be kind to her, look after her—that goes without saying. But neither of us were brought up to know what a happy family looks like. Her father is a self-centred obsessive, you know that. And then he hit her.'

'Does she realise how much you have in common?' Cris asked.

Gabriel shook his head. 'And she won't.'

'She will when she sees your back. Or has she already?'

'Not yet.' He moved uneasily as though the pressure of the chair back might chafe the old scars into active life again and shifted the subject. 'How do you do it, you and Alex and Grant? You all make your wives happy.'

'Love,' Cris said simply. 'It is a novelty for men raised as we were. For most aristocrats, I suppose. But we married women who understood about love and family and *warmth*, I suppose. Do you love Caroline?'

'No.' Gabriel was certain about that. He had no idea what loving a woman in the emotional sense would feel like, but he was very certain he would know it if it happened to him. It had changed his friends and he was the same man that he had been before Caroline had erupted into his life. Absolutely the same.

'Does she love you?'

Lord, I hope not. The thought of hurting Caroline appalled him. He would try his best, but he felt he was embarking on a journey with no road maps, no compass. 'I told you. She's resigned to marrying me, but that is all.'

'If you want my advice, and you probably do not, tell her about your family.'

'You mean so she can conclude that I will turn out like my father and flee screaming?' Gabriel enquired.

'You never would. You wouldn't be worrying about it if there was any danger of that.'

'What a comfort you are,' Gabriel retorted to cover the

fact that, yes, it *was* a comforting thought. 'I hardly recognise you.'

'I know it. It must be the effects of marriage. What do you say, shall we see if Alex can join us and we'll have a bachelor night out on the town?'

'Perfect. I'll call in on him on my way home.' He got to his feet, but stopped at the door. 'Did I tell you I found a new hell just off Hill Street?'

'I am not playing cards with you! Have you any idea how expensive wives are?'

Gabriel was still smiling when he collected his hat from Benson. *Thank heavens for my friends.* 'Would you give my compliments to Lady Caroline and tell her I will call tomorrow? I imagine she is closeted with Lady Avenmore at the moment.'

He tipped his hat to a rakish angle, pulled on his gloves and sauntered along King Street, passing Almack's with a faint shudder. Yes, thank heavens for his friends. There was no one else he could talk freely about his demons to, no one else he would admit weakness or anxiety to either. Certainly none of those things were to be discussed with a wife, a woman who needed only his strength and his protection, not his doubts and fears and secret nightmares.

'Madame Fleur, this may be a quiet wedding, but I can assure you it will be an important one,' Tamsyn said with a steely determination that sent a shiver down Caroline's spine. It looked as though it was having a similar effect on the modiste who stood in the middle of Tamsyn's bedroom surrounded by what appeared to be the entire stock of her shop, a number of half-finished gowns and several twittering assistants.

'You are being given the opportunity not only to provide the wedding gown for the new Countess of Edenbridge, but her entire wardrobe. And to demonstrate that I was right to select you to dress me exclusively,' Tamsyn continued.

The calculation was plain on the dressmaker's face: upset a number of clients who were waiting for gowns or seriously displease the Marchioness of Avenmore *and* lose the publicity surrounding what might well be the most talked-of wedding of the summer.

'But of course, my lady.' Madame rose to the occasion, gathered up her tape measure. 'My hesitation was merely while I acquainted myself with Lady Caroline's colouring and style. If you would condescend to disrobe and to stand here, my lady, we will begin. The entire wardrobe, you say?'

'Everything except a court dress. That can wait,' Tamsyn said, brushing lightly past the fact that one might never be needed.

Two hours later Tamsyn was still talking of lists as they descended the stairs. 'Millinery, shoes, stockings, corsets, lingerie, ribbons, hairdresser…I need more paper. I will go and jot all this down while I think of it. Why don't you go and have a rest in the drawing room for a while? Do ring for the tea tray.' She swept on, leaving Caroline feeling like a wilted nosegay in her wake.

'Never mind tea, I need brandy,' she murmured as she walked into the front reception room.

A young man clutching a leather portfolio rose to his feet. 'Lady Caroline? Benson said I might wait for you in here.'

Sandy hair, green eyes, half a head shorter than Gabriel and not yet twenty. 'Are you by any chance Mr Louis Stone?' she enquired, holding out her hand to him. *At last, a glimpse into Gabriel's home life.*

'Yes, I am.' He peered at her myopically. 'We haven't met, have we?'

'No, Gabriel described you. I was just about to take tea. Will you join me, Mr Stone?' She rang the bell, then gestured to the sofa and sat down beside him so that he did not have to squint across the room at her. 'I am delighted to meet one of Gabriel's family at last. Are you in London permanently?'

'No, just for the vacation. I go back to Cambridge at the beginning of October for the Michaelmas term,' he explained. 'But I am staying with Gabriel for the moment and helping him as much as possible.' He was flushed with earnest enthusiasm and Caroline was reminded painfully of Anthony, even though Lucas was almost a young man. 'I finished today's tasks, so I have come to see if I could be of any assistance to you, Lady Caroline.'

'Caroline, please.' She smiled at him, liking his earnest manner. The contrast with Gabriel was almost amusing. 'We will be brother and sister very soon.' He grinned at her, suddenly a student and no longer the earnest man he was trying to be. 'Tell me how you assist Gabriel.'

He talked readily, even when the tea tray had been brought and he had to juggle cup, saucer and a plate of cakes.

Why, he worships his brother. This was far from the distant relationship that Gabriel's few references to his family had left her imagining. 'Do you see much of your brothers?' she asked. 'I have not yet been to Edenvale and I am looking forward to that very much. I imagine you all get together there as often as possible.'

It was as though he had brought a shutter down over his face. Louis said stiffly, 'No, not often. Ben is with his regiment, of course, and George has his parish and Gabriel avoids the place like…I mean, he prefers London. I usually visit friends during vacations, but this summer Gabriel has started teaching me about the estates so I have seen much more of him.'

'Tell me more about Edenvale,' she encouraged him. 'Gabriel has hardly mentioned it. It must hold wonderful childhood memories for you.'

This time the shutters positively slammed down. 'I was never very fond of it. I have written to Ben and George and I have every expectation that they will be able to come to the wedding. Can I help with anything here? Place cards, perhaps? I have a good hand.'

So what on earth was wrong with Gabriel's country house that he avoided it? And it certainly seemed to hold no good memories for Louis either. Yet Gabriel had made no mention of any problems to her and she assumed that was where they would go after the wedding. It occurred to her abruptly that the subject had never even been discussed.

There was no point in pressing Louis, nor should she. 'I am certain Lady Avenmore would be delighted if someone took on that task. The marquess's secretary is already loaded down with all the work we are finding for him. Ah, here she is. Lady Avenmore, may I present Mr Louis Stone, Gabriel's youngest brother. Louis, the Marchioness of Avenmore.'

Louis made a very proper bow and shook hands and they all sat again while Caroline explained about his offer of help and Tamsyn accepted gratefully.

'Lord Edenbridge, my lady.' Benson ushered Gabriel in.

'Tamsyn, Caroline.' He stopped halfway across the carpet. 'Louis? What are you doing here?'

'I came to offer my assistance as I have completed everything you left me.'

'Have you indeed? And you have made yourself right at

home, I see.' Gabriel cast a jaundiced eye over his brother's crumb-strewn plate.

'We are very glad to see him, and I am delighted to make his acquaintance,' Caroline said. 'We were just talking about Edenvale.'

In the silence that followed she thought she could hear her own heart beating.

'What about it, exactly?'

'I was just saying that I couldn't tell Caroline much because I hardly ever go there,' Louis said.

'I don't even know where it is,' she added in an effort to ease the strained atmosphere. 'I am looking forward to seeing it very much.'

'We will drive over when we are in Brighton,' Gabriel said with no marked enthusiasm.

'We are not going there for our honeymoon, then?'

'Brighton, yes. Edenvale, no. It needs work doing to it,' he added. 'I thought you would like Brighton. Have you been before?'

'No, never.' *And I know a* No Trespassing *sign when I see one.* 'I am sure it will be delightful if this weather holds.'

'It looks set fair. Excuse me, I must go and discuss wine with Cris. Make yourself useful here, Louis, and I will see you for dinner at Mount Street.' He paused with one hand on the door. 'I have asked Cris to be my best man. I wondered if you would like Alex to give you away, Caroline.'

'Oh, yes, I would.' He nodded and went out as she said to Tamsyn, 'I cannot think of anyone better qualified to soothe a nervous bride's nerves.'

'Are you nervous?' Louis asked, then blushed violently. 'I do beg your pardon, I am sure that is the sort of thing one does not ask.'

He was so charmingly dismayed that she laughed. 'It is merely the scandal, that is all.'

'The scandal? You know about...?' His voice trailed away. 'Oh, you mean the scandal about the elopement. If you will excuse me, I will go and find Lord Avenmore's secretary and offer to help with the place cards.'

'And what was that about?' Caroline asked Tamsyn whose bemused expression must be a match for her own. 'What scandal?'

'I have no idea. You will have to ask Gabriel.'

'No, Gabriel has enough to worry about. If he wants me to know, he will tell me.'

'You are very trusting. Anyone would think you were in love with the man,' Tamsyn said slyly. 'Have another cake.'

Chapter Seventeen

'Deep breath, chin up.' Alex said, settling her hand more firmly in the crook of his elbow. 'You look ravishing, you'll bring Gabriel to his knees, every man in the place, including the vicar, will want to run off with you and all the ladies will be green with envy over your gown.'

If the laugh that escaped her was shaky it did release some of the tension, which was presumably why Alex was laying on the flattery with a trowel. 'Thank you,' Caroline said, answering the intent, not the words.

'Off we go then.' Alex set off at a slow walk for the head of the stairs, then paused for her to lift the hem of her skirt a little and get a grip on the spray of cream-and-pink roses and ferns she carried.

At the foot of the great sweep of staircase the household staff were arrayed in formal ranks and, as she came down the final curve, Caroline could see heads turning in the drawing room. Goodness knew what strings Cris and Alex had pulled, what wiles Tess and Tamsyn had employed, to get such a number of guests there. And such influential ones, too. Two Patronesses of Almack's, the Swedish ambassador and his wife, one ancient duke, a marquess, a scattering of countesses, an archdeacon…

Tess had briefed her about each and every guest and it had all fled what passed for her brain now the wedding was actually happening. She had hardly slept last night, tossing and turning with nightmare visions of everything that might happen to stop it—her father appearing with a shotgun, the archbishop refusing the licence, Gabriel coming to his senses. And when she had fought all those phantoms down she was racked with worry that it *would* happen and that the marriage would be a disaster and—

'*Breathe*,' Alex murmured as they entered the drawing room. For a second her knees turned to jelly and then she looked up through the gauzy veil and saw Gabriel standing at the far end of the room. He was a stranger, a well-groomed gentleman in a beautiful tail coat and silk breeches, his hair fashionably cropped, his expression severe. And then he saw her and everything was all right. She had no idea what tomorrow might bring, but here, now, the man she loved was smiling at her, was, against all convention, holding out his hand to her, and she was conscious of nothing more than his voice speaking the vows, the warmth of his grip, the caress of his lips as he put back her veil and kissed her.

'You make a very lovely countess,' Gabriel said as they processed back between the rows of guests.

'It is this gown.' She was walking on air now in her pretty French kid slippers, ready to believe he thought her *lovely* as the cream silk whispered behind her, as the tiny crystals and pearls caught the light and sparkled like snow in summer, as the diamonds he had given her flashed defiant fire at her ears and throat, wrist and in her hair.

'It is you, my lady. You would have this room at your feet even if you were wearing sackcloth. You make me proud to be your husband.'

Hold this moment a little voice inside her urged. *You will need this memory, you will need its strength.*

'How married do you feel?' Gabriel asked as the chaise rattled over the cobbles past Brixton church and Caroline took off her bonnet and sat back with a sigh. They had a six-hour journey ahead of them, it was already well past noon and his bride was a trifle wan. She was still beautiful, but pale now and her smiles were beginning to look artificial. She would regain her spirits, he had confidence in her resilience, but for now he would try and keep things light.

'I feel very married. But I am not certain about being a countess,' Caroline confessed, with a dimple appearing that looked perfectly natural. 'I will have to get Harriet to address me as Lady Edenbridge with every sentence until I become accustomed. How married do *you* feel?'

'Exceedingly. The sight of my beautiful bride might have been a dream, but I have been comprehensively lectured by Cris and Alex on the subject, I have signed numerous legal papers, much to Louis's delight, and I have seen an alarming amount of luggage loaded on the coach this morning. That all feels very real.' So did the pleasure he felt when he looked at her, caught one of her smiles. It was almost easy to believe that he could make her happy. That she could make him happy.

'Wait until the bills arrive, then you'll most definitely know you have a wife,' she said darkly. 'Tamsyn and Tess insisted that you had given them *carte blanche* to buy whatever they felt was necessary, but it seems like a great deal to me.' Glancing down, he saw that the dimple had vanished. 'I wish my father would release my dowry, I do not like coming to you empty-handed.'

'You bring yourself. That is all I need. I am a rich man, Caroline. I can well support a wife in style.'

She slipped her hand into his. 'Thank you.' Caroline was silent almost as far as Streatham village and he was wondering if she had fallen asleep. Then she said, 'I do like your brothers.'

'You do?' He had kept a wary eye on them, as far as he was able amidst the demands of an early wedding breakfast.

'Ben is a good officer, I imagine. He has that same knack of leadership that you do, but allied to military discipline. And I imagine that he takes good care of his men, for all his seeming rather abrupt. That is like you, too.'

'Me? I lead no one anywhere except into trouble and I have no one to take care of. Except you now.' A sweet duty.

'And your brothers. And your friends. But if you are going to be foolishly modest I will tell you that I also liked George and I consider him quite indecently good looking for a clergyman. The poor man will spend his entire career evading heart-struck spinsters in the vestry. He will make a very beautiful bishop, which Louis informs me he intends to become.'

'I am prepared to admit that he resembles me in looks,' Gabriel said, fishing to see just how truthful she would be.

'George is better looking than you are. His nose is straighter and he has a very engaging smile.'

'That puts me in my place. And what about Louis?'

'Oh, Louis is a darling. He is anxious to do well in his studies so that when he graduates he can be of the greatest use to you. He hero-worships you, of course.'

'Nonsense. They all avoid me like the plague unless they need money. Or, in Louis's case, employment.'

'They are in awe of you,' Caroline said, tipping back her head to frown at him. 'They look up to you. I never spoke to them all together, but they all said the same thing, that they owe you so much. They love you, you know.'

Gabriel shifted on the seat, the plush upholstery suddenly as hard as planks. They could only have been referring to their childhood, but none of them knew just what lengths he had gone to in order to protect them. And none of them had witnessed that final crisis, only Louis, for whom the memory had been blanked out by shock.

He had sneered at Caroline's devotion to Anthony, her total commitment to putting his welfare above her own. But he knew now why it had made him so uneasy and defensive. He had felt the same, had made his own sacrifices. But all this flummery about love… No. Even if his brothers did know, all he had done was his duty to them. He was the eldest and they were his responsibility.

'You will invite them to stay, won't you?' Caroline rested her head on his shoulder. 'There is room for guests at Mount Street and I imagine Edenvale is large enough for proper house parties. Now what have I said?' She sat up again. 'You have gone all stiff.'

'None of us likes Edenvale.'

'Then we must fix whatever is wrong with it. It is a wicked waste to have a large house uninhabited. It should be giving employment to the entire district, for one thing.'

She sank back against his shoulder and Gabriel wondered why that gesture was quite as pleasing as it was. This was his wedding day, he should want kisses and caresses from his wife, not confiding snuggling. Then she nudged him in the ribs. 'Ouch!'

'What about Edenvale? What is wrong with it?'

'You are quite right about the employment. And I had meant to open it up for you as I imagine you would be happier down there when the children come along.' Now it was her turn to stiffen, but he judged it unwise to ask why. 'We did not have very happy childhoods there, that is all. A familiar enough tale, I suppose. Our mother died when I was fourteen. Ben was eleven, George ten and Louis only four. Our father was not an easy man.' And that was all he was going to say on the subject.

'And I suppose it is entailed, so you cannot sell it,' Caroline mused as they entered Croydon. 'But as I assume you did not intend depositing me, and our hopeful family, down there and never visiting, we must change it enough to reconcile you to it.'

'As you say,' he temporised, choosing to ignore the soft snort that produced. 'Tell me why you have never been to Brighton. I would have thought your father was entranced by the Pavilion.'

'Oh, yes, he much admires it. But he did not believe in taking the family on holidays when we had a perfectly good country house for fresh air and recreation. Tell me all about it. Where will we stay and what is there to do?'

'I have taken a house overlooking the Steine. We were lucky to get it at this date, but apparently Lady Maltravers, who was renting it, had a violent quarrel with her bosom friend Lady Feldrake over a young man and has flounced off to Weymouth, declaring that the company there is far less vulgar.'

Gabriel talked about assemblies and libraries, drives and public breakfasts, the dubious aesthetics of the Pavilion and, of course, the opportunities for sea-bathing, until Crawley was behind them. 'This is Pease Pottage,' he said, expecting a murmur of amusement at the name. 'We will change horses at the Black Swan.' A soft, lady-like snore greeted this intelligence so he made no move to get out, instead settling Caroline more comfortably against his shoulder and gesturing away the landlord who came busting out while the grooms changed the horses and the postilions vanished into the taproom for a hasty pint of ale.

She was exhausted, and no wonder, he thought, surprising himself when he realised he was feeling no impatience at being trapped in the chaise instead of being able to get out, stretch his legs and take refreshment. It was a novelty to have a woman to take care of, one that he was discovering an unexpected tenderness for.

Caroline woke with a start and found they had drawn up abruptly because a young man was struggling to turn his gig and half-blocking the road. 'I am so sorry.' She sat up, uncomfortably aware that the shoulder of Gabriel's coat was creased where her head must have rested, that her hair was in disorder and that she had slept at a time when any other bride would have been wide awake and paying close attention to her new husband. 'Where are we?'

She had expected Gabriel to be irritable with her, but his smile was the rare one that reached his eyes and made her want to hug him. The smile she had seen at the altar. 'Hand Cross, thirty-three miles from London. We'll stop at the Red Lion, I expect you would like some tea.'

'I would, definitely. I am sorry I went to sleep.'

'Why be sorry? You are tired, which is no surprise, given what has transpired over the past few days.'

'It is not very wifely behaviour,' she said primly, which made him burst out laughing as the chaise turned into the inn yard.

'And what do you know about wifely behaviour?'

'About as much as you, I imagine. Or were you in the habit of driving down to Brighton with young ladies in the guise of Mr and Mrs Smith of Scandal on Thames?'

'*Ladies?* One at a time, Lady Edenbridge, please. You have a flattering notion of my stamina.' When she shook her head at him he smiled. 'I am not in the habit of travelling with females.'

'Are you not?' she quizzed him, but he got down from

the chaise and helped her out. She did not like to tease
when there was the chance they might be overheard.

To Caroline's surprise, Gabriel returned to the subject
when she joined him in the private parlour after seeking
out what the landlady coyly referred to as, 'The ameni-
ties, ma'am.'

'Did you think I travelled with a bevy of light-skirts and
opera dancers?' he enquired as she poured tea.

'I have no idea.' Caroline passed him his cup and surveyed the assortment of dainties that had been brought in
with the tea. 'I have no knowledge of that sort of thing,
but you *do* have a reputation.'

'For a sequence of *chères amis*, all of whom were, shall
we say, ladies rather than professionals. And note I did say
sequence. One at a time is quite adequate.'

Caroline digested this along with a cake that was turning to sawdust in her mouth. 'Who is the current one?'

Gabriel choked on his tea. 'No one!' He recovered himself and added with his old, mocking half-smile, 'Terribly
bad *ton* for a newly married man.'

'So you gave the lady her *congé*?' She tried to gain some
comfort from this, although the implication of his words
only confirmed his earlier remarks about the likelihood
he would stray from his vows.

'I did. All very amicable, I assure you.'

Caroline almost believed him, but she was beginning
to be able to read Gabriel, just a little, and there had been
a betraying tightness about his mouth for a moment. So,
the mistress of the moment had not been pleased. She repressed a little shiver, then assured herself that pride, if
nothing else, would prevent whoever it was from making
an unpleasant scene when she next encountered Gabriel
in public. All the scandals about this marriage were going
to be the ones she was responsible for bringing with her.

I will be a good wife, she promised herself. *I will make him happy if it kills me. And I will not give him any excuse to chase other women,* she added grimly. *If he does then I will not be a complacent wife, even if Gabriel thinks that would make me a good one. I love him and I do not intend to share.*

'This is an excellent inn,' Gabriel observed, looking round at the warm glow of the polished panelling. 'It has been a long day. Shall we ask if they have a decent room available to go with this parlour? We could break our journey here.'

'But we are only about twenty miles from Brighton, surely?'

'Yes, but that is another two hours and there will be all the business of arriving at a hired house which is never straightforward, however early one sends down the staff. We could rest and then have dinner and go to bed early.' His eyes had the heavy-lidded look she had seen before, the one that sent an answering *frisson* of desire through her.

'*Rest*, my lord?' Caroline pushed away the niggling little doubt that it was talking about his former lovers that had made Gabriel think about bed now.

'A convenient euphemism I have learned from my married friends. It is amazing how weary marriage makes some couples. It is, after all, our wedding night.'

'Then, yes, let us take a bedchamber. You have warned me, after all, not to overestimate your stamina.' She widened her eyes at him in mock-innocence and felt a certain return of confidence when he got immediately to his feet and strode from the room.

There *was* a chamber, charming and old-fashioned with a great oaken four-poster bed, a thick Turkey carpet on the uneven floor and a ceiling that bulged and dipped so that Gabriel banged his head as he straightened up after dragging the curtains part-way across the window. Caroline bit her lip with sympathetic amusement, then felt the laughter die as she saw his face, recognised the heat and the desire. He wanted her and she wanted him, wanted him with a fever that had consumed her for days, ever since he had shown her what they could be together.

'No, leave it all,' he said as she lifted her hands to open the catch on her necklace, a fine double string of pearls left to her by her mother. They lay warm and comforting against her skin, now she arched her neck so he could lift her hair away from the nape and manipulate the delicate fastening.

Gabriel seemed in no hurry. His fingers played along her hairline, making the fine hairs stand up in response to his touch, then he bent and kissed her nape, his lips slightly open so she felt the heat of his breath, the tiny touches of his tongue.

The pearls curled on to the dressing table, then he unhooked her earrings, kissing behind each ear. Caroline leant into the delicious, teasing caress as he nibbled his way down the tendon at the side of her neck and gasped as he closed his teeth over it and bit down gently.

'Mine,' Gabriel murmured, his voice possessive. 'My bride to unwrap like a particularly delicious parcel.'

She had changed into a walking dress of deep sapphire, worn under a pelisse of paler blue that she had removed when they sat down to tea. Now Gabriel had unobstructed access to the row of tiny enamelled buttons down the back, which had taken Harriet her maid minutes to fasten, but which seemed to evaporate under his touch. The gown vanished, so did her petticoats, chemise and shoes, which left her in a corset, stockings and garters.

Gabriel stepped back from the bed and surveyed the result, like some pasha viewing the latest slave girl brought from his harem, she thought with mingled excitement and indignation.

She reached for her garters and he growled, 'Leave them.'

'But this feels more indecent than when I was wearing nothing,' she protested, flustered.

'I know.' The growl became the purr of a large cat. 'That's because it is. Very arousing. Look.' He tipped the glass on the dressing-table mirror so she could see herself sprawled on the pale-rose coverlet, her breasts pushed up by the tight lacing, her legs looking longer with the white stockings and the blue of the garters drawing the eye…

Caroline closed her legs abruptly and curled up against the headboard. 'You are still wearing all your clothes.'

Gabriel sat down, hauled off his boots and stockings together, shed his coat, waistcoat and neckcloth, unbuttoned his shirt and then his falls. The breeches slid down his long flanks, taking his smallclothes with them. 'Better?'

His shirt, open for the first ten inches, showed a tantalising amount of chest and hid a tantalising amount of everything else. Without troubling to remove it he sat on the edge of the bed and pulled her towards him.

She wanted to say, *No, take it off, let me look at you in daylight,* but the words stuck to the roof of her very dry mouth and then Gabriel was running his finger along the top edge of the corset, teasing her nipples in their tight confinement. He pushed at the edge until they were free, then bent to blow gently on the tips.

'Like cherries on a plate being offered up for me to nibble,' he said, and did.

The corset was tight, the pressure seeming to tip both her pelvis and her breasts towards Gabriel, into his clever hands and wicked mouth. She was breathless, racked with tension and delicious, terrifying sensation, desperate to touch him, to have his skin against hers. She tugged at the hem of his shirt, but it was crushed between them, then her hands found the neck opening and she jerked the sides apart, heard the fabric rip, then burrowed down to fasten with lips and teeth on to his right nipple.

Everything happened very quickly then. Gabriel was inside her and her body remembered him, responded without her having to think or do more than cling to him as he swept her up into the storm of his own powerful urgency. Her fingers knotted into the shirt over his shoulders, her heels locked into the small of his back, she heard her own voice gasping his name, heard the sound of their bodies meeting in hot, wet, desperation and then he reared up on his knees, lifting her with him so that he sank impossibly deep and she buried her face against his neck as the pleasure exploded, spinning her into fragments and she was lost in him.

Chapter Eighteen

Gabriel woke her by trailing deliberately sloppy kisses and licks around her right ear.

'Beast!' Caroline sat up, batting him off.

'It was the only bit of you I could get at,' he grumbled, falling back on to the pillows. 'You were curled up like a hedgehog.'

He was still wearing the ripped shirt and nothing else. When she leaned over and ran her fingers into the dark curls on his chest he caught her hand and pressed it flat until she could feel the beat of his heart under her palm. 'Caroline.' She looked up to meet his gaze and saw he was suddenly serious. 'Did I hurt you? I was too rough, I forgot that this is still new for you.'

'No, you didn't hurt me, although, frankly I doubt I would have noticed. And I was rough, too, I ripped your shirt.'

'That was exciting, my little hellcat. No one has ever done that to me before.'

She turned her fingers into claws beneath his hand and raked gently down his chest, following the trail of silky hair. When his eyes narrowed she whispered, 'Do you know what I want to do now?'

Gabriel shook his head, his gaze as intent as a hawk watching a vole.

'Get out of these stays and have a bath. Oh, no—we haven't any luggage!'

'Yes, we have. Look.' In the corner were three valises and her dressing case. 'I thought it was unwise to send everything ahead of us.'

'Yes, but it has only just occurred to me, Harriet and your valet will be wondering what has become of us. They will be so worried.'

'I expect they will guess we have been held up on the road.' He was looking so innocent as he straightened up from the bags with their robes in his hands that Caroline was immediately suspicious.

'You planned this, didn't you? You told them we wouldn't be in Brighton tonight.'

'I thought you might like something more spontaneous, more like a scandalous elopement,' Gabriel said as he shrugged on a heavy amber silk banyan over the tattered shirt. 'Let me untie that tight lacing before we ring for baths.'

'Why, I do declare you are a romantic, Gabriel Stone,' she said on a sigh of relief as her stays tumbled to the floor.

He held the peignoir for her. 'No, I am not, merely a rake. That's why we are so dangerous to innocents.'

Caroline blinked hard as he crossed the room to tug on the bell pull. *That's what you get for being romantic yourself, you fool. He doesn't love you, he is merely displaying his usual repertoire of seduction and lovemaking. And he is very good at it. The benefit of experience as he says.*

Caroline had her smile stitched firmly in place as her husband turned back. He had spoken in jest with no intention of hurting her, she was certain, for he would have to know that she loved him for that comment to have been meant to wound. She'd had no illusions about who and what she was marrying and she was not going to start their life together with tears and reproaches.

The cheerful expression was still intact as the maid came in and Gabriel gave orders for baths, shaving water, dinner. *The years of practice hiding my feelings from my father are bearing fruit now,* she thought and then had to turn away abruptly as the tears slid down her cheeks. Of all the bitter ironies, to have to use the deceit learned in her early life in order to hide her true feelings from the man who had rescued her from it.

'I am so enjoying Brighton.' Caroline tightened her grip on Gabriel's arm for a second and he glanced down at her, his expression amused.

'You haven't exhausted all the entertainments in a week?'

'Of course not. After all, this is the first time we have been swimming.' She gave him a sidelong look from under her lashes. 'It is the first morning I have been able to drag you out of bed in time.'

'You were not so unwilling to stay there,' he murmured, lowering his voice because Harriet and Corbridge were walking behind them, the valet carrying towels and the maid with Caroline's swimming outfit and hairbrushes.

It was true that she was easily persuaded to stay in bed for just one more kiss, which usually led to more than kissing. On the other hand Gabriel appeared to consider any time of the day or night suitable for lovemaking, so getting up on such a glorious morning as this would hardly deprive either of them.

'Mrs Wilberforce is waving from her carriage,' she said, drawing Gabriel's attention to the passing matron and her daughters. He lifted his hat, Caroline exchanged slight bows with the other ladies and they walked on, passing several new acquaintances and others whom Caroline or Gabriel knew from London.

'Everyone is so friendly,' she said. 'I did not expect it. We eloped, so I thought many of the matrons would poker up and that they would not welcome me associating with their daughters.'

'I suspect our friends have been busy on our behalf, although I must admit to being pleasantly surprised. Probably your father's eccentricities are so well known that no one blames you for escaping. And we did come to London and marry at once from a most respectable address. You are a countess now and although I have got a reputation, as you very well know, I have always been received.' He doffed his hat to a handsome lady in an open carriage who dimpled back at him.

'Stop flirting,' Caroline said lightly. She might as well tell a cat to stop chasing mice. Gabriel noticed pretty women, looked at pretty women and smiled at them, too. *And* he had spent two evenings at the Castle Inn assembly rooms deep in card play. But there was no sign that he went any further than smiling and as for the cards, he kept an eye on her and tossed in his hand the moment he noticed her looking tired.

'I am male, I have a pulse and I am under ninety and given that I caught you in Donaldson's circulating library using the telescope to study the west beach, I have to tell you, my lady, that was a case of the pot calling the kettle black.'

'I was not studying it! I only happened to swing the telescope in that direction. How was I to know it was the men's bathing area?' *Or that they all bathe stark naked?* None of the Brighton machines had the all-enveloping hoods that she had read about. It made her blush all over again just thinking of it.

'I will bespeak two bathing machines, mine at the eastern edge of the men's beach and yours at the western edge of the ladies' beach and then I can keep myself between you and any more assaults on your modesty.'

They were approaching the bathing house where those wishing to be 'dipped' booked their machine. Down on the beach the mules were trundling up and down the shingle, dragging the bathing machines and from the water came faint shrieks as ladies were ducked by the muscular female dippers.

'I do not want to be dipped, Gabriel.'

'A dipper is a fixture with the ladies' machines, I'm afraid. Besides, if you haven't been in the sea before then it is easy to be swept off your feet. I do not want you drowned, my dear. Just tell her you want to keep your head above water.'

He thinks I am nervous of being forced under the surface. I never told him I can swim, she realised, almost blurting it out, then thinking again. It might be fun to surprise Gabriel if he really was going to be close enough to reach without the risk of encountering any of the other men. Her mother, hearing of a tragedy where an entire family had been drowned on a boating trip, had insisted that her daughter as well as her sons were taught to swim before they were allowed to row on the lake. Lucas had taught her, surprisingly patient as she doggy-paddled around in the shallows in a voluminous shift over a pair of his old breeches.

She was still smiling at the memory as Gabriel paid the one shilling and three pence for her and the one shilling for himself without a dipper.

'There are two machines free now, just where I wanted

them. Apparently the ladies prefer not to be so close to the men and the gentlemen are inhibited by the thought of appearing to spy on the ladies.'

Caroline went down the ladies' steps to the beach with Harriet to be met by a woman with her sleeves rolled up over brawny arms. Her stout form was clad in a voluminous and soaking wet black-bombazine gown with numerous flannel petticoats dripping below the hem.

'I am Mrs 'Uggins, marm, and I'll be your dipper. No need for any alarm, marm, I've dipped them all from dairy maids to duchesses and never lost one yet. If you and your woman just step along and climb aboard, 'Uggins will take you down to the briny, smooth as silk.'

They clambered up the steps, through the door and into a narrow box with wooden benches on either side, a door at the far end and louvered slats letting in some light and the sound of the sea.

'It is a good thing I spoke to Mrs Chamberlain's maid yesterday and got some advice,' Harriet said as she began to unfasten Caroline's walking dress. 'It would be far too difficult getting fully dressed and undressed in this, my lady.'

She had the simple gown and one petticoat off without any trouble and was just attacking the strings of the pair of short stays that was all the corsetry Caroline was wearing when the machine gave a lurch and began to move. Harriet sat down with a thump on one bench and Caroline on the other.

She was still giggling when she emerged through the door on to the steps into the sea to find Mrs Huggins at the foot of them, the waves rising and falling around her vast hips, her impressive bosom emerging like sea cliffs from the foam.

'Down you come, marm. Lovely and warm it is. We'll have you dipped three times before you can say Neptune!'

Caroline took advantage of the dipper's bulk as a screen as she descended the steps, stifling a shriek as the water hit her stomach. Then she was in, her Bathing Preserver, as invented by the modiste Mrs Bell and widely advertised, shrouding her in its folds. The weighted hem kept it from billowing up and once she had arranged it evenly around her she felt quite decently covered and surprisingly unhampered.

'I do not require dipping, Mrs Huggins. I can swim quite well.' And in fact it was quite difficult to keep her feet on the bottom in the buoyant salty water.

'It's more healthful to be dipped,' said the bathing woman doubtfully. 'Not many ladies swim. Are you used to the waves, marm?'

'I am perfectly confident, thank you. I can see my husband over there.' And sure enough Gabriel's dark head was visible as he swam powerfully out to sea from the next bathing machine. He dived under and re-emerged to swim back towards the hut and when he reached the steps he rolled on to his back and began to float.

Caroline struck out, put her head under, blinked at the salt, then, suddenly confident, dived and swam submerged towards him. Being beneath the sea was different from the still cloudiness of the lake and clouds of bubbles released by the breakers and the swirls of sand disorientated her for a moment. Then she saw Gabriel's legs and surfaced close behind his back, ready to splash and startle him.

The sunshine was directly on him, gilding the water on his skin, emphasising the muscles, the beautiful masculine taper from shoulders to waist, the dip of his spine. *The scars.*

Gabriel turned at her gasp and his face, for once unguarded, was stark with shock and anger in equal parts. 'Get back over there,' he snarled. 'Are you mad? If anyone saw you behaving like a hoyden the word would be around Brighton before you have dried your hair.'

Blindly she dived back under the water and came up within the shadow of her own hut. Mrs Huggins was calling across to one of the other dippers and seemed not to have seen her and she realised that the incident had been over in seconds. No one was looking across from the men's swimming area, the ladies were too preoccupied with their own rigorous dippings to peer through saltwater-laden lashes in her direction and as far as she could see the few telescopes in evidence on the promenade were trained at the horizon.

She had not been seen, and if someone had spotted one head popping up too close to the invisible dividing line, then there was no reason to suppose she could have been recognised. And Gabriel knew that. His anger had been because of what she had seen, not what she had done.

Those scars. In the unforgiving light his back had been a tracery of thin silvery lines, dead straight, criss-crossing like intricate lace created by some demon. He had been whipped, often and often, and he had tried to hide the fact from her. When they made love the curtains were always at least partly drawn, or the candles away from the bedside. When he got out of bed he reached for his robe, or his shirt, before turning his back to her and always took his bath behind a screen. She had thought it simply a courtesy to preserve any modesty she might feel once the intimacy of lovemaking was over.

But he could not have thought he could hide them from her for ever, surely? As her confidence grew she felt an increasing desire to sometimes take the lead in bed, to explore Gabriel's body, to push the robe from his shoulders or to see what erotic games might be played in a bath. And in the day-to-day intimacy of married life, surely he might expect her to walk in on him unclothed and unaware?

Unless he did not expect their intimacy to extend much beyond this honeymoon trip. Unless domestic closeness was the last thing he intended.

'Marm, are you all right? You've gone all white-like. Knew you should have had a good dipping and then got out.' Mrs Huggins surged towards her like some amiable sea monster. 'Up you go now, your girl's waiting for you with a nice big towel.'

Her legs were tired which must be why she was so clumsy. Stumbling up the rough wooden steps, she stubbed her big toe painfully enough to bring tears to her eyes. Harriet, anxiously fussed over the bruised toe, worrying as she swathed Caroline in towels and did her best to get her dressed in the gloom.

'Oh, my lady, that must hurt so much. I can't see if there are splinters. We must send for a doctor directly, you might have broken it, for you to cry so.'

'I'm not…' *Yes, I am.* With an effort she pulled herself together, scrubbed at her eyes with the edge of the towel, and did her best to get her clothing in order over her damp skin. 'It was the shock. You know how things always hurt more when you are cold? I'll just slip my foot into the slipper and not fit it right on.'

Harriet was down the beachside steps before her when they finally jolted to a halt. She ran over the shingle to where Gabriel waited, his face once more his impassive card-player's mask. Caroline, hobbling down the steps with the assistance of Mrs Huggins, could hear her talking.

'…broken toe, my lord…doctor…'

Gabriel came striding down the beach and scooped her up from the bottom step with a curt nod to the dipper.

'Harriet, find a coin in your mistress's reticule for this good woman.'

He took the steps up to the bathing house without pausing, passing an interested group of ladies at the top. 'My wife has a slight injury to her foot, that is all. Thank you for your concern, Lady Oxenford. Mrs Hughes, too kind, I am sure it is nothing serious. If there is a retiring room where she can rest while we wait for a doctor to come—'

Through sore eyes Caroline could see that no one was looking censorious as the manager ushered them through to a small room with a *chaise longue* and assured them a doctor would be with them directly. Her *hoydonish* prank had not been observed.

'No one saw me,' she said the moment the door was closed.

'What did you do to your foot?' Gabriel was stripping off her stocking, ignoring her words.

'I stubbed my toe on the steps.'

'It is beginning to bruise. It might be broken.' He looked up. 'Your eyes are red.' It sounded like an accusation.

'They were watering with the pain. I rubbed them too hard, that is all. Gabriel—' The knock on the door silenced her.

'Lady Edenbridge? My lord. I am Dr Foster, I was with one of my patients using the warm baths, so I am most conveniently on hand, am I not? Now, ma'am, what seems to be the trouble?'

'The trouble *seems* to be a severely stubbed toe and possibly a broken bone,' Gabriel said. He set an upright chair by the head of the *chaise* and took Caroline's hand in his.

It should have been an affectionate gesture but, glancing up at his set jaw, Caroline wondered if it was simply to prevent her babbling out any more indiscretions. She was glad of it for support when the doctor, keeping up a constant flow of inane chatter presumably intended to soothe her, manipulated the toe, announced that it was not broken and bandaged it.

Gabriel thanked him punctiliously, handed him his card and invited him to send in his account to the London address. He walked out with him and came back with the information that he had a sedan chair for her. 'Should I carry you to it? There is a throng of interested ladies outside.'

'Then I see no reason to give them any more opportunity to gawp at you displaying your muscles,' Caroline snapped. She had no wish to find herself carried, to lie back and revel in the romantic thrill of being carried by her strong husband. Not now, with him so angry at her.

Chapter Nineteen

Gabriel escorted her back to the house on the Steine, striding beside the chair in total silence. He gave her his arm to hobble into the hall and up the stairs and instructed Harriet curtly to look after her mistress.

'Where are you going, my lord?' Caroline enquired as he turned to the door.

'Out.'

'Harriet, please leave us.' She waited until the maid had gone, then got up from the chair where Gabriel had deposited her. 'You are not running away from me until you tell me what you are so angry about. And do not tell me it was because I approached the men's part of the beach. No one saw me and they would have had a hard time recognising me if they had.'

'Madam, I do not require your permission to come and go in my own house.' But he stayed where he was.

Caroline drew in a silent breath of relief for that small mercy at least. 'You were never a common soldier. You were never a criminal. And if you have a desire for pain along with your sexual pleasure, then you are hiding the fact exceedingly well. Therefore those scars on your back were put there by your father when you were under his control. And that means he was a vicious man who should have been ashamed of himself. It does not explain why you feel you have to hide them from *me*.'

'Marriage does not mean I have to confide every detail of my past to my wife.'

'*Detail?* You call receiving savage whippings a *detail*, Gabriel?'

'I call it the past and I have avoided this because I knew it would end up with you becoming ridiculously over-emotional about it.'

'I am not over-emotional,' she snapped.

'Then what are you crying about?'

'You, you idiot.' She threw up her hands in frustration, wising she could pace up and down the room, or thump the man to get some reaction from him. 'The boy you were, because those scars are not recent. And you now, because it is plain they still hurt as much as they ever did.'

'My father was subject to uncontrollable rages and the conviction that his word was law. He demanded perfection. That made him demanding and difficult to live with. You can no doubt understand that from your own experience. I did not want to remind you of what you had suffered, that is all.' As though realising that his very rigidity betrayed his feelings Gabriel moved away from the door with his habitual relaxed prowl. Anyone who did not know him well—*anyone who does not love him*—would have seen nothing amiss.

'My father is a deeply selfish man with a number of eccentricities who loses his temper when he is thwarted. He lashed out at me and that was very wrong of him.' She paused while she got her breathing back under control. 'But he had never done it before and, although I know he has chastised Lucas and Anthony, just as every school-boy in the country must have been punished, it was never the kind of systematic whipping that produces scars like those. And you were the eldest. What on earth did he do to your three younger brothers?' She thought of Ben, big and bluff, George, scholarly and ambitious, and Louis. Earnest, studious Louis.

'Very little. He rarely found them at fault,' Gabriel said with his mocking smile. 'I was the flawed one, the wicked, provoking one.' When she opened her mouth to protest he said, 'You wanted to know where I was going? To Edenvale. You may come, too, if you wish, provided I am not subjected to any more maudlin tears about the past.'

'You can be quite hateful when you choose, Gabriel Stone.' And it was a deliberate choice to be so, she was certain of that. He wanted to push her away. Or perhaps the word was *needed*.

'Are you only just discovering that, my dear?' He paused at the door, as cool as she was heated. 'You had best change if you are coming with me, I have hired a curricle.'

His mood was communicating itself to the hired pair who fidgeted and sidled as he kept them waiting for Caroline to emerge from the house. Gabriel forced himself to relax his hands, to speak to the horses until they calmed. He only wished he could exert the same soothing influence over his knotted guts. The memories of the past were bad enough. Not the pain, that he had learned to lock away, but the flashbacks to his father's body at his feet, strangely pathetic in death, all that power and fury reduced to nothing but flesh and bone and expensive tailoring. He had been glad he had died, he had to bear the guilt of that as well.

The images flooded in as he fought them. Louis, a white-faced child, mercifully unconscious; Ben and George, just boys themselves, stammering questions; and further back, his mother as white as the sheet she lay upon and the doctor sweeping a bottle into his case with one hasty brush of his hand. *A tragic accident*, he had said, and fourteen-year-old Gabriel, shivering with dread behind the curtains, had known with absolute certainty that he lied.

But that was the past and he had learned to live with it, contain it. His marriage was the present and he had allowed the poison to leak from that sealed room in his mind to hurt Caroline. And what had he done this for, this marriage, if it were not to save her from hurt?

She came down the steps using her parasol as a cane, her weight on her heel, waving away the footman. 'Thank you, Robert. I can manage.' But she let the man help her into the curricle and settled herself with perfect composure beside Gabriel.

His wife was a lady through and through, he told himself as the pair moved sedately out into the traffic bordering the Steine. Whatever had passed between them, whatever hurts she had, mental or physical, she would not sulk and she would not show anything but a pleasant face in public. His mood softened, he felt himself grow calmer, just because she was beside him.

'I had expected a high-perch curricle,' she said as he gave a wide berth to the fishermen drying their nets on the end of the greensward nearest the beach and then turned eastwards along the seafront.

Play the cards as they were dealt, he reminded himself. You didn't win at cards by cursing every poor hand that came your way, but by working with what you had. And just now he had a wife who was apparently forgiving enough to drive out with him.

'The roads around Edenvale are more lanes than anything. One needs a carriage built with substance rather than style. I had no wish to deposit you in a ditch when an axle broke.'

'Then you had planned for us to make this expedition today?' Unspoken was the question of why he had not mentioned it before.

Cowardice was probably the correct answer, but he left that unspoken also. 'Yes. It is less than an hour's drive.' Which was no answer at all.

Caroline maintained a flow of intelligent conversation as they drove, commenting on the landscape, the boats to be seen along the coast, the state of the tide, the occasional picturesque cottage or view. None of it was taxing, none required an answer beyond the occasional monosyllable. Gabriel decided he was probably being managed and that he deserved it. That he welcomed it. He did not want to be at odds with his wife.

He turned inland when they reached Saltdene, wending his way through narrow lanes up on to the rolling downland. 'Access is better from the north, but this is a more attractive route,' he added as he made the sharp turn into the park through the gate to the Home Farm.

She was silent as they drove across the parkland, past the famous herd of fallow deer, past the lake and the great stable block and, finally, to the front of the house.

'Queen Anne,' Gabriel offered when she was still silent. 'Not over-large and the rose-red brickwork is considered rather fine.'

'It is beautiful and seems very well kept up.'

'I have excellent staff here.'

As he spoke the front doors were opened. Two footmen appeared and a groom came running from the stables. Gabriel helped Caroline down and offered his arm as she limped across to the steps. 'Does it pain you very much?'

'Just the bruising coming out. If I did not have to wear a shoe it would be trivial.'

'My lord.' Hoskins, the butler, stood waiting, permitting himself one of his rare smiles. 'Welcome home, my lord. And, my lady?'

'Indeed yes. My dear, this is Hoskins, who has been with me for ten years. Hoskins, Lady Edenbridge, your new mistress.'

Caroline smiled warmly at the man and then looked around the great double-height hall. 'I see you manage the house in fine style, Hoskins. What a magnificent staircase!'

'It is one of the showpieces of the house, my lady. That double sweep, the ornately carved newel posts, the painted ceiling—students of architecture frequently call just to admire it.'

She stood at the foot where the two arms of the stairs came together on the pure white stone and Gabriel could see, beneath her feet, the pool of crimson slowly spreading, spreading... Then he blinked and all was clean marble again.

'Refreshments for her ladyship in the Chinese Drawing Room, Hoskins. And no doubt Mrs Hoskins will make certain the countess's suite is in readiness should she wish to rest.'

'Thank you, but I feel the need for tea more than anything else.'

'You have the butler charmed, which is a good start,' Gabriel observed as they seated themselves in the drawing room. It was in good order, but then it should be: he had written before they had set off to Brighton to tell Hoskins that he would be opening up the house again.

'A good start for when you leave me here by myself, you mean?'

'There is little to entertain you in London just now, I would have thought. Naturally you will want to return when the Season starts, but in the meantime I assumed you would want to order this place as you see fit.'

'While *you* will have plenty to entertain you in London?'

'Probably. My clubs… It is pretty much a bachelor society at this time of year. And then when hunting starts I expect to receive invitations to various people's boxes in the shires.' *The clubs, the hells, the safe, solitary evenings.* The loneliness that had seemed like peace before he had become used to Caroline's presence.

'I see. You no longer require my company?' Caroline's colour was up. 'Or my presence in your—' She broke off as a footman came in with a tea tray and thanked him as he set it at her side. 'Bed,' she finished when the door closed again. 'I cannot say you did not warn me. But I also warned you, Gabriel, that I take marriage vows seriously. I am not prepared to simply acquiesce to this. I will not nag, I will do everything in my power not to mention it again, but I will not be closeted in the depths of the country while you commit adultery all over London.'

'Adultery?' It took him so much aback that he stared at her. 'Who said anything about adultery?'

'You did. Before we were married. You said you would not keep your vows, you as good as instructed me to take a lover once I had provided you with the requisite number of sons. Well, Gabriel Stone, I am not prepared to be stabled down here in the country like a brood mare awaiting the attentions of the stallion. I will be faithful to you because *I* take vows seriously, but I will live in London or here or visit friends as I wish.'

He could not deny what he had said, fool that he was. 'I have no desire to be with another woman.' *When had that happened?* 'Nor would I force myself on you. If you allow me to your bed then I would be…honoured. There will be no other women in my life.'

'Then why do you want me away from you?' Caroline attempted to pour tea, sloshed it into the saucer, said a word he had no idea she knew and banged the teapot back down again.

'Because I thought you would want your freedom to do the things that interest you. I want… I am not used to this intimacy, of living with someone, sharing thoughts.'

'The day you share a thought with me, an intimate, important thought, without it being forced from you, will be a first, Gabriel.' Caroline lifted the teapot again and this time managed to pour two cups. 'I do not want to pry, I do not expect you to share every passing thought, every private contemplation with me. I do not want to force your secrets out of you. But I do not want to spend the rest of my life alone and I find it hard that you seem to want loneliness. Aloneness.'

'Everyone is different,' Gabriel said harshly.

'Your brothers love you. Your friends and their wives love you. What are you afraid of, Gabriel? That I might love you, too?'

'You love far too many people for your own safety, Caroline. That is your nature and I cannot prevent you including me in the band that you take to your so-loyal heart. But to fall *in love* with me? You have far more sense than that. It would be a tragedy, would it not?'

He could accept love now, he was learning that. The changes in the lives of his three closest friends had made those friendships richer. His brothers, rallying round at the wedding, welcoming Caroline without hesitation, had stirred something deep inside him. He was their older brother and it had always been his duty to protect them as well as he could, and, at the end, he had so nearly failed.

Caroline was a woman who had turned to him for help and it was his duty to give that, whatever it took.

But he had always known there was something lacking in him, some spark that some other men seemed to have, the willingness to expose himself to the risk of pain that love, accepted and returned, brought. Had brought. He *would not* think of his mother. 'I fear hurting you,' he said now, as gently as he knew.

'Deliberately?' she asked, watching him with a frown line between her brows as though he was a puzzle to be solved.

'No. Never that.'

'Then do not shut me away. This is a lovely house and I would like to spend time here with you. But not now. We will go back to Brighton, finish our honeymoon, learn to co-exist a little better, if you can bear that. Then we will decide what each of us does next and discuss it.'

Caroline was making plans. He was beginning to recognise that when she was under pressure she felt better for having a strategy. 'Very well. Shall I show you around now we are here?' He could manage that, surely? He had the courage to face a duel, wade into a street fight. Take a beating. He could summon up the guts to show his wife around a house.

They drove back to Brighton in a state of wary truce. Something had gone very wrong in that house, Caroline knew that for a certainty, and she felt as certain that Gabriel had built high walls around the memories. But the poison was seeping out like the miasma from a vault. She shivered convulsively, appalled at the ghoulish image that conjured up. She was becoming emotional lately and every little feeling seemed heightened.

'Are you cold?'

'No. Just a goose walking over my grave.' *Stop thinking about graves.*

'I have upset you. I am sorry for my temper and my secrets. I want whatever compromise is best for the both of us, whatever will work for us.'

'Compromise is a word that does not come often to your lips, I think.' She ventured a teasing note and, glancing up, was rewarded with a smile.

'Not often enough, I am sure.'

Reassured by the smile, Caroline tucked her gloved hand under Gabriel's elbow and was not repulsed. *We must look the perfect just-married couple,* she thought as they reached the Parade and passed the grassy length of Marine Square, its new houses sparkling white in the sunshine. 'There is Lady Carmichael. She was so pleasant when I spoke to her in Donaldson's the other day.' Caroline waved. 'Oh! Gabriel, she *cut* me.'

'You are imagining things. She must not have seen who we were.'

'But she did, I saw her recognise me and then she just went blank. Gabriel, slow down, there is Mrs Wilberforce, walking with her daughters.' As the curricle drew level she smiled and waved. 'Good afternoon, Mrs Wilberforce.'

The matron who had beamed at her only that morning gathered her three girls closer as though to shield them from contagion and hurried on.

'Stop!' Caroline made a grab for the reins and when Gabriel brought the pair to a halt she half-scrambled, half-jumped down, gasping in pain as she jarred her sore toe. 'Mrs Wilberforce, wait, please.'

The older woman turned. 'Lady Edenbridge, I will thank you not to accost me, or my daughters, again.'

'Why not?' Caroline demanded, keeping her voice moderate with an effort. Even so, heads were turning. 'You acknowledged me this morning.'

'I was prepared to make every allowance for you, given your blameless record since your come-out and the fact that, despite your shocking elopement, you married immediately and with such distinguished sponsors. But I am not prepared to give countenance to the wife of a murderer. A *patricide*.' She turned on her heel. 'Come, girls.'

'No, you will not turn your back on me after making such an accusation.' Caroline caught at her sleeve, jerking her to a stop. 'Where did you hear such lies?'

'Why, today's *Morning Post* and a letter from London from my good friend the Duchess of Brancaster. Now, unhand me, Lady Edenbridge.'

She marched away and Caroline turned, aghast. People were slowing, someone pointed and just in front of where Gabriel was backing the team, a couple crossed the road to the other side, heads averted.

'What the devil?' he demanded as the curricle drew level with her.

'She said…she says the newspapers say…that you are a *murderer*.'

Chapter Twenty

'Get in.' Gabriel held out a hand to help her. 'Smile. Don't cry.'

'I am not crying,' Caroline said between gritted teeth. 'I am furious. How dare she? How dare the *Morning Post*? It is libel, you must sue them. Who are you supposed to have murdered, for goodness sake?'

'My father, I assume,' Gabriel said as he drew rein outside their rented house. 'Can you manage to get down? Go straight inside and wait while I return this to the mews.'

That was enough to knock the anger clean out of her. Caroline limped up the steps, back straight, chin up, and the door swung open before she could knock. James, the footman, closed it, virtually on her heels.

'My lady, the newspapers—is his lordship coming back soon?'

'Yes.' Ebbing fury left her sick and weak and it took a conscious effort to speak calmly. 'Take the decanters to the drawing room. Is there any post?'

'Yes, my lady.' He hurried after her with half a dozen letters on a silver salver and three folded newspapers.

Most of the letters were for Gabriel, but she rec-

ognised Tess's neat black handwriting and broke the
seal without sitting down.

> *My dearest Caroline,*
> *I hope this reaches you before the news is abroad in*
> *Brighton, but I doubt it. Your father has descended*
> *on London telling all who will listen that he had the*
> *man who 'abducted' his daughter investigated and*
> *has found a witness who swears that Gabriel mur-*
> *dered his own father twelve years ago.*
> *Cris tells me that he knows about the accident*
> *and that it cannot have been anything else, and of*
> *course we, and all your friends, are countering the*
> *rumours wherever we hear them.*
> *Cris is writing and will do nothing more until he*
> *hears from Gabriel whether he wants him to secure*
> *the services of the best lawyers or whether he is*
> *coming back to London himself. He says to tell you,*
> *'Courage!' and to do your best to stop Gabriel com-*
> *mitting murder in reality.*
> *Tamsyn and I stand ready to come to you, if that*
> *would help, or to do whatever you ask.*
> *Your loving friend,*
> *Tess*

'It was my father,' she said the moment Gabriel walked
into the room. 'He is telling everyone that he has a witness
who says you murdered your father.' She thrust the letters into his hands. 'Cris has written and I think that one
is from Alex.' When he took them she went and poured
brandy into two glasses and brought one to him. Then she
sat and waited, fighting the churning panic. This was her
father's revenge, she had brought this down on the man
she loved.

Gabriel put the letters down unopened and ignored the brandy. 'Are you not going to ask me if I did it?' His eyes were dark and steady as he watched her face, but lines bracketed his mouth and his voice was harsh.

'Of course you did not.' But a tiny worm of doubt stirred. Something dreadful had happened at Edenvale, something that had made the place hateful to Gabriel and his father had whipped him unmercifully. Surely not…

'It was brought in at the inquest as an accident. There were no witnesses. He fell down the stairs, smashed in his head on the marble, broke his neck, but no one could account for why,' Gabriel said. He had his composure again and his voice was devoid of emotion. 'Your father's investigator has turned up the old case.'

'Was he drunk?' she managed.

'At four in the afternoon? No. Stone-cold sober. None of the servants would admit to being in the hall or near the head of the stairs. By the sound of it there must have been someone after all and your father's money has loosened their tongue.'

She wanted to ask whether he meant that someone's tongue had been loosened to tell lies, or the truth, but she could not bring herself to show such disloyalty. 'But there was no one you know about?'

'Louis,' Gabriel said as though the name was being dragged out of him. 'But he had fallen at the top of the stairs and knocked himself out. He could remember nothing, not then, not to this day. You saw those carved newel posts. It was a bad blow and it made his sight worse.'

'There must have been some conclusions drawn, surely?'

'Oh, yes. The jurors found that my father had tripped over the riding whip he was carrying, that Louis had seen him begin to fall, rushed forward to help, tripped himself and hit his head. When the butler came on the scene I was at the foot of the stairs standing in a pool of blood, the broken whip in my hands. The coroner was prepared to accept that I had heard the fall, rushed to the scene from the study on the ground floor and automatically picked up the whip in my shock.'

'Then there is nothing to it but wicked fantasies created by my father. A good lawyer will sort this out, force him to retract under threat of legal action. The original coroner's report can be republished. I will never forgive him for this, never.'

'The slight problem is, my dear, that it did not happen as the coroner stated. I was not downstairs when my father fell, I was on the stairs. And there was a slash on his cheek from the whip that was never accounted for.' Finally Gabriel picked up the glass. He drained it in one swallow and sat down. 'The coroner concluded that somehow the whip had hit him as he fell.' Caroline pushed her own untouched brandy glass towards him, but he shook his head. 'It would only take one servant who did in fact see me going down those stairs with the whip in my hand and I will discover whether the old tale about silken nooses for peers is true.'

The whip, Gabriel's back. How many vicious thrashings did it take before a young man snapped, hit back? Killed his tormentor? No. But Gabriel had not denied it.

'Stop trying to make light of this,' Caroline said, amazed that her voice was steady. 'There is more to it than you told me, certainly more than you told the coroner's court. If they found it was an accident, then that was what it was and you cannot have been responsible.'

'You believe that? I saw your expression when you heard what I said about the whip and his face. You were thinking about the scars on my back, weren't you?'

'Yes.' She would not lie to him. 'I do not understand it

all and I do not know what you are hiding, although I think you are protecting Louis in some way, but I do not believe you could kill in cold blood, nor hot blood either. Not and intend it. And unless my father withdraws this accusation and publically apologises, then I will stand up in court and swear that he is mentally incompetent.'

'You will *not* get involved.' Gabriel slapped one hand down on the table, making her jump, then stood up and began to pace, as though movement helped him think. 'Murder is not treason, therefore the title and the estate are safe for Ben, whatever they find. I can make provision for you. The problem is the damage this will do to your reputation, but the lapse of time from the death is in our favour there. Everyone will assume you were taken in by me, that you are simply a victim in all this.' He sounded perfectly calm, as though working through a problem that his steward had brought to him.

'I will surrender myself to whoever is the chief magistrate here, not wait to be dragged out of the house. That will create a better impression and may allow me a little more freedom to manage my affairs. It will certainly make less of a scene here and may divert any sensation-seekers from the house and from you.'

'Gabriel, stop it.' Caroline found she was on her feet, too. 'You are frightening me. You must fight this, prove your innocence.'

'I cannot. I am very sorry, Caroline, but I cannot. I was a fool to believe that I actually had a chance of real happiness with you.' He caught her by the shoulders and kissed her, taking her mouth with a savage desperation that stole her breath and filled her with fear. 'Now, stay here. Order the servants not to answer the door to anyone. Write to Cris, tell him to come and fetch you, send you to Grant in Northumberland. You'll be away from the public eye there.' He released her as suddenly as he had seized her, leaving her to stagger back into a chair, her hand to her mouth. His smile as he turned back from the door was gentle. 'Goodbye, my love.'

'No. Gabriel, I must tell you, I am— *No!*' But he was gone. *A chance of real happiness with you. He called me my love.*

Caroline jumped to her feet and yanked the bell pull. When James entered, so quickly that he must have been lurking outside, she snapped, 'Answer the door to no one but the Marquess of Avenmore or Lord Weybourn. Be ready to take letters to the receiving office in a minute and send Corbridge to me.'

The valet came in as she was addressing the first letter to Cris. 'Corbridge, I must write to his lordship's brothers, most particularly Mr Louis. Have you their directions?'

'Yes, my lady.'

'Were you with my husband when his father died?' she asked as she scribbled the next note.

'I was a footman at Edenvale, my lady.' There was something in his tone that made her glance up sharply. The valet tightened his lips as if on some outburst, then said in his normal, quiet voice, 'It was an accident, my lady. I have seen the newspapers, but nothing will make me believe otherwise.'

'Could anyone have witnessed the fall who has not come forward before now?' She wrote Louis's name on the next letter and reached for a fresh sheet of paper.

'I cannot think so. Let me address those, my lady.' He gathered up the letters as she finished them. 'They will catch the post to London and be with the marquess, and Major Stone, tomorrow morning. Mr Louis may receive his in the evening, I believe.'

'Thank you, Corbridge. Then come back, please.'

He was away perhaps two minutes, long enough for Caroline to take a small mouthful of brandy and to wipe all trace of tears from her eyes. She had suspicions, she also had, if not a plan, at least the outlines of a strategy and she would not give way to despair. Besides, there had been that smile, those words. *He loves me, even if he does not quite believe it, even if there is some other loyalty that is stopping him from telling me the truth.*

'Corbridge, your master has gone to seek out the chief magistrate of the town and intends to surrender himself to him for the investigation of these accusations.' Perhaps it was only shock that allowed her to sound so calm and collected, but if it was, then she would use whatever advantage it gave her. 'I want you to find him. I have no idea what that will involve, but I need to know where my husband is and what he needs.'

Waiting was the worst thing. Or perhaps uncertainty, she could not decide which. Caroline moved into the back parlour when people began to walk slowly past the house, staring, and waited there as James answered the door time and again with the same message. 'My lady is not at home. My lord is not at home.'

She hated the wallpaper in that room. She hated the pattern of the carpet. She absolutely loathed all the novels she picked up and tossed aside in the two hours it took for Corbridge to return.

'I have seen his lordship. The magistrate, Sir Humphrey Potter, feels it is best if he remains at his house for the moment because of the interest the matter is arousing, my lady. As his guest, Sir Humphrey asked me to assure you.' Corbridge brushed at a smear of green on his sleeve. 'Forgive my appearance, my lady, but it was necessary for me to climb over several garden walls and to enter through the back garden. James has already evicted one man who climbed in through the coal hole and was attempting to bribe the kitchen maid for information.'

'Will the magistrate allow you to stay with his lordship, Corbridge? No? Then I trust he will accept it if we pack a valise for him. Come.'

While Corbridge laid out a change of linen and Gabriel's shaving gear, Caroline fetched her new travelling case and took one of the razors to its lining. Under the leather she slid thirty guinea coins, all she could find in the safe, and six hairpins, tied in a handkerchief. Corbridge set out a pair of evening shoes and she wrapped the little pistol from the safe in the stockings and tucked that into the toe of one of the shoes. It would all come right, she had to make herself believe it, but just in case…

'Please tell his lordship that this is my newest valise and to be particularly careful of it. He can be so careless.'

'As you say, my lady.' Corbridge took the bag and Caroline was left with nothing to do but wait and try to find some comfort in the fact that Gabriel was not languishing in Brighton's lock-up.

Cris and Tamsyn reached Brighton at ten the next night, bringing with them a second coach containing four burly men. 'Some of my grooms,' Cris said as he straightened up from kissing her cheek. 'I guessed you might need the barricades manned.'

'People are such vultures,' Tamsyn said as she hugged Caroline. 'Tess and Alex send their love and they are staying in London to do anything needed at that end. Where is Gabriel?'

Caroline told them everything while they ate supper. 'Do you know what happened?' she asked Cris. 'Gabriel is hiding something, but I cannot believe he would kill his own father.'

'You have seen his back, of course,' Cris said. 'A court might well feel that evidence of such harsh treatment shows motive enough, especially as he was holding a whip when the body was discovered. But I do not know the truth. What he told me is what he told you. Like you I do not believe he did it and also that he is withholding something.'

'I have sent for Louis,' Caroline said and took a sip of the port she and Tamsyn were sharing with Cris.

'Yes? Then you share my instincts about this. But I have always understood he remembered nothing of the accident.'

'I cannot think of anyone other than his brothers whom Gabriel would shield at the hazard of his own life,' Caroline said. 'But we cannot expect to see Louis until late tomorrow at the earliest.' The doorbell rang. 'Oh, for goodness sake! Who is that at this hour? People have no decency.'

'Major Stone, Mr George Stone, Mr Louis Stone, my lady.' James opened the door wide and Gabriel's three brothers walked in, heavy-eyed and travel-worn.

'Where is Gabriel?' Ben demanded the moment they were inside.

'Residing with the magistrate,' Caroline said. 'How did you all get here? I am so glad to see you, but I only wrote to Louis yesterday. Come in, sit down. James, fetch food and wine.'

'I never got your letter. I saw the papers and left Cambridge immediately.' Louis was pale and behind the lenses of his spectacles his eyes were red with exhaustion. 'I found the others in London at Lord Weybourn's house.'

The brothers ate while they listened to the news, but Caroline noticed that Louis soon put down his knife and fork. He looked as though he might be sick at any moment.

'So, either someone saw something at the time that

seems incriminating and have only just come forward in response to my father's probing for scandal in Gabriel's life, or he is making bricks without straw. But Gabriel is not telling me the entire truth, of that I am certain. If only someone we can trust actually saw what happened.'

There was an aching silence, then Ben put down his cutlery with a clatter. 'I saw and George, too. Gabriel doesn't know.' He looked across the table at his brother sitting beside Louis. George's face as was white as his clerical bands. 'He would be furious if he knew we had spoken.'

'Gabriel can kick you from here to London for all I care,' Caroline snapped. 'I only want him alive to be able to do it.'

Louis snatched up his glass, gulped the contents and banged it down again. 'I did it. I killed Father.'

Chapter Twenty-One

'Lady Edenbridge has sent this valise by your valet, my lord.' The magistrate's man set the bag down on the ottoman at the foot of the bed. 'He asked me to pass on her message to please be careful of the leather as it is her ladyship's new case.' He passed a professional hand over the surface and nodded approval of its quality. 'Sir Humphrey is dining alone this evening and requests the pleasure of your company at dinner, my lord. I will come up to assist you at seven o'clock, if that is convenient.'

Such a polite gaoler. 'Thank you, yes. Please convey my thanks to Sir Humphrey.' Gabriel waited until the valet had bowed himself out then opened the valise.

It was not like Caroline to fuss over her possessions, let alone send chiding messages at a time like this, which meant she was up to something. He lifted out the carefully packed clothes, then almost dropped one evening shoe in surprise at its weight. The little pistol designed to be carried in a pocket gleamed up at him dangerously. Gabriel shook his head, checked that it was loaded and uncocked and slid it into the breast of his coat. What else had she done?

Even empty the bag was heavy. It did not take him long

to find the money and the hairpins. He sat on the edge of the bed, the little twists of wire on one palm, wondering at the strange tightness around his heart and the absurd, inappropriate urge to laugh. He was hysterical… *No, I am happy. Oh, Caroline, you will never give up, will you?* Presumably she imagined him in some dank cell, picking the locks, fighting his way to freedom, and she would give him the tools to escape whatever the cost to herself. 'I love you, you brave, loyal, beautiful woman.'

How long had he felt like this and not recognised it for what it was? Those unguarded words as he had left her had come from somewhere deep inside, a blinding revelation that the way he felt when he was with her, when he thought about her, was *love*.

The urge to laugh left him as suddenly as it had come, but the grip around his heart did not ease. Of all the times to discover that he could fall in love—and with his own wife, the most unlikely of miracles. Gabriel stamped down on the hope that Caroline might one day come to love him, too. She was as open as she was loyal and honest. She had admitted her physical attraction to him, a daring thing for a young lady to do, so it seemed impossible that she would be reticent about the much more respectable emotion of love.

Better that she never did, given that all he could look forward to was disgrace at the best and death at the worst. He could not, would not, tell the truth about what had happened. Of all the times to find his loyalties stretched on the rack. He could hear his mother's voice in his head as clearly as he had that day when he had been fourteen and had found her weeping in her bedchamber. *Promise me you will look after your brothers, Gabriel. Swear to me.* And he had sworn, not understanding. Not then.

* * *

Dinner with the magistrate was surprisingly civilised. Sir Humphrey was a widower in his early sixties, a burly, down-to-earth man.

'You're better off here,' he remarked as he gestured to Gabriel to refill his wine glass with the good Burgundy they had drunk with the beef. 'It will do no harm for it to be known that you surrendered to me of your own free will the moment you heard the rumours. Makes a good impression, that sort of thing. Lady Edenbridge will be safe in that house with all your servants around her, I have no doubt.'

Nor had Gabriel. He would not have left her otherwise, but Corbridge had his orders, and Gabriel's pistols, and he would lose a large wager with himself if Cris de Feaux wasn't on her doorstep by tomorrow.

'Sunday tomorrow,' Sir Humphrey observed. 'We won't see the coroner before Monday, I imagine. He lives in Lewes, of course, you'll recall from the original inquest, it being the nearest town to the house. You'll not want to go to church tomorrow, I presume?'

'I have no desire to disrupt a service, which is no doubt what would happen.'

'Quite. Should I ask the vicar to call in? Perhaps you would welcome some quiet contemplation and prayer with him.'

'Thank you, no.' The last thing he needed was quiet contemplation. What he *needed* was to be alone with Caroline, a large bed and a *Not Guilty* verdict. What he *wanted* was his hands around her father's throat. Neither of those ambitions could be confessed to the vicar. 'The use of your library would be much appreciated.' If nothing else the sight of his unwilling guest calmly reading might help convince the magistrate that he had no bloody crimes on his conscience. It was likely to be a long day.

* * *

'Who the devil?' Sir Humphrey enquired the next morning as the sound of the knocker reached the breakfast room. 'We have hardly finished our meal. This is no time to be making calls.'

'The coroner, perhaps?' Gabriel suggested, moving aside the London Sunday papers that the footman had placed between the two men. Time enough for the first stagecoach to bring Monday's budget of gossip, speculation and lies. He was not going to ruin his breakfast with yesterday's.

'He'll still be at his own table. Yes, who is it?'

The footman looked decidedly flustered. 'The Marquess of Avenmore, Sir Humphrey. And a lady, a clergyman, an army major and a young gentleman and they all say they want to speak to you. I told them you would not be available yet and they said they would wait.'

'They want to speak to me, you mean,' Gabriel interrupted. His brothers as well? And he had thought things could not get much worse.

'No, my lord. They were very definite, it is Sir Humphrey they want to see.'

'Put them in the study, fetch them refreshments and tell them I will be with them shortly.' He waited until the man went out and turned to Gabriel. 'Well? What is this delegation?'

'A close friend, my wife and my brothers, I assume.'

'With evidence?'

Gabriel shrugged. 'I very much doubt it. As I have said all along, there were no witnesses to my father's fall.'

'Then if it is not evidence I do not need to wait for the coroner and I see no harm in you joining me. I haven't had so much excitement since the last time Prinny's entourage kicked up a riot in town.'

The party waiting for them in the magistrate's study was certainly more tastefully dressed, and considerably more sober, than the new king's cronies. Caroline, thank heavens, was pale but perfectly composed, the fine veil thrown back over her bonnet apparently her only concession to the fact that her husband was under house arrest and their name a byword over the nation's breakfast tables. She was wearing the newest and most fashionable of her London walking dresses and smiled at him in a way that made him catch his breath.

At her side Cris, as elegant and cool as ever, stood to exchange bows with the magistrate. 'Sir Humphrey? I am Avenmore. May I introduce Lady Edenbridge. Major Stone, the Reverend Mr Stone, Mr Louis Stone. I apologise for this early interruption to your morning, but we have evidence in the matter of the late Earl of Edenbridge's death.'

'Evidence? In that case I feel I should wait for the coroner.' The magistrate looked none too happy.

'There is none. There can be none,' Gabriel said. Louis was white and he saw Caroline reach out and touch his hand for a moment.

'Excuse me, Sir Humphrey.' It was the nervous footman again.

'Yes? What now?'

'Mr Barton, the coroner from Lewes, sir.'

'Already? Well, send him in, this cannot become much more irregular than it is already.'

Gabriel barely recognised the coroner, but then it had been ten years since the inquest and the man must have been in his fifties then. He stalked in like a dyspeptic heron, peered around and snapped, 'I've come on the Edenbridge matter, Sir Humphrey. What is this? Trying the case already?'

'Certainly not. Allow me to introduce you.' The magistrate made the introductions and everyone sat down again, making the study feel uncomfortably small. 'Apparently Lord Avenmore believes that some of those present have evidence to present.'

'Do you indeed?' Barton seemed unintimidated by the presence of a marquess, even Cris at his most arctic. Gabriel felt an unwilling twinge of admiration and an equally unpleasant lurch of apprehension. This old bird was going to show neither fear nor favour.

'I wish to speak to my brothers in private.'

'Collusion? I think not, my lord. If they wish to address me, they may do so.'

Louis stood up and Ben, magnificent in full scarlet regimentals, waved him back to his seat. 'Let me. Lord Knighton has a grudge against my brother because of Gabriel's elopement with his daughter. He has spread it about that his investigations have revealed a witness to my father's death, but I know who did witness it and I can attest to the fact that none of those present that day have spoken to any investigator. In other words, he is inventing evidence.'

'And who were those witnesses?'

Witnesses, plural? Gabriel looked at Louis again and saw that Caroline had put her hand on his forearm.

'My eldest brother, the present Lord Edenbridge, you know about, sir. There were also myself and my other two brothers.'

'You were not there,' Gabriel interrupted. 'And Louis was unconscious.'

'Allow Major Stone to finish, if you please. Where were the servants? As I recall, we were told they were all below stairs or in various rooms not within sight of the hall and landing.'

'Yes, sir. There was to be a dinner party that evening. The staff were either in the kitchens, or in the dining room or preparing the drawing room. My brother George and I were in the room where we studied because our tutor had left us an exercise in Latin translation before he went into Lewes. We heard a loud crash.'

'Yes, I knocked over a valuable Chinese vase that stood at the head of the stairs,' Gabriel stated. 'You were nowhere in sight.' He felt Caroline's gaze on him as though she had prodded him with her finger, but he did not look in her direction. He wasn't under oath, not yet.

'That is not true,' Louis said and all eyes turned to him. 'I knocked it over and I was trying to hide the pieces, which was stupid of me. But I knew if I didn't then Gabriel would take the blame like he always did and he would be the one who was whipped.'

'Louis—'

'No. We should have spoken up long ago, right from the beginning, but we were all too afraid. We let you pretend you were the clumsy one, or the one who had done something out of mischief. Father soon believed you were wicked—you didn't have to try very hard to fake the evidence and protect us.'

'Damn it, Louis! *Will you be quiet?*'

George, Ben and Sir Humphrey all began to speak at once.

'No, Gabriel,' Caroline said, her quiet voice stilling the noise like one chime of a bell. 'No, Louis will not be quiet. He is going to tell the truth and so, finally, are you.'

At a stroke she was going to uncover all the wounds he had spent such pain and misery covering up, would shatter his brothers' memories of their childhood, would make him break his vow to his mother. He knew why—she had a passion for truth, she had a fierce loyalty to him as her husband. But his loyalties were older than their marriage and he could not allow how he felt about her to shake them.

'You are my wife and you will do as I tell you. Now, be silent.' He had never spoken to Caroline like that before, had never thought he would. In his own voice he heard echoes of his father, of hers, and he saw her go white even as he felt the stab of nausea in his gut.

'No,' she said again. 'We are all going to disobey you. Your wife, your brothers and your friend. We have made a conspiracy against your secrets. The truth matters and, besides, our child is not going to grow up believing she or he had a murderer for a father. Go on, Louis.'

It took perhaps two seconds for her words to hit home, then the rest of the room vanished from his consciousness. *Our child? Caroline is expecting our child? But that is impossible.*

He came back to himself to find everyone, his wife included, had their attention fixed on Louis, who must have simply carried on with his story. '…it was idiotic to try to hide the damage, but I was in a panic. Then I heard Father coming. He had heard the crash, of course, and he had his whip. I expect he thought it was Gabriel again. He rushed towards me, shouting.'

'We'd heard the noise and we were just coming out of the corridor when we saw you running up the stairs, Gabriel,' Ben said. He stood at attention as though he was making a report to his commanding officer.

'Father slashed at Louis, who grabbed at the whip. Father jerked it back and Louis let go, so it flew back and it hit Father's face. Louis crashed into the newel post and Father tripped over his body—he was going too fast and was off balance because of the blow to his face. He went down the stairs, hit the banisters on the curve—I think that was what broke his neck—tumbled past you, Gabriel, and hit the floor. I saw you run back down to him, then all hell broke loose. George started retching and I dragged him away so he couldn't see. By the time I came out again you were telling people the story you told at the inquest. I couldn't contradict you, and besides, there was all the fuss over Louis.'

He turned to the Coroner. 'If there had been any danger of Gabriel being blamed I would have spoken at the inquest, sir. But George and I were frightened for Louis. He was only a child and when he came round he couldn't recall anything about it. Provided Gabriel was safe, we thought it was best to say nothing.'

'And now you conveniently recall it all, young man?' the Coroner said to Louis.

'Now, yes. For years I just had nightmares, flashes of memory that I thought were a kind of waking dream. Then it all began to get worse about six months ago when I started working closely with Gabriel.' He looked round at Ben and George. 'When I read the newspaper accounts, I suspected it was real memories and went to talk to my brothers. I suppose you'll want to arrest me now, Sir Humphrey.'

'And me,' Ben said, making to draw his sabre from his belt in formal surrender.

'For what?' Sir Humphrey enquired. 'No perjury was involved. Neither of you was called to give evidence and you were both schoolboys. It is up to my colleague, of course, but I can see no legal reason to reopen the inquest. No new evidence has been brought forward that would make the verdict of Accidental Death unsafe in my opinion.'

'Nor mine,' Barton said. He looked at George. 'Reverend Stone, can you confirm what has been said?'

'Yes, sir. Every word.'

'Then Sir Humphrey and I will issue a report stating that we have interviewed three new witnesses to the death of the late earl and that their evidence supports the original verdict of accidental death. The newspapers will get their teeth into that, I have no doubt. I suggest, my lord, that you take legal advice and issue your father-in-law with a strongly worded warning of what will happen if he does not withdraw his slanders. Major, Reverend, Mr Stone, I will take down your evidence with Sir Humphrey as witness. I see no reason to detain you, my lady, my lords. Good day.'

Gabriel found himself outside a firmly closed door. 'I can't leave my brothers.'

'They are grown men.' Cris gave him a decidedly unfriendly shove towards the front door. 'I would suggest you cannot leave your wife.'

There was a considerable crowd in the street outside, far more than could be explained by the sight of Cris's magnificent coach and team of matched bays. 'Get in.'

'Cris—' Gabriel realised that he was confused, relieved and, quite simply, furious.

'Damn you, accept some help from your family for once. The last time you were this aggravating I knocked you on your backside and I swear if you do not get in that carriage with Caroline in the next twenty seconds I'll do it again.'

Gabriel offered his hand to Caroline and she got into the carriage. She had put down her veil and he could not see her face, but her chin was up, he could tell.

Cris slammed the door on them. 'Now go home. I'm walking.'

'Gabriel?'

'How could you?' he asked, hearing his own voice cold and hard. 'How could you do that without asking me? All my life I have protected my brothers and you tossed them to the wolves.'

'They told the truth, finally, and everything is all right.' Caroline threw back the veil. 'You are safe, they are safe, my father's horrible scheme has been checkmated. Can't you be happy about that?'

'Not when you lie to me in front of a room full of people, try to manipulate sympathy by telling falsehoods. You cannot know that you are pregnant, it is barely a month since that first night.'

Chapter Twenty-Two

So, this is what you get for loving a rake. Accusations and ingratitude and anger. Caroline took a deep breath and saw they were drawing up at their own front door where there was another, smaller, crowd with Cris's grooms holding them at bay. This was not the time to lose all control and scream at the man, tell him how much he hurt her, how much she cared for him.

'I may not have to tell our child his father is a murderer,' she said as she lowered her veil. 'But I *am* going to have to explain to the poor little soul that he is an ungrateful idiot.'

The groom holding the door for her lost his composure for a moment, then got his face under control as Caroline swept out of the carriage and up the steps to the front door that, thankfully, opened as she reached it.

'*I* am an idiot?' Gabriel slammed the door behind him, shaking the silver tray on the hall table. 'I was not the one smuggling hairpins and firearms and sovereigns into a magistrate's house. Why not go the whole nine yards and bake a cake with a file in it?'

'I didn't think of that.' She paused on the bottom step of the stairs and swung round. 'Perhaps because I am a poor feeble woman with my brain turned to porridge by pregnancy. Or perhaps because I knew there were no bars, but that you might need to get out of the house and bribe a boatman to take you across to France. For some reason, which is escaping me now, I did not want you to hang.'

Caroline stalked upstairs, ignoring the throbbing in her toe, and found a little comfort in the fact that she could close the bedchamber door without slamming it. She turned the key and sat down at her dressing table. Men were the very devil, all of them. But she loved one, was married to one and she was carrying his child, whatever the stubborn creature believed.

She had expected Gabriel to come to the door and ask her to open it. She had half-expected him to kick it down, but when the tap came half an hour later it was Tamsyn.

'May I come in?' When Caroline opened the door Tamsyn caught her in a hug, then held her at arm's length. 'Cris says we are to pack and go back to London straight away. He says, and I quote, "Gabriel always was the one with the brains, if he could only be brought to realise it. Let him work this out, because it is beyond me."'

'Oh. If Cris is abandoning us…'

'I think he is simply putting a safe distance between himself and the urge to hit Gabriel. Personally I think it would be an excellent idea to punch him, but men are strange.' She cocked her head on one side. 'This isn't just about his father, is it?'

'I told him I was expecting his baby.'

She could see Tamsyn doing some mental arithmetic. 'Er…'

'It is very, very early. But it is his. I am certain, but he thinks that I lied to the magistrate just to get sympathy.'

'Oh, so you…before the wedding?'

'Yes, not long before. The night my father found me,

after we agreed to marry. I don't understand why he is so upset, I thought he wanted children.'

'Don't be a cloth-head,' Tamsyn said inelegantly. 'You blurted it out in the middle of that meeting, in front of his brothers and the magistrate and the coroner? My dear, that might not be the best time and place to tell a man he is going to be a father.'

'I was becoming angry with him,' Caroline confessed miserably. 'And frustrated that he would not tell the simple truth. He is so protective of his brothers, he seems to feel that he has total responsibility for them, whatever they have done.'

'He is protective of you, too. Look what he did for you,' Tamsyn pointed out.

She didn't need reminding. 'But his oldest loyalty is to them. He actually worked it all out, how if they hanged him I would be looked after and how Ben would get the title. He is angry with me because I acted without telling him, exposed Louis's part in their father's death.'

Tamsyn shivered. 'So cold blooded.'

'He is a gambler. And I think that being like that helps him cope. He has pushed all his emotions right down so they can't hurt him.'

'Are you going to leave him? You can come back with us.'

'Would you have left Cris?'

'Yes. I did.' Tamsyn looked bleak. 'I thought it was the best thing for him. It was horrible. But he didn't agree with me and came and got me, thank heavens.'

'You were not married then?' The other woman shook her head. 'Well, I am. For better, for worse. I promised.'

'When he calms down he'll want to do the right thing because of the baby,' Tamsyn suggested.

'I don't want him doing the right thing because that is

his duty. I want him to trust me and to love me. And, yes, I know I am wishing for the moon.'

'Good luck.' Tamsyn got up and pressed a kiss on Caroline's cheek. 'I would offer to stay, but I think you two need to work this one out for yourselves.'

Caroline clung for a moment. 'Thank you. You have been such a good friend. And Cris and Alex and Tess. Give them my love.'

A carriage pulled up outside, then away again. *Cris and Tamsyn*. The sound of voices in the street ebbed to its normal level and when Caroline tilted the dressing-table mirror to reflect the view outside she saw the crowd beginning to disperse across the Steine. They had heard the news about Gabriel's innocence and were off to discuss the whole intriguing scandal over the tea cups, she assumed. The house was quiet, the servants were tiptoeing about while their master brooded behind closed doors.

She could go down, insist that he listen to her and then he would accept that she was telling the truth about the baby, that it wasn't simply a ploy to attract sympathy from the Coroner and that would be that. She could forgive him being angry to have that sprung on him in public, he'd had a lot on his mind, to put it mildly.

'But I love him,' Caroline said into the silence.

And I want him to love me. I want a real marriage, a love match, a family. I want him to be happy, not just content with an arrangement.

But how? If she marched in and explained and then announced she loved him Gabriel might very well be feeling guilty enough to pretend he loved her, too, and that would be…awful. She would have to think and hope her instincts would guide her, because just at the moment her brain was not helping in the slightest.

The front door slammed and she jumped to her feet

and went to the window. Gabriel, hatless, gloveless, was striding across the grassy expanse of the Steine towards the sea, anger in every uncoordinated, jerky step. She had never seen him move like this, without elegant, careless grace. He was hurting.

Well, so am I, Gabriel Stone. So am I.

The wind had got up and the clouds, a ragged grey threat of rain, scudded across the sky. The sea was already showing white horses in a vicious chop of small waves and the last bathers were being towed up the beach towards warmth, dry clothes and their luncheons.

A few brave souls were promenading along Marine Parade, but the ladies were furling their pretty parasols and clutching the arms of their escorts who were hurrying towards their lodgings before the rain fell, free hands clamped to the top of their hats.

Gabriel went down the steps on to the beach, his feet sinking into the shingle, walked almost to the water's edge and then began to follow it. The tide was on the ebb and he was walking in sodden pebbles, his boots already wet. He hunched his shoulders, thrust cold hands into his pockets, the wind whipping his hair into his eyes, stinging with the salt-laden air.

He walked on, the loose footing, making each step as much effort as ten on hard sand, walked until he lost track of time and found himself beyond even the newest developments that were spreading Brighton along the coast. There were dinghies pulled up clear of the high-water mark, like so many turtles, and he sat down on one with his back to the town and tried not to think.

Not that his mind would clear, that was the problem. His brothers, his parents, Caroline, his friends. *A baby.* Everything was churned up and nothing made sense.

The threatened rain came in a sudden, spiteful shower that whipped against him like handfuls of thrown grit. It was gone in moments, leaving him damp and cold, but at least it had shocked him into vaguely rational thought.

It must have been that very first time, that night at Springbourne when all that had seemed to matter had been persuading her to marry him and finally losing himself in her. The time before he realised he loved her, the time when he had complacently thought of children as some theoretical, abstract outcome of their marriage. But they were not an abstract. They were real, important, and he had thrown the miraculous news that he was to be a father back in her face along with his anger and ingratitude at being saved from the gallows.

He got to his feet, raked the wet hair off his forehead and turned to walk back. Apologise. Thank her. Try to understand his own feelings about his past, about their future. Hope against hope that somehow he could understand hers, because Caroline was his wife and he loved her. Somehow, with no model of how to do it right, he was going to have a family to look after. For the first time in his adult life he felt fear, gut-clenching, knee-weakening fear. *What if I can't do it? Can't be a decent father and husband? What if...?* The doubts raged in his head like the wind that was battering the coast now.

It seemed like a hundred miles back along the shore, the shifting pebbles dragging at his feet until his legs began to feel like lead. He should cut up towards the coast road. Gabriel stopped and assessed the ways up the low, crumbling cliffs and saw, in the distance, a figure coming towards him, laboriously battling wildly blowing skirts and hampering shingle. As he watched her bonnet whipped off her head and out to sea and her hair broke loose as she clutched for the ribbons, the blonde streamers in the wind like a flag. *Caroline.*

Gabriel began to run, heedless of the strain on his tired legs. It was like a nightmare where every step seems to be mired in mud. She was carrying a child, she shouldn't be struggling along this damned beach. She was coming to him.

He realised the moment she saw him and recognised who it was, because she stopped walking and bent over, hands on her knees, out of breath. When he reached her, breathless himself, she had straightened up and only the high colour in her cheeks and the rise and fall of her bosom revealed the speed she must have been walking at.

'Caroline. You shouldn't be out here, not exerting yourself like this.'

'I am pregnant, not sick.'

'Why did you follow me?' He took her arm and steered her, unresisting, up the beach to where a fisherman had constructed a rough shelter out of driftwood and old planks. 'Sit down, it is going to rain again in a moment.'

'I saw you leave, so angry you could hardly walk straight. And I saw where you were heading and I thought...'

'That I was going to throw myself in the sea?'

'No.' She smiled faintly. 'But I thought you might need me.'

'If I did, why should you care? This is the man who is so damned thoughtless and insensitive that a shock is enough to make him cruel and ungrateful.'

'You are my husband.'

'And you take your vows very seriously,' he said, feeling the weight of despair on his shoulders. He was a duty to her and she was going to do her duty if it killed her.

'So do you. To whom did you make a promise to always look after your brothers? Your mother, I suppose.'

He nodded, unable to find the words. When she did not press him he managed to say it. 'She killed herself. Took poison. I'll never know whether my father beat her or whether it was the unkindness of words or neglect. I was fourteen, too young to really understand. Such a good little boy.'

'Were you?' That little smile had deepened, made soft dimples in her cheeks. He wanted to kiss them.

'I was the heir. It was my duty to be good,' he said, mocking the earnest child he had once been.

'And then you turned into a miniature hellion to deflect your father's anger on to you.'

'Yes.'

'Clever, as well as brave. Your mother would have been very proud of you.' When he shrugged, embarrassed by the praise, appalled to find it mattered so much, she asked, 'But why did you become so remote from them that they were unable to come to you and tell you what they had seen?'

'If I had shown I was fond of them then he would have suspected.'

'So you made yourself be alone with no one to love you.' To his horror Caroline burst into tears, just as another squall hit, lashing them with icy rain. Gabriel curled himself around her, sheltering her, and let her sob on his shoulder until the squall and the tears ceased together. 'Oh, I am sorry. I feel so weepy at the moment. Harriet says it is because of the baby and her sister was a complete watering pot for months.'

He found a handkerchief and mopped her eyes, but she took it from him and blew her nose briskly. 'I am too stunned to add up.'

'I have only just missed my courses, but I am always so regular and I am absolutely convinced that something has changed.' Caroline took a deep breath. 'It is far too early to have said anything. Many pregnancies don't go beyond the first month or two. But somehow...'

'Somehow you are sure.' He stood up and held out his hand to help her to her feet. 'Shall we start out before the next rain squall comes?' When she nodded and slipped her hand into his he felt a shock of fierce protectiveness. 'I'll do my level best to be a good father, Caroline. At least I've plenty of experience of what makes a bad one.' She said nothing, but tightened her grip for a moment. 'I'll do my best to be a good husband, too. I'm not good at emotion, Caroline.'

'I noticed.' She was teasing him, he thought. Hoped. 'I understand. It has never been very safe for you to feel, has it?'

He thought that was all she was going to say. They walked back slowly in silence, then, as they reached their own front door, she said, 'Promise me something?'

'Anything.'

'Rash!' She was serious again in a moment. 'Promise never to lie to me. I won't probe your secrets, I won't expect you to open your heart to me. But do not lie to me, Gabriel. Not about how you feel. You told me you do not obey vows, but you do, don't you?'

'I do when they are to you. Yes, I promise.' It felt very serious, very heavy, that promise, but her smile was suddenly light and gay.

He insisted on walking her upstairs. 'Call Harriet, lie down and rest.'

'I will.' Caroline stood in the bedchamber, her hand on the edge of the half-open door. 'I love you, Gabriel.' Then, softly, she closed it, leaving him on the far side. Alone.

* * *

Half an hour later Gabriel was sitting in the drawing room nursing a glass of brandy he was not drinking and trying to remember what his life had been like on the first day of June at eleven in the morning. He had been single, heart-free and with no responsibilities in the world other than three brothers who were either independent of him or on the verge of being so. He owned estates that were run efficiently by excellent employees, a house full of memories that he could close the door on and walk away from and three close friends whose own lives had recently been turned upside down in a way that he had been certain would change their relationship with him for ever.

He'd been comfortable, self-indulgent, vaguely uneasy and…bored.

Now those locked doors had been flung wide open and it had been his brothers who had come to stand shoulder to shoulder with him. His friends had rallied to guard his back just as they always had. He had a wife, a child on the way and a secret lifted off his neck.

He had a wife who loved him. That promise she had extracted from him made sense now. She was afraid that he would take pity on her and mouth the words in response, pretend a depth of emotion he did not truly feel. Clever Caroline. She knew he would lie *for* her, but now, not *to* her.

There was a bang on the door and Gabriel put down the untouched brandy, cursing under his breath and got to his feet. *What now?* His brothers came in, filling the room with their energy and their excitement.

'It is all over town.' Louis, grinning like an idiot, threw his arms around Gabriel and hugged him fiercely. Startled, he found himself hugging back, then both Ben and George piled in to.

When they finally broke apart Ben picked up the brandy glass and knocked it back in one gulp. 'The gossip mill is in full swing and your father-in-law's name is mud. The ladies are swooning with the romantic delights of the elopement and you rescuing Caroline from what was some sort of Gothic house of horrors and the gentlemen are assuring each other that they always knew Knighton was queer in the attic and that you are as good a man as our grandfather.'

'And they got all this from the statement that witnesses had been examined and the fact of an accident has been confirmed?' Gabriel asked, suspicious.

'We have been elucidating the situation,' George pronounced, looking pious. 'Naturally we did not want anyone to retain the wrong impression.'

'And we've done a damn good job,' Louis said, straightening his spectacles. 'Ben stuck his chest out, rattled his sabre and looked manful while commending your honourable reluctance to call out your father-in-law. George has been murmuring about the chivalrous rescue of a lady in terms which, frankly, were fairly sickening when he got round to comparing you to Lancelot, although it did make Lady Hesslethwaite weep. And I've been muttering about having my advice about suing for slander turned down. In fact, Brother, you are probably not safe to go out alone or you'll be mobbed by the ladies and have your hand shaken off by the men.'

Gabriel stared round at them. Ben was smirking, George was smug and Louis was grinning and suddenly they were all laughing and he was, too, and they were just his brothers. Not responsibilities to sacrifice himself for, not a constant aching worry. Simply his brothers whom he loved and, startlingly, appeared to love him. Not that a gentleman talked about such things, so, still gasping with laughter, Gabriel filled four glasses and raised his own in a toast.

'The Brothers Stone.'

Chapter Twenty-Three

The bed dipped and warm lips began to kiss their way down the back of her neck. It was a dream…but did dream lovers rasp their stubbled chins on your more delicate areas of skin and did they smell of brandy?

'Gabriel?' Carolyn wriggled back and there was a moment of tugging and flapping before there was a male body under the covers for her to snuggle into. Definitely not a dream. Dream lovers did not have to fight the bedding.

'No, the Archbishop of Canterbury. Who were you expecting?'

'Are you drunk?'

'Surprisingly not.' He wrapped an arm firmly around her waist and Caroline realised that he was as naked as she was. 'Did we sound as though we were carousing downstairs? I'm sorry if we disturbed you.'

'You sounded happy. That was good to go to sleep hearing.' She twisted round until she could burrow her head under his chin and pressed her lips to his collarbone.

'I sincerely hope I usually sound happy when we finally do go to sleep,' Gabriel grumbled into her hair.

'You don't laugh then. I have never heard you laugh before.'

'Never?' He bent back and pushed up her chin so he could frown at her, their noses almost touching.

'Never. Not a proper, letting-everything-go laugh because you are happy rather than because something amuses you.'

Gabriel tucked her head down against his shoulder again. 'I must be a misery to live with.'

'No, merely rather intense sometimes.'

There was silence and she was content to lie there against his warmth, feeling his heart beating close to hers, his breath stirring her hair.

'I have no idea how to be a father,' Gabriel said abruptly.

'And I have no idea how to be a mother, so we will just have to work it out as we go along. You know what makes a bad father.'

'That's true.' By some miracle he sounded amused. 'And you already know how to be a wife.'

'I do? I suspect I am rather a disobedient one.'

'Dreadfully so,' he agreed. Caroline felt him take a deep breath and the long body cradling hers became tense. 'Not letting yourself feel emotion is like taking laudanum when you've got a broken leg. You know there is a vast amount of pain out there somewhere, but it is behind shutters, quite safe unless you are foolish enough to let it out by stopping the dose. But you have to stop the dose because otherwise you become addicted to the medicine.'

'You have to want to stop,' Caroline suggested.

'Yes. You caught me at just the right moment.'

'I caught you? That makes me sound like a designing hussy.'

'You are a hussy.' She could hear the laughter in his voice. 'You proposition notorious rakes, you drug unwanted suitors, you hide up chimneys, you order marquesses about and invade the homes of respectable magistrates. No wonder I love you. Such a rakehell as I am needs a wicked wife to love.'

'You...' Her heart seemed to have stilled to a slow, almost painful, thud. 'Gabriel, I know you desire me—' Just at the moment there was absolutely no ignoring the physical evidence of that.

'Have you such little faith in my promises?' Gabriel rolled over on to his back as though to stop himself clouding her thoughts with his touch. 'I had no idea that was what I was feeling and I didn't want to dig and find out, coward that I am. I have always controlled risk. People think gamblers are reckless, but successful ones are the exact opposite. We calculate risk, we know just what we can afford to lose. Loving gives a hostage to fortune, doesn't it? I did not dare to hazard my heart on you. How have you so much more courage than I do?'

Caroline turned to rest on her elbow and smiled at him. 'I have been practising loving all my life. My mother, my brothers. I even worked hard at loving my father. And I suspect women find it natural to take the risk, because if we have children then every moment we could be in fear for them and if we couldn't face that, then the human race would die out.'

She loved Gabriel's face when he was thinking hard. Every ounce of intelligence, every scrap of ferocious concentration showed in those dark eyes, in the set of the sensual lips, in the line that formed between his brows. He was so good at putting on the mask that hid his feelings that she knew it was only absolute trust that let him relax so in front of her.

'I can't promise I'll always get it right.'

'Nor me. How dull if we did,' Caroline teased. 'No arguments, no drama, no lovely making it up afterwards.'

'Hmm.' Gabriel's eyes had lost their brooding intensity. 'Are you tired still?'

'No,' Caroline said demurely. 'I am wide awake. Oh!'

Gabriel tossed back the covers and began to smooth his hands down over her body. 'Nothing shows yet.' He sounded ridiculously disappointed.

'Of course not! It will soon enough and then I'll be lumbering about like a whale.'

'More lovely curves.' Gabriel's tongue drew a lingering trail of liquid fire down over the swell of one breast, into the valley between them and up over the other. He explored her body as though it were new to him, murmuring with appreciation over the curve of her hip, the dimple beside her knee, the elegance of the curl of her ear until he almost had her believing herself that she was the most beautiful woman in the world. *Perhaps I am to him*, Caroline thought in wonder. *I think he is the most handsome man. And the kindest and the...*

'Wickedest!' she gasped as Gabriel slid down the bed and began to do outrageous things with his tongue.

'You called?' He lifted his head and looked at her with such an innocent expression that she laughed and was still laughing, joyously, as he came up the bed and abandoned gentle teasing for a passionate possession that sent her spinning from laughter into blind ecstasy in moments.

'You are thinking,' Caroline said much later, as she lay with Gabriel watching the light fade out of the sky. 'I can hear the wheels turning.'

'So are you. A guinea for them?'

'You may have them for free. I was wondering what you wanted to do with Edenvale.'

'Turn it into a home,' Gabriel said without hesitation. 'I won't let my life be ruled by memories and secrets any

more and I certainly won't allow my father's ghost to drive
me out of what should be our family home. And we'll have
my brothers and yours to stay, often, and Alex, Cris and
Grant and their children and make so much noise that not
a single spectre dare linger.'

'I do like the idea of ghosts and ghouls fleeing gibbering in the face of a house full of happiness. And what was
on your mind?'

'What you wanted to do about your father. Louis wants
to sue the boots off him, I favour leaving him to stew in
his own juice.'

'I will write to Lucas. I do not want to be estranged
from him and I suspect if he and Anthony encourage my
father to start a new building project he will soon retreat
from reality into that. And perhaps one day he will be…
stable enough to want to see his grandchild.'

'So we have put the world to rights between us.' Gabriel
stretched, languorous as a big cat.

'We have put our corner of it to rights at least,' Caroline leant over to kiss his smiling lips.

'Our new world,' her husband said. 'And it will take us
a lifetime to explore it, my love. Beginning now.'

Epilogue

Half Moon Street, London—February 14th, 1821

'We are definitely going to have to move house. We cannot even hold a christening party without it resembling the crush at a royal Drawing Room and Alex's valet is becoming fretful over the dressing room becoming a nursery.'

Tess sank down on the end of the sofa in the window alcove, the only available seat left in the drawing room, and tucked Dominic Alexander Hugh Tempest and all his yards of christening robe snuggly into the crook of her arm.

'Perhaps this fashion for huge skirts and ridiculous puffed sleeves will subside.' Kate, the Countess of Allundale, squashed her own skirts up to make more room. 'Although that will only help with parties, not bedchambers. I worry that our new house in Brook Street isn't big enough.' She laid one hand over the spot where a myriad of heaped ruffles concealed the third of the Rivers' brood, due to make an appearance in July. 'Grant has become so enthusiastic over suffrage reform that he keeps throwing political receptions and dinners so the downstairs guest bedchamber must be sacrificed to extend the drawing room.'

'You don't mind London life and parties any more? No, don't move, I'll just slide round and prop myself up on the back of the sofa which is inelegant, but does wonders for my back.' Caroline sighed with relief. 'Don't say anything, but I have just taken off my slippers.'

'*What* a good idea,' Kate said. There was some surreptitious rustling and two more sighs. 'How we suffer for fashion. And parties. But, no, I enjoy them now. I've even become used to being a countess. Almost. I still keep thinking people are going to point at me and cry "Imposter", but it hasn't happened yet. I can hardly believe how much my life has changed. Do you know, I even found myself arguing with the Prime Minister about married women's property rights the other evening?'

'Goodness. What did he say?' Tamsyn arrived, set a footstool in front of the sofa and sank down in a cloud of amber silk and blonde gauze, careless of what anyone might think of a marchioness virtually sitting on the floor.

'He huffed and puffed and called me *dear lady* and escaped as soon as he could, but I'll corner him yet. We've all taken our slippers off,' she added in a whisper to Tamsyn who promptly did the same.

'My ankles are swelling,' she grumbled. 'No one tells you these things.'

'You— You're not expecting, too?' Caroline managed to keep her voice down to a muted shriek.

'Shh! Yes, but I haven't told Cris yet. I saw how Alex fussed and Gabriel and Grant seem almost as bad. But today is St Valentine's Day, so I have ordered a special supper and I am going to tell him then.'

'You are looking smug,' Kate observed. 'I assume a new negligée is to hand?'

'Definitely. Sea-green silk. That should keep his mind off fussing.'

'So the four Lords of Disgrace are going to be the proud and respectable fathers of four babies within a year,' Tess mused. 'Just think, if one of you has a boy and two have girls, perhaps in twenty years' time we could be sitting down and planning two weddings.'

'Tess, you are a hopeless romantic,' Caroline teased. 'But what a wonderful thought. We all had such a rocky path to finding our true love and the men were there for each other...'

'Here they are.' Tamsyn waved to Cris, who stood with his friends, the four of them making the room seem crowded with masculine energy.

'And so beautiful, all of them,' Kate said with a sigh as their husbands crossed the room to them. 'And not looking in the slightest bit respectable, thank goodness.'

'What are up to, my ladies?' Cris asked, stooping to kiss his wife.

'We were just saying how handsome you all were.' Kate batted her eyelashes at Grant as he stretched out a hand to her.

'And what else?' Alex demanded. 'You are scheming, I can tell. I've come to claim my son for five minutes,' he added as he took the sleeping baby from Tess.

'Yes, we are,' Caroline agreed. 'But you can all relax. You will not need to worry for, oh...twenty years at least.'

Gabriel looked from his wife to his friends. 'Gentlemen, I suggest we retreat to the study and take young Dominic with us. I have no idea what our wives are up to, but he is going to need all the advice we can give him if he is to end up as happy as we are.'

* * * * *

If you enjoyed this story make sure you don't miss
the other three books in Louise Allen's
LORDS OF DISGRACE *quartet:*

HIS HOUSEKEEPER'S CHRISTMAS WISH
HIS CHRISTMAS COUNTESS
THE MANY SINS OF CRIS DE FEAUX

COMING NEXT MONTH FROM

H HARLEQUIN®

HISTORICAL

Available July 19, 2016

HER SHERIFF BODYGUARD (Western)
by Lynna Banning
Caroline MacFarlane's one mission in life is votes for women. But when her safety is threatened, suddenly protective sheriff Hawk Rivera is glued to her side—day *and* night!

SHEIKH'S MAIL-ORDER BRIDE (Regency)
Hot Arabian Nights • by Marguerite Kaye
The world believes Constance Montgomery lost at sea, but Murimon's ruler, Kadar, knows the truth. She's honor-bound to leave, but can the brooding prince tempt Constance to stay?

MISS MARIANNE'S DISGRACE (Regency)
Scandal and Disgrace • by Georgie Lee
Excluded from society, Miss Marianne Domville finds solace at her pianoforte. That is, until author Sir Warren Stevens brings a thrill of excitement into her solitary existence...

ENSLAVED BY THE DESERT TRADER (Ancient Egypt)
by Greta Gilbert
Hardened desert trader Tahar knows he could—and *should*—sell his new captive for a handsome price. But can Tahar find a way to keep Kiya as his own?

Available via Reader Service and online:

ROYALIST ON THE RUN (English Civil War)
by Helen Dickson
Years ago, Colonel Sir Edward Grey broke off his engagement to Arabella. But now that they're thrown back together, they must take a chance on their rekindled passion once again!

HER ENEMY AT THE ALTAR (Regency)
by Virginia Heath
When Lady Constance Stuart is discovered in the arms of Aaron Wincanton, scandal abounds. And an unexpected marriage is just the beginning for these two former enemies...

**YOU CAN FIND MORE INFORMATION ON UPCOMING HARLEQUIN® TITLES,
FREE EXCERPTS AND MORE AT WWW.HARLEQUIN.COM.**

HHCNM0716

SPECIAL EXCERPT FROM

⒣HARLEQUIN®

⒣ISTORICAL

*Hardened desert trader Tahar knows he could—and
should—sell his new captive Kiya for a handsome
price. But when a wild heat explodes between them,
can Tahar find a way to keep Kiya as his own?*

Read on for a sneak preview of
ENSLAVED BY THE DESERT TRADER
by *Greta Gilbert*.

When she saw him unwrapping his headdress and stepping
out of his long tunic she knew she had overestimated the
power of her own will. He stood to his full height and
gazed at her from the bank, and already she yearned for
him. His luxuriant mane hung about his face in thick,
wavy ropes, and it was the only thing he wore.

He was a man. That was clear.

Stunningly clear.

But as she appraised the whole of his body, she realized
that he was also a god. Every chiseled bit of him radiated
strength and masculinity. There was not even a hint of
the softness of age or leisure, not a single inch of fallow
flesh. He was as taut and ready as a drum.

And he was coming for her.

The strong sinews of his lower legs tensed as he
stepped barefoot into the water. He began to walk toward
her, and his upper leg muscles bulged and contracted,
creating rings of small waves that radiated out from his

body. Those waves traveled slowly across the pool, and when they crashed into her body they made her shiver.

If she had seen him among the tomb workers she would have thought him a loader. She pictured him bare chested and sweating in the sun, lifting some large boulder, his dense muscles flexing. He would have been the most irresistibly handsome loader that ever was.

And he wanted her—nothing could be clearer.

She had thought that she repulsed him. Now it seemed he was making the opposite known.

Just the sight of him made her heart thump wildly.

He continued toward her, his narrow hips sinking beneath the velvety water, his muscular arms stretching out to caress its still surface. With the moon above him, the contours of his massive chest cast shadows upon his pale skin. It was as if he had been carved in alabaster, a temple relief showing the picture of an ideal man. Only this man was real—very, very real—and he was advancing toward her.

Don't miss
ENSLAVED BY THE DESERT TRADER
by Greta Gilbert, available August 2016 wherever
Harlequin® Historical books and ebooks are sold.

www.Harlequin.com

Copyright © 2016 by Greta Gilbert

HHEXP0716

Turn your love of reading into rewards you'll love with

Harlequin My Rewards

**Join for FREE today at
www.HarlequinMyRewards.com**

Earn **FREE BOOKS** of your choice.

Experience **EXCLUSIVE OFFERS** and contests.

Enjoy **BOOK RECOMMENDATIONS**
selected just for you.

PLUS! Sign up now
and get **500** points
right away!

Earn
FREE
REWARDS
HarlequinMyRewards.com
Join
Today!

MYR16R

Love the Harlequin book you just read?

Your opinion matters.

Review this book on your favorite book site, review site, blog or your own social media properties and share your opinion with other readers!

Be sure to connect with us at:
Harlequin.com/Newsletters
Facebook.com/HarlequinBooks
Twitter.com/HarlequinBooks

HREVIEWS

JUST CAN'T GET ENOUGH?

Join our social communities
and talk to us online.

You will have access to the latest
news on upcoming titles and special
promotions, but most importantly,
you can talk to other fans about your
favorite Harlequin reads.

Harlequin.com/Community

 Facebook.com/HarlequinBooks

Twitter.com/HarlequinBooks

Pinterest.com/HarlequinBooks

HSOCIAL

THE WORLD IS BETTER WITH
Romance

Harlequin has everything from contemporary, passionate and heartwarming to suspenseful and inspirational stories.

Whatever your mood, we have a romance just for you!

Connect with us to find your next great read, special offers and more.

f /HarlequinBooks

🐦 @HarlequinBooks

www.HarlequinBlog.com

www.Harlequin.com/Newsletters

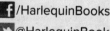 **HARLEQUIN®**

A 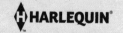 FOR EVERY MOOD™

www.Harlequin.com

SERIESHALOAD2015

REQUEST YOUR
FREE BOOKS!

◊ HARLEQUIN®

ℋISTORICAL

Where love is timeless

2 FREE NOVELS PLUS 2 **FREE GIFTS!**

YES! Please send me 2 FREE Harlequin® Historical novels and my 2 FREE gifts (gifts are worth about $10). After receiving them, if I don't wish to receive any more books, I can return the shipping statement marked "cancel." If I don't cancel, I will receive 6 brand-new novels every month and be billed just $5.69 per book in the U.S. or $5.99 per book in Canada. That's a savings of at least 12% off the cover price! It's quite a bargain! Shipping and handling is just 50¢ per book in the U.S. and 75¢ per book in Canada.* I understand that accepting the 2 free books and gifts places me under no obligation to buy anything. I can always return a shipment and cancel at any time. Even if I never buy another book, the two free books and gifts are mine to keep forever.

246/349 HDN GH2Z

Name _____ (PLEASE PRINT) _____

Address _____ Apt. # _____

City _____ State/Prov. _____ Zip/Postal Code _____

Signature (if under 18, a parent or guardian must sign) _____

Mail to the **Reader Service:**
IN U.S.A.: P.O. Box 1867, Buffalo, NY 14240-1867
IN CANADA: P.O. Box 609, Fort Erie, Ontario L2A 5X3

Want to try two free books from another line?
Call 1-800-873-8635 or visit www.ReaderService.com.

* Terms and prices subject to change without notice. Prices do not include applicable taxes. Sales tax applicable in N.Y. Canadian residents will be charged applicable taxes. Offer not valid in Quebec. This offer is limited to one order per household. Not valid for current subscribers to Harlequin Historical books. All orders subject to credit approval. Credit or debit balances in a customer's account(s) may be offset by any other outstanding balance owed by or to the customer. Please allow 4 to 6 weeks for delivery. Offer available while quantities last.

Your Privacy—The Reader Service is committed to protecting your privacy. Our Privacy Policy is available online at www.ReaderService.com or upon request from the Reader Service.

We make a portion of our mailing list available to reputable third parties that offer products we believe may interest you. If you prefer that we not exchange your name with third parties, or if you wish to clarify or modify your communication preferences, please visit us at www.ReaderService.com/consumerschoice or write to us at Reader Service Preference Service, P.O. Box 9062, Buffalo, NY 14240-9062. Include your complete name and address.

HH15